The Inspector sighed. H......
disposition; he had the s............. ....-beaten
face of a countryman and something of a countryman's
stoicism, but the evening always found him at a low
ebb . . .

Someone switched on a torch and swung it round in an
arc. In the unexpected, moving light, branches and tree
trunks sprang suddenly forward. The white tapes were
startlingly clear, showing the outline of a human form,
with the legs bent and one arm flung out.

Not One Of Us, *originally published in 1972, is the first in
June Thomson's extremely popular and successful series
featuring the patient and intuitive Inspector Finch.*

Also by June Thomson in Sphere Books:

SHADOW OF A DOUBT
TO MAKE A KILLING
SOUND EVIDENCE
A DYING FALL
THE DARK STREAM

Not One of Us

JUNE THOMSON

SPHERE BOOKS LIMITED

SPHERE BOOKS LTD
Published by the Penguin Group
27 Wrights Lane, London W8 5TZ, England
Viking Penguin Inc., 40 West 23rd Street, New York, New York 10010, USA
Penguin Books Australia Ltd, Ringwood, Victoria, Australia
Penguin Books Canada Ltd, 2801 John Street, Markham, Ontario, Canada L3R 1B4
Penguin Books (NZ) Ltd, 182–190 Wairau Road, Auckland 10, New Zealand

Penguin Books Ltd, Registered Offices: Harmondsworth, Middlesex, England

First published in Great Britain by Constable & Company Ltd 1972
Published by Sphere Books Ltd 1988

Copyright © June Thomson 1972
All rights reserved

Printed and bound in Great Britain by
Richard Clay Ltd, Bungay, Suffolk

Except in the United States of America,
this book is sold subject to the condition
that it shall not, by way of trade or otherwise,
be lent, re-sold, hired out, or otherwise circulated
without the publisher's prior consent in any form of
binding or cover other than that in which it is
published and without a similar condition
including this condition being imposed
on the subsequent purchaser

1

"He'll be in soon, for this," said the woman behind the counter, waving an envelope which the postman had just left in the shop. It was a plain, buff-colored envelope with the name and address typewritten.

"I'm off then," said the woman she was serving. "He gives me the creeps, he does. Just give me the marge and the large cornflakes for now and I'll come in for the rest tomorrow."

When the woman had gone Mrs. Bland, who ran the village general store, put on her glasses to examine the envelope more closely. Every Friday, for over a year, a letter had come addressed to him at her shop. She had not, at first, objected when he asked if letters might be sent care of her address. After all, he was new to the village and she liked to oblige people, especially a customer. He had taken a cottage, he explained, a mile out of the village and he wanted to be sure of getting his letters regularly. So she had agreed. There seemed no harm in it. He had not been so odd, either, in those first few weeks; a bit shabby, it was true, and not very talkative, but anyone could see he came from a good background; he was well-spoken and polite. There had been speculation about him, of course. People wondered where he had come from and why he had chosen to live in Stokes' cottage, which had been empty for two years because nobody wanted to live up that lane, half a mile from the main road with only old Stokes himself for a neighbor. They came to the conclusion that the newcomer was from London and had been ill or perhaps recently bereaved. He had the withdrawn faded look of illness or grief.

As the months passed, however, Mrs. Bland was not so sure she had made the right decision. The oddness in the man's behavior and appearance became accentuated. He grew a beard and kept his hair long, so that it touched the collar of his coat, and he became less and less talkative as the time passed. He would stand silently in the shop, looking out the window, if another customer was being served. No one could draw him into a conversation and in the end people ignored him. Some of them even avoided coming into the shop while he was there, he made them feel so uncomfortable. But, as Mrs. Bland said to them, what could she do? He only came in once a week, on a Friday morning, and she couldn't refuse to serve him. You can't turn a man away because he doesn't like talking.

"Besides," she added to her husband, who had a weak chest and sat coughing quietly all day in the hot little living room behind the shop, "I don't want to lose his custom. He spends above a pound a week in the shop sometimes and I'm not turning away trade."

She wondered about him, though, as everybody else did, and every week looked at the envelope that came for him, hoping to find out something. It was her opinion that it contained money, although he had never opened it in her presence. It was something thin and flat anyway. The postmark, when it was legible, never varied, London, SW 5, and the name and address were always typewritten: Mr. John Smith, c/o The General Store, Frayling, Essex.

Mr. John Smith, indeed!

"He must think we're a pack of fools," she muttered and in a fit of exasperation thrust the envelope into the back of the till.

It had begun raining again before he came up the road. Mrs. Bland had run to put down newspapers on the floor to save the lino from the worst of the wet and mud when she saw him coming. He was trudging along with his head bent against the downpour, the dog at his heels. She hurried to get behind the counter before he came in. For some reason that she could not explain she preferred to be isolated from him by the three feet of brown-painted deal. Behind this barrier she could smile and serve him.

He paused at the door to tell the dog to remain outside on the step. It took only one word "sit" and the dog obeyed instantly. He would have sat there forever, mild-eyed, soft-eared, his brown and black coat bedraggled by the rain, flapping his tail up and down to show his good will, but never for an instant taking his eyes off the door through which the man had gone. When Smith entered the shop Mrs. Bland felt the need to begin a conversation immediately, although she knew he would not respond.

"Good morning, Mr. Smith. What dreadful weather we're having. Nothing but rain. You were unlucky, getting caught in it. Your letter's come."

She ran the sentences together, talking to show good will.

"Yes," said Smith. He took the envelope she handed him and put it, without looking at it, into his inside pocket, handing her in exchange the shopping list he always had prepared, written in pencil in a thin, slanting hand.

She read through it, saying each item aloud as she fetched it from the shelves. She liked talking. Even when alone she kept up an interior monologue, but she was afraid of serious conversations. She left that sort of thing to her husband, who was clever with words and sometimes alarmed her with

3

the force of his opinions. You had to be so careful what you said to people in a shop. She would have hated to cause offense, so she limited herself to pleasant chat that said little and harmed nobody. And when Smith was in the shop words formed a barrier against him. She did not notice his silence if she talked, but her thoughts ran alongside her speech like the alto part of a song, deeper and more somber.

"Half a pound of cheese. It's nice and fresh, came in yesterday. Packet of dog biscuits. Isn't he good, your dog? Never a whine or a bark. Lifebuoy soap."

Well, they can't say he doesn't wash. Whatever else he may be, he keeps himself clean.

"Small brown loaf. Jar of marmalade. You like the chunky, don't you? Tin of condensed milk."

She smiled and talked and moved about the shop, walking well clear of him when she had to emerge from behind the counter. All the time she tried to keep her eyes off his face, but she was constantly aware of him; of his beard, the reddish-brown hairs of it glistening with rain; of his mouth within the beard, the lips thin, well-defined, closed in a line and yet with an upward flicker at the corner; of his ears, small for a man and close against the head with the long pieces of wet hair, as long as a woman's, brushing forward over them as he bent his head.

He kept his eyes down, intent on putting his groceries away in the plastic bag which he had taken from his pocket. He had thin hands with prominent knuckles and dry, ridged nails. Mrs. Bland saw his hands moving on the counter, gathering up the tins and packets, and she waited, unable to concentrate on adding up the bill, until he had finished, rolled up the neck of the bag and put it under his arm.

"That's one pound four and sevenpence, Mr. Smith," she said brightly, smiling the moment just before she looked up at him.

He had to put the parcel down again on the counter while he took the money from his jacket pocket. There was a crumpled pound note and two half crowns. Mrs. Bland smoothed the note out before putting it into the back of the till.

"Your fivepence change," she said, slamming the till drawer shut to make the bell ring hard enough for Mr. Bland to hear it in the back room. He liked to note the number of times it rang during the day and comment on it when she had time to go in to him. "You've had a lot in this morning, Glad." Or, "Been a bit quiet, ain't it?"

She handed Smith the change and he put it into his pocket, picked up the parcel and half turned toward the door.

"Thank you," he said. They were the only words he spoke voluntarily.

"Thank you, Mr. Smith," cried Mrs. Bland, with relief that he was going and with something of pity too for the man. God knows what kind of life he must lead, all alone in that cottage.

Outside he snapped his fingers at the dog, which stood up, its tail wagging. Mrs. Bland stayed in the shop long enough to watch them walk up the road together in the rain; the man walking slowly, the parcel under one arm, stoop-shouldered because of its awkward shape, and the dog padding along behind him, his nose an inch from the man's heels.

Well, at least he keeps himself clean, said Mrs. Bland again to herself. All the same she washed her hands thoroughly at the kitchen sink before putting on the kettle to make tea.

As soon as he was clear of the village, Smith began to walk faster and to whistle under his breath. It was so soft that it was more a musical breathing out than a recognizable

5

tune. The dog heard it, though, and sensed the feeling of relief. He broke from the man's heels and began to run forward, sniffing along the hedge and the grass verge at the side of the road. Smith walked faster after the dog, whistling louder and looking about him as he walked. He took in everything in quick, darting glances: the sky across which great banks of dark clouds were moving swiftly; the fat buds glistening on the hedges and trees; the surface of the road, polished by the rain; the dog ahead of him, thrusting its nose into the wet grass.

Farther down the road, the hedge was broken by a five-barred gate. When it came to the opening, the dog stopped and sat down on its haunches, wagging its tail with great sweeping flourishes that sent the water drops flying. It knew the man always stopped there.

Smith tumbled the dog's head and ears with his hand and then, resting the parcel on the top bar, he stood in the rain, looking out across the open country.

The fields sloped away toward a valley. It was a view of meadow and plowland, broken by the irregular lines of hedgerows and here and there the dark clump of a wood, misted over with green where the new leaves were breaking. Beyond, the fields sloped up and again on a clear day the houses on the farther slope were visible, scattered about near the line of telegraph posts that marked the road leading to the next village, Framwell. But the rain, driving across the valley, had blurred everything into a general gray, hazy background. Only the horizon showed up clearly with a line of bright, almost liquid, light running along it where the clouds were dispersing.

When he had looked his fill Smith picked up his parcel. There was no need to whistle the dog, which had anticipated his going and was already trotting along the road ahead with its ears pricked up. They were going home.

Halfway down the hill a lane turned off to the left. Smith and the dog turned along it. It had been tarred at one time but the surface was now broken up and deeply rutted. On each side high hedges shut out the fields. They passed a farmhouse, set sideways on to the lane, its brickwork darkened by the rain. The gate to the yard was set open and from somewhere in the yard a dog set up a fierce barking as they went by. Smith's dog kept close to his heels until they had passed and then ran on again.

Farther on they came to another gate; a small one made of wooden palings which were stained greeny-brown between the patches of old white paint. Smith shoved it open and went up the short path to the front door of the cottage. The door needed a good push, too, to get it open, because it had dropped on its hinges.

Inside the cottage the air was damp and musty. There was the smell of old plaster and wood which was always strong on a wet day when the cottage had been closed up for a time. Smith set the door open, propping it back with a large stone that stood ready for this purpose on the doorstep. The dog ran in ahead of him and sat down on a sack which was spread out on the floor by the empty fireplace.

The cottage had been built for farm laborers and their families. It was a simple, basic construction; two rooms downstairs and two up, with a tiny windowless lobby between the downstairs rooms from which a narrow, steep staircase led upward. Smith never used the bedrooms. The roof leaked and big pieces of plaster had fallen from the ceilings. Buckets and pails stood about in both rooms on the bare wooden floors to catch the water as it dripped through. Smith occupied the two downstairs rooms only: the living room, into which the front door opened directly, and the kitchen, beyond the little lobby. The living room also served him as a bedroom. It was sparsely furnished with a camp bed, a deal table which stood under the window, with an oil lamp standing on it, a folding wooden chair of the kind used in public halls, and a deck chair which was drawn up to the fireplace. The kitchen was even more simply furnished. There was an old shallow brown stone sink with a single cold water tap over it, a two-burner oil stove, and a long wooden shelf which contained food and cooking utensils. Beside the stove stood a marble-topped wash-hand stand on which Smith prepared food and there was an old-fashioned boiler built into one corner near the back door, made of bricks with a little firedoor at the base of it and a big round wooden cover over the top.

Both rooms had bare stone floors and two windows, one in the front wall facing the high hawthorn hedge that screened the cottage from the lane, the other overlooking a narrow back area, paved with bricks, which contained a privy of creosoted wood, and beyond that the fields, the same fields that Smith had looked across from the gateway outside the village.

Smith took the parcel of groceries into the kitchen and came back into the living room with a piece of old, rough towel. He began to dry the dog's coat. The dog was sitting on the sacking shivering, partly from cold, partly from excitement at being home again. The task was a routine it knew and it lifted each paw in turn for Smith to dry, wagging its tail all the time. Smith knelt on the sack, absorbed in the task, his wet beard and hair, rough and springy, close to the dog's fine silky fur.

When the dog was dry Smith went back into the kitchen to fetch wood and paper from a cardboard box under the sink. He crouched down to light the fire and remained there for several minutes, watching the little bright flames threading through the tent of twigs he had made. The smoke whirled and then was sucked upward and the burning wood spat and crackled. The dog sat beside him, so close that its head was almost under his arm, and after a moment Smith put his arm round the dog's neck. They sat together like this until the twigs were well alight and then Smith leaned over to get the logs which were stacked to dry in a corner of the hearth. There were only a few left. The woodpile behind the privy was, Smith knew, also getting low.

"We'll go wooding this afternoon, Cairn," said Smith to the dog, which wagged its tail in response and stretched itself out, with a grunt of satisfaction, in front of the fire which was now blazing up and filling the room with the smell of warm wood smoke.

Smith changed his wet clothes next, taking clean trousers and shirt from a large leather suitcase which was kept under the camp bed. He rough-dried his hair and then went through to the kitchen to prepare a meal for himself. All his movements as he cut bread, buttered it, and sliced up cheese were precise and deft. He had an easy way of using his long, thin hands. The expression on his face as he performed any task—drying the dog's coat, lighting the fire, cutting up bread—was one of complete absorption and peace. The odd upward quirk at the corner of his mouth deepened as he carried the plate through to the living room and saw the dog stretched out before the fire, the dark mouth of the fireplace opening now bright with flames. The rain still fell outside and bright drops slid off the dark twigs and little budding leaves on the hawthorn hedge just beyond the window. As he ate Smith kept glancing out at the rain and then back to the fire.

When he had finished eating he took the plate into the kitchen and washed it, then came back into the living room and sat down in the deck chair by the fire, stretching out his legs and giving a deep sigh of satisfaction as the dog had done. He read for a while from one of the books that were piled up on the high mantelshelf above the fireplace.

It was the dog that stirred first. It grunted, roused itself, and got up, stretching, and came to sit by the man's side, looking up into his face with bright, expectant eyes. Smith smiled and put down the book.

"All right," he said. "We'll go out. We'll go to the wood but first I must go to the farm."

He spoke to the dog as one might speak to a child who has not yet any knowledge of the meaning of words, only of the inflections and tones of the voices. Smith's voice rose on the word "wood," fell again on the word "farm." The dog watched the man's face closely and responded to the voice, its ears sharpening and then drooping again.

Smith bent and patted its head sympathetically.

"I know," he said. "But we must go to the farm. I have to pay the rent."

He took from his inside pocket the envelope that Mrs. Bland had given him and flapped it gently across the dog's ears.

"The rent, Cairn. The rent has to be paid."

At the sound of its name the dog began to wag its tail vigorously and to paw at Smith's legs.

"Wait!" he said, laughing. "I must get it ready first. Down, Cairn. Sit!"

Cairn sat at once, its head on one side, watching what the man was doing. First, he opened the envelope and took out the money it contained, three pound notes and two ten-shilling notes. There was nothing else in the envelope, no letter, only the money. One of the ten-shilling notes he replaced in the envelope, putting the rest of the money in the back of the book he was reading and replacing it on the mantelshelf. From the shelf he took a cocoa tin, into which he put the change he had received that morning at the shop,

10

extracting from it two half crowns which were placed in the envelope with the ten-shilling note. He crossed out his own name on the envelope and wrote on it in pencil, "Mr. Stokes. Rent. 15/-."

The fire had burned down to a glowing heap of small wood and ashes. He raked it over carefully, scattering the embers so that they would die out, and then, taking his brown plastic raincoat which had been hanging to dry on the back of the door, he thrust the envelope into one pocket and set off down the lane again, with Cairn running ahead eagerly.

The wind had dropped and the rain had eased to a fine drizzle. There was a luminosity in the sky, the veiled light of the sun behind thin clouds, which gave a clarity to everything. The rain-soaked trunks and branches of the trees stood out very dark, the wet leaves and grass were sharply green. Water drops hanging from every twig and blade held, suspended and trembling, globules of brightness and the puddles in the ruts of the lane reflected the luster of the sky.

Smith walked briskly toward the farm. As they approached it, Cairn slunk back to his heels, anticipating the farm dog's outcry.

"Wait," said Smith when they reached the gate. "Sit."

He went into the farmyard alone. The house and buildings surrounding the yard had the appearance of neglect. There was a sagging barn with broken wheels and pieces of rusty farm implements piled up against the wall. The farm dog, barking itself into a frenzy, leaped and choked at the end of its chain.

Smith was about to push the envelope through the letter box in the front door when the farmer, Stokes, a short man with broad shoulders and a bad-tempered face, came stumping across the yard from one of the outbuildings.

"Bugger you, shut up!" he shouted to the dog. "Brought the rent?" he asked of Smith.

"It's here," said Smith, handing him the envelope which Stokes stuffed into his pocket. Neither man said any more, Stokes going on toward the back of the house and Smith turning to walk back toward the lane.

"I'll get that bloody roof of yourn fixed one of these days!" shouted Stokes as Smith reached the gate. It was a promise he made every time Smith came and it was raining. Neither of them believed it, but Smith acknowledged it with a wave of his hand all the same. With Cairn running free again in front of him he went on a little farther where there was a break in the hedge and, scrambling through it, they set off across the fields toward the wood.

The sun had cleared the clouds and was shining in a pale dazzle. A man was plowing the field beside the wood, the tractor garishly orange against the shimmer and iridescence of the trees. The bright plowshare, caught by the sun, bit into the earth and turned it, as rich and as moist as fruitcake. Suddenly exuberant, Smith laughed out loud and threw sticks for the dog, which leaped and ran and barked, filled also with sudden joy.

2

The body of the dead girl was found in the wood on the following Monday by the driver of the tractor, Reg Meyrick. He was plowing in the field beside the wood, work which had been constantly delayed throughout the early spring because of the wet weather. That Monday morning was sunny at first but at about quarter past twelve great black clouds began to gather over the village. Then they broke and came sweeping across the sky, driven by a rising wind, the rain streaming from them in a dark curtain.

Meyrick saw it coming and, abandoning the tractor, grabbed up the haversack containing his sandwiches, and ran before the storm for the shelter of the trees.

He broke through the hedge at the center of the wood, jumping the ditch and scrambling up the bank that lay on the other side. The wood here was open, with large trees standing solitary in grassy spaces. The leaves were only beginning to break so there would be little shelter from overhead but it would be better there than in the open field. There was a large oak tree with a massive trunk and thick twisted roots that grasped the ground like hands. Meyrick squatted down in the hollow between the roots on the lee side of the tree, opened his haversack and began to eat the sandwiches his wife had prepared for him. As he chewed he looked about him. Facing him was a wide, grass-grown

13

bridle way that ran through the center of the wood, emerging at the one end of it into a stony track known as Romans Way, which in turn led past Leverett's farm where he was employed. On the far side of the bridle path the large, widely spaced trees gave place to a thicket of birch saplings and hazel bushes where the timber had been felled some years before.

As the rain fell, broken and scattered by the branches and twigs overhead, it formed a misty fume of water that blurred the farther view. All the same, Meyrick's attention was caught by a patch of red which stood out even through the rain vapor and the tangled twigs of the bushes in the thicket. As there was nothing else to look at, he studied it, chewing thoughtfully. It was too large an area of color to be merely a piece of paper. It could have been the clothing of a courting couple, lying there under the bushes, only it did not move and Meyrick thought it unlikely that anyone would be daft enough to go courting in a downpour of rain. He decided finally that it was probably a bundle of rags which might be worth having a look at when the rain stopped. Ever since he had found in a ditch a perfectly good piece of wire netting, big enough to mend the front of his ferrets' cage, he had taken a hopeful interest in other people's rubbish.

The storm blew over at last and Meyrick stood up, easing his aching back and knees which were stiff from squatting for so long. Slinging his haversack over one shoulder, he walked across the bridle path to the thicket and, using his boot, crashed an opening in the intertangled twigs and thin branches, holding back those above with his right arm.

What was lying beyond, huddled in a little clearing between the bushes, he saw and yet did not see. His eyes took in, in a single, horrified glance, a red coat, a twisted leg spattered with earth and dead leaves, a mass of tumbled brown hair, and a face, purple and swollen with pulpy lips and open eyes.

Meyrick was never able to remember the next few seconds. He must have backed away and begun to run. But he only became aware of running when he reached the end of the bridle path where it emerged from the wood and where his boots began to slide on the wet pebbles of the lane leading to the farm. He slowed down to a jog trot, his haversack bumping on his back and his breath rasping painfully in his chest. Slithering and clattering on the stones, he reached the gate which opened into the farmyard. His bicycle was there, propped up against the barn wall. There was a telephone at the farm but it did not cross his mind to make use of it. He had never used a telephone in his life. The only thought that occurred to him was to get up to the village and tell Bob Russell, the local policeman, what he had seen. Mounting his bicycle, he rode out of the gate, down the short length of lane and, turning right at the bottom, pedaled off up the road toward the village.

The policeman's house was the last in a row of council houses, all identical, with drab, pebble-dashed walls and flat windows with metal frames. The police house differed from the others only in the blue globe over the front door, the police notice board by the gate, and a single-story addition on the side of the house, which was Russell's office.

Leaving his bicycle at the gate, Meyrick went round to the back of the house and knocked on the kitchen door. Mrs. Russell opened it. She was a pretty, fair-haired woman whose looks were already beginning to fade. When she came to the door she was carrying a child, straddle-legged, across one hip.

Meyrick said, "I want to see Mr. Russell."

The child began to whimper and she jogged it up and down on her hip.

"Is it important?" she asked. "I've just dished up his dinner."

Russell himself appeared behind her, wiping his mouth. He was in his shirt sleeves with his collar undone.

"Anything up, Mr. Meyrick?" he said.

"There's a girl in the wood," said Meyrick. "She's dead."

"Dead?" said Russell. He seemed about to ask something. His eyebrows went up and his mouth opened interrogatively. Then he changed his mind and said quickly, "Come inside."

Meyrick followed him into the living room. The table was set for a meal with Russell's dinner served out on a plate.

"I'll put it in the oven," said his wife, and she returned to the kitchen with the plate, still carrying the child on her hip.

Another door led into the office. Russell opened it and motioned Meyrick inside, slipping his arms into his uniform jacket that had been hanging on the back of his chair.

The office was tiny. There was a desk, its surface cluttered with papers, and a board on the wall with official notices pinned to it.

"Sit down," said Russell. There was only one chair, drawn up to the desk and he had brought one of the dining-room chairs for Meyrick to sit on. Meyrick sat down awkwardly.

"Tell me about it," said Russell, seating himself at the desk.

Meyrick could not think how to put into words what he had seen. He knew Bob Russell well; he had seen him often about the village; the two men had exchanged pleasantries about the weather, their gardens, village affairs. It was Russell who had come immediately to Meyrick's mind as the person to tell about the dead girl. But the little, cluttered

16

office, the notices on the wall, the signs of officialdom silenced him. He was aware, suddenly, of the law that Russell represented. He was no longer just an affable, red-faced young man in a blue uniform.

Also, Meyrick had only a confused image in his mind of what he had actually seen. On his way up to the village he had made no effort to clarify that image, one of hair, swollen lips, sprawled legs, staring eyes. Indeed, he had deliberately concentrated all his attention on riding as fast as he could, putting out of his mind the reason for his haste. The dead girl's image had become lost in the need to pedal hard, in the urgency of driving the wheels forward and getting to Russell's house. Now he was there he found that he could not easily say why he had come.

Russell was looking at him. "What did you see, Mr. Meyrick?" he was asking.

Meyrick said slowly, "I found this girl. She were dead."

By patient questioning Russell managed to draw the facts out of him; where he had discovered the body; whether she was known to him; at what time this had occurred. He wrote briefly on a piece of paper. Then he said:

"I'll be telephoning the police at Wrexford. They'll know what to do. If they need to contact you, where will you be?"

"I'm going home," said Meyrick. A thought suddenly occurred to him. "I ain't told Mr. Collins at the farm. I just come straight here. And the tractor's still in the field."

"We'll get in touch with him," said Russell kindly. He felt sorry for the man. He was shocked and the effort of telling about the body had affected him. He sat inert, heavy, like a sack, slumped forward in his chair.

"You go on home," he said, "and have a bit of a lie-down."

Meyrick got to his feet.

"I expect they'll find the body all right," Russell continued, "without having to ask you to show them where."

"I ain't going back there," Meyrick said, with an unexpected flash of spirit. "Not for you nor nobody else."

He set his jaw stubbornly. Russell said soothingly, "There'll be no need, I'm sure."

He took Meyrick to the back door. Mrs. Russell was in the kitchen, setting out cups on the draining board. The child wailed in a high chair.

"He's teething," said Mrs. Russell apologetically. "Are you going? I was just making tea."

Russell said, "I think Mr. Meyrick would like to get home. He's had a bit of a shock."

She gave Meyrick a look of quick sympathy, dashing a piece of hair out of her eyes. But the kettle was boiling, the child was crying, and she turned away.

Meyrick went round to the gate, collected his bicycle, and pushed it across the road to his house opposite, a clapboard cottage, one of a pair, with a front door that was never used and a long path that led from the gate to the back of the house and a range of outbuildings: washhouse, privy and coal shed, where his cage of ferrets stood against the end wall. Leaving his bike just inside the gate, propped up against the hedge, he walked heavily down the path to the back door. As he passed the living-room window, a dark form bobbed up behind the net curtains. It was his wife who was at the back door and had it open before he reached it. She had taken out her teeth and had been sitting down, resting and reading the *Daily Mirror* after dinner and she was not pleased to see him.

"What are you doing home at this time?" she cried accusingly.

He did not answer but pushed past her through the kitchen. There were dirty plates on the draining board and a smell of mutton stew hung about the house.

18

Meyrick sat down in the armchair by the living-room fire and began to unlace his boots. His wife, who had found her teeth and put them in with a snap, stood over him with her fists on her hips. She was a thin woman with a hard jaw.

"What's up then?" she asked. "You ill or something?"

A sudden thought came to her.

"Here, you haven't got the sack, have you?"

Meyrick eased off one boot and held his foot between the palms of his hands, massaging it gently.

"I been to the police," he said. "I found this girl in the wood. So I went to see Bob Russell. I had to leave the tractor."

"What girl?" asked his wife.

"I dunno," he said. "I didn't look at her more than half a second. But she were dead all right. I could tell that. Russell said he'd ring the police at Wrexford."

He took off his other boot and looked shyly up at his wife. She did not know how to take the news or what to say. Her jaw moved once or twice as if she were chewing slowly.

"It fair turned my stomach," Meyrick said, after a moment's silence. He offered the remark as a kind of appeasement between them. "I could do with a cup of tea."

His wife went through to the kitchen and began clattering about.

"You'd best stay home the rest of the day," she called out through the open door. There was the sound of a saucepan lid being lifted. "Do you want your dinner, now? I could warm it up."

She came to the doorway, holding the saucepan. The smell of the stew was very strong.

"I couldn't face it," he said. "A cup of tea'll do me."

"What about them sandwiches?" she asked sharply. "You didn't leave them?"

"No, I ate them. It was when the storm come over. I took them into the wood and stood behind a tree."

The wood and the dead girl it contained silenced them both. Mrs. Meyrick poured a cup of tea from the pot that she had made for herself just before her husband's return. It was still hot but stewed and she put in an extra spoonful of sugar to take away the bitterness. Nudging her husband's shoulder with one hand, she passed him the teacup. He gulped the tea down, ducking his head away from her. She drew one of the straight-backed chairs from the table and sat down, folding her arms on the chenille cloth.

"That girl," she said. "Did you know her? Was it anyone local?"

"No," he said. "Leastways, I don't think so. I only took a quick look." He paused and then added slowly, "She were strangled."

"Strangled! Are you sure?"

"I think so. She had marks . . ." He put one hand up to his own throat. The teacup rattled in its saucer in his other hand.

"Did you tell that to Bob Russell?"

"No. I've only just remembered it."

The memory of the girl's face had returned indeed vividly, with the swollen, discolored lips and the dark bruising on the throat.

"I'd biked all the way up from the farm," he said, by way of explanation. "It'd come as a shock, finding her. I couldn't think straight. D'you think I ought to over and tell him?" he added, in a panic.

"No," she said. "You stay where you are. They'll see for themselves soon enough."

Her jaw chewed rhythmically again, then she said, "If she were strangled, it'll be murder."

He looked up startled. The thought had not occurred to him, but he did not answer and turned away his head to gulp down the rest of the tea. Wiping his mouth with his hand, he passed the empty cup to her. She took it and then got up with sudden resolution.

"I'm going through to see," she announced.

He knew where she was going; into the front room that was hardly ever used. Its window looked out into the road and one could watch, from behind the thick lace curtains, the comings and goings of the village without being seen. She had watched weddings and funerals from this vantage point; chimney fire in one of the council houses opposite and the Sunday afternoon incident that was never referred to but had never been forgotten when Mrs. Dawson had turned her future daughter-in-law out of number 16 and had come to the gate to shout "bloody whore" after her. But her son had married the girl, after all, in the registry office at Wrexford and they had never been seen in the village again.

Meyrick could hear his wife moving the little round table that stood in front of the window in order to get a better view. Presently she came back into the living room, rubbing her forearms with her hands, to get a cardigan.

"It's like an icehole in there," she said.

When she went back, he got his tobacco tin out of his jacket pocket and rolled himself a cigarette. He sat smoking and watching the small fire that burned in the range, the door of which was let down so that the fire was visible behind the bars. It burned sluggishly, choked with dust at the bottom, and he took the poker and with the tip eased the ashes away. Despite his care, the coals fell, showering dust into the hearth. The coal bucket was empty and he lacked the energy or the interest to go outside to the coal shed to fill it.

After ten minutes his wife returned.

"There's been a couple of cars go through," she said. "Big cars, like police cars. They'll be from Chelmsford."

21

She noticed the fire and added sharply, "You've been poking that fire about."

"It was full of ash," he explained.

"Shift yourself," she said, leaning angrily over him to get the coal bucket. "The fire'll be out before you'd lift a finger. And there's the washing-up not done either. They'll be round any minute, I shouldn't wonder."

"Who will?" he asked, surprised.

"The police of course; asking questions. You found her, didn't you? Stand to reason they'll want to ask about it."

He had thought his part of the case finished when he had seen Bob Russell. He had told his story once and that, he imagined, would have been the end of it. The thought of telling it again, to strangers, to policemen from Chelmsford, frightened him.

"I can't tell them nothing much," he said stubbornly.

"All the same . . ." She left the sentence unfinished and went out to fill the coal bucket, leaving him sitting, brooding, by the fire. Bringing it back full, she banged it down by his side on the hearthrug.

"You can make that fire up," she said. "I'm washing up and then I'm off, down the shop."

While she washed up in the kitchen, he got up slowly and moved the kettle over from the hob and, lifting out the center ring, began to drop pieces of coal into the fire. It looked dead and he opened the damper in the chimney pipe to get a draft through it. Then he sat down again and stared at the coal through the fire bars.

Mrs. Meyrick came in to clear the cups and the teapot. She shook the tablecloth into the hearth, folded it and put it away in the drawer in the table, moved a vase of plastic daffodils from the top of the sewing machine to the center of the table, and then, shoving her husband with her elbow to make him move back, bent down to sweep up the hearth.

22

"There!" she said. She sounded satisfied. All was tidy. Let them come. She was ready for them. Taking down her coat from the hook on the back of the door, she put it on, buttoning it up to the neck so that no one should see she was still wearing her overall. She felt for her purse in her pocket. "I'm off down the shop, then," she said. "I need a quarter of tea, anyway. If they come when I'm out, I shan't be long."

She would find out what they were saying in the shop. She might even be the first with the news. It would be something worth telling and the shop would be busy at that time in the afternoon, with women coming in to collect their bread before the children came home from school. She liked an audience and she began to rehearse in her mind how she would tell the news.

"A quarter of tea," she would say. "I'm running a bit low and I'll be needing a fair bit, I shouldn't wonder, with the police coming round."

"Police?" they would say, not quite knowing how to take it.

She smiled grimly to herself as she looked in her purse. She had half a crown which would be enough.

"Yes," she would reply. "Haven't you heard, then?"

"No," they would answer. "What's up?"

"Well," she would say, "I'm not sure I ought to be telling you, but it's bound to come out sooner or later. Well, Reg went into the wood, back of the farm, when that storm come over and he found this girl lying in the bushes. Strangled she were. He come straight up to tell Bob Russell. I'm surprised you didn't see the police cars go past. Two of them from Chelmsford, I would reckon."

"Where was she, by the way?" she asked her husband offhandedly.

He looked up.

"Alongside the bridle path, in the bushes. She had a red coat on, that's how I spotted her."

He spoke reluctantly and then said in a sudden burst of anguish, "They won't think it's me as did it?"

His wife looked at him with genuine astonishment.

"You!" she said. "Don't be daft!"

"They might," he said.

"I'll soon settle them if they do," said his wife. She looked as if she meant it. Meyrick avoided her eyes. He hated rows and there had been several in the past, with people in the village. He could not see the point of them. He liked a quiet life and when his wife got into one of her moods there was no peace.

"Don't forget that damper's open," she added, going to the door. "You remember to close it or the fire'll be roaring up the chimney, once it catches."

The back door slammed behind her and her footsteps went clicking purposefully up the concrete path at the side of the house.

Meyrick sank back into his chair and watched the fire burn up. He thought miserably of the police coming and what he would say to them and he thought, too, of how his wife would go on and on about the dead girl, giving him no peace. Murder, she had said. He supposed it must be. He shivered slightly and drew his chair nearer to the fire. He did not want to think about it. He did not want to talk about it again, but he would have to and he knew that between them, the police and his wife, they would drag out of him every detail, force him to go over it all, again and again, until forgetting it would be an effort and remembering it too easy.

3

Inspector Finch stood with his hands in his pockets, gloomily watching the various activities of the policemen and detectives in Leverett's wood. There seemed very little more to be done for the moment. The photographers had finished their work and had gone away. The police surgeon had made a preliminary examination and had also left. The ambulance had lurched up the lane and the body, decently covered, had been carried to it on a stretcher and been driven away to the mortuary. Sergeant Boyce had been sent to make inquiries at the farm at the end of the lane. The stooping figures of the policemen were searching the undergrowth and the ditch for anything that might be helpful, with special instructions to try to find the girl's shoes, which were missing.

The light was fading fast. The white tapes which marked out the position of the body under the hazel scrub glimmered faintly in the gathering dusk. The abandoned tractor in the field beyond showed as a vague red shape, whose color and outline were losing their intensity. It would soon be useless to continue the search which, in any case, had produced nothing of value to the investigation.

The Inspector sighed. He was usually a man of cheerful disposition; he had the stocky figure and weather-beaten face of a countryman and something of a countryman's stoicism, but the evening always found him at a low ebb, both emotionally and physically, and he had, moreover, an intense dislike of woods, especially at dusk, when the crowded branches and sense of secret, hidden life seemed to him both melancholy and sinister.

Someone switched on a torch and swung it round in an arc. In the unexpected, moving light, branches and tree trunks sprang suddenly forward. The white tapes were startlingly clear, showing the outline of a human form, with the legs bent and one arm flung out.

She had been young, about sixteen, with thick, brown hair and a red coat and someone had choked the life out of her.

Finch walked forward, stamping his feet to get the blood moving again. Boyce had just returned. Finch could hear him cursing as he stumbled over a root.

"Any luck at the farm?" he asked.

Boyce and Finch had built up a good working relationship between them. The sergeant, a big, burly man with a deep voice, understood Finch's way of working. He rarely needed to be given detailed instructions.

"None," he replied. "They were watching television on Sunday evening and the sitting room's at the far end of the house. There is a dog that's kept in the yard but it doesn't usually bark unless someone actually comes into the yard. They said they didn't hear anything."

"No line on the girl either?"

"Blank there too. I described her fully but they didn't seem to know her. Neither of them wanted to come to the mortuary. They're knocking on a bit . . ."

"Leave it, then," said Finch. "Somebody'll miss her sooner or later, I hope. But we can try them with a photograph tomorrow. We'll pack this lot in for the night too," he added, indicating the searchers. "We'll start again in the morning. You'd better organize a guard, though, or we'll have half the locals traipsing about here, gawping. I'm going up to the village if you want me."

Leaving Boyce to arrange these matters, Finch beckoned to Russell and walked with him down the bridle path toward the lane.

"I want to talk to the man who found the body. Where can I find him?"

Russell was full of quick information. After all, it was his area and he knew the people.

"Meyrick, sir, the tractor driver. He lives in the end one of a pair of clapboard cottages, left-hand side of the road as you enter the village, opposite the council houses."

"What's he like?" asked Finch.

Russell thought seriously, puckering up his forehead.

"Very quiet type of man, sir. Keeps himself to himself. Married. No children. His wife's got a bit of a reputation."

Finch paused with his hand on the door handle of his car.

"What do you mean, reputation?"

"Well, a bit sharp-tongued, like. Doesn't say much generally, but when she does she can let fly. People in the village don't care to get on the wrong side of her."

"Thanks for the warning," said Finch, getting into the car. "I'll watch out for her."

He drove off down the lane, leaving Russell wondering whether he had been ironic or serious.

As he turned the car into the road, Finch noticed the cluster of youths on bicycles, circling slowly round and round. They had been there all afternoon, like vultures at the scene of the killing. He blew his horn savagely at them and they scattered as he drove up the road.

He had no knowledge yet of the countryside. He passed, without knowing it, the lane that led to Smith's cottage. Half a mile farther the scattered lights of the village appeared and he slowed down and looked out for somewhere to park the car. There was a wide grass verge on the outskirts of the village and he drove onto it and walked the rest of the way.

The dusk was deepening rapidly. The windows in the row of council houses were all lit up. Some with their curtains still undrawn presented glimpses of interior life; a family having tea at a table; a woman stretching up to hang clothes on an airer over the living-room fire.

The front windows of both the cottages were dark, however, but Finch, who understood the pattern of life in these small, old-fashioned houses, did not doubt that there would be someone at home. There would be a back room where all the living was done. He had himself been brought up in a cottage like this and it was a familiar action to fumble at the wicket gate for the latch and to walk up the path to the back door.

Mrs. Meyrick opened the door to him and showed him silently into the living room, where Meyrick still sat, where he had sat all afternoon, in the armchair by the fire, his boots on the fender beside him.

"Here's the police," she announced with an odd note of triumph in her voice. She was angry with her husband, who sat there, sunk in obstinate apathy, not bothering to shift himself.

"You'd best sit down," she added to Finch, indicating the other armchair by the fireside. She herself sat down at the table, facing them on one of the straight-backed chairs, her arms folded on the dark-red chenille cloth, like someone presiding at a meeting. Her jaw worked ominously.

Finch, who was aware of the tension, nonetheless sat down with equanimity, folding the skirts of his raincoat over his knees. He felt quite at home. The cottage, with its high, cluttered mantelshelf, the kitchen range with the door

28

let down and gray ash spilling out between the bars, the pot holder hanging on a nail, the treadle sewing machine under the window, reminded him of his own childhood home. He had done his homework at a round table like the one at which Mrs. Meyrick was sitting and had carried the same kind of heavy coal bucket into the backyard to fetch coal for his mother.

There had been tension, too, especially for a clever boy who, at an early age, had realized the limitations of such a world. But in his case it had been his father who had been sharp-tongued and frequently heavy-handed. His mother had been the one who withdrew, with folded lips, into silence.

Finch looked at Meyrick. The man, he guessed, was in his late forties and was not bad-looking in a mournful, long-featured way. At the moment, though, his expression was sullen and Finch realized the discovery of the body had shocked him deeply.

"It's a bad business," said Finch.

"Ah," replied Meyrick, not lifting his eyes.

"It must have come as a shock, finding her."

"Ah. It were."

"Can you tell me about it?" asked Finch.

"She were there," said Meyrick, adding as an after-thought, "lying in the bushes."

"Have you any idea what time this was?"

Meyrick rolled his eyes toward his wife, who said snappishly, "It must have been close on half past twelve. He said he went into the wood when that storm come on and he found her after. Well, the storm let up by just on half past twelve."

"What made you notice the body?" asked Finch.

"It were that red coat she had on," answered Mrs. Meyrick.

Finch turned to Meyrick, leaning deliberately forward to fix the man's attention.

"What did you do after you found the body?"

"I fetched my bike and came up to the village and told Bob Russell."

"You didn't touch the body?"

The effect of the question was startling. Meyrick flung himself forward in the chair, his eyes staring, his face suffused with blood.

"No, I bloody didn't! I didn't lay a finger on her! And anybody as says I did's a bloody liar! I ain't ever seen her in my life before."

"No one's suggesting you killed her," said Finch calmly, although he had been taken back by the outburst. "I only asked if you touched the body, moved it or turned it over."

"No," said Meyrick, lapsing back in his chair and resuming the sullen expression. "I never touched it."

Mrs. Meyrick got up from the table and came between them to fetch the teapot from the hob, but also, Finch guessed, to divert his attention from her husband.

"I'll make some tea," she said. Her profile was inscrutable.

She took the teapot into the kitchen and Finch heard her emptying it into the slop pail under the sink. She returned to pour water from the kettle which she had set to boil over the stove. Stooping between the two men, her eyes intent on her task, she said to her husband, "Tell him about that man."

"What man?" asked Finch.

"You tell him," she repeated and carried the kettle out to the kitchen where she began filling it at the tap.

"What man?" asked Finch again.

Meyrick shifted uncomfortably. He had spent a miserable two hours when his wife had returned from the shop, going over and over unwillingly the circumstances of his discovery of the body. He had let slip the fact that he had seen Smith go into the wood a few days before and he had not liked the way his wife had pounced on this piece of information. He knew and feared her capacity for making trouble.

"Ain't much to tell," he said, "It'd be last Friday. I was plowing the same field and I saw this man go into the wood, about the same spot as I did. The ditch ain't so wide there. You can jump it. He had a dog with him."

"What time was this?" asked Finch.

"Can't say to the minute, but it'd be round about half past two."

"Did you see him come out again?"

"No. I packed up early. It started raining again and the light was bad."

"Do you know this man?"

Mrs. Meyrick, who had entered the room again and had been silently pouring out tea, handed a cup to Finch with a bowl of sugar.

"He's called Smith," mumbled Meyrick. "I don't know much about him."

Finch spooned sugar into his tea to take away the bitter taste of the dark-brown brew.

"Smith?"

Mrs. Meyrick spoke suddenly. Her outburst had none of the unexpected vehemence of her husband's but there was a suppressed venom in her voice and a hard glitter in her eyes.

"If that's his right name, which I doubt. He's a stranger to the village. A Londoner, I should think. Looks like one of them artists, long hair and a beard. Never speaks to a soul. But he has letters. I've seen them. They come every week to the shop. Now what's a man like that doing wandering about at a wood at this time of the year? You answer me that."

Finch looked interested.

"Does he live around here?" he asked.

But Mrs. Meyrick had said her piece. She stirred her tea and would not look up.

"You ask at the shop" was all she would say. "Mrs. Bland'll tell you about him."

"Thanks," said Finch, swallowing his tea and standing up.

"I'll go and ask her."

He buttoned up his coat and then turned back to Meyrick.

"I shall have to ask you to come down to the station to put your statement into writing," he said. "I'll arrange for a car to pick you up, perhaps tomorrow."

He noticed how Mrs. Meyrick looked across quickly at her husband, who avoided her eyes.

"I'll see myself out," said Finch.

The shop was farther down the road. It was closed but a light was still burning inside and Finch could see a woman sweeping the floor. He tapped on the glass and she came to the door, putting one hand over her eyes to see past her own reflection. She was a short woman with neat gray hair, newly permed, flattened under a hairnet. Finch smiled and held up his police card. She nodded in recognition and, drawing the bolts on the door, let him in.

"You're from the police," she said. "I expect you've come about that poor girl."

"Inspector Finch," said Finch, introducing himself.

"Inspector!" Her eyes widened. "Well, we are honored. I don't know what we can do to help you but you'd best come through. Mind the dustpan. I was just having a bit of a sweep-up."

32

She led him through the shop, every shelf and flat surface of which was crowded with packets, jars, tins and boxes, to a door behind the counter which led into the living room. Finch followed her, ducking his head to avoid the hanging cards of bobby pins and erasers.

The little room behind the shop was bright and hot. A powerful bulb in a white plastic ceiling shade cast a hard brilliance into every corner of the room and glittered back from the brass ornaments and the surfaces of polished wood. A huge fire, with a red and gold brilliance of its own, roared in the fireplace.

"Take your coat off," said Mrs. Bland. "You'll be more comfortable. I have to keep a good fire going because my husband has a bad chest."

Mr. Bland was seated in a low chair with wooden arms next to the fire. He had the thin, delicate face and hollow chest of an invalid. He sat like a well-behaved child, his hands folded in his lap, his hair nicely brushed, neat and clean in a hand-knitted pullover whose pattern clashed with the cretonne cover on the chair. But his eyes were quick and bright, darting to and fro between Finch's face and his wife's. They reminded Finch of the eyes of a bird, eager, acquisitive, knowing.

"This is Inspector Finch, Harold," said Mrs. Bland. "He's come about that poor girl, although, as I said to him, I don't know what we can tell him that would be any help. Have you found out who she is yet? Oh, do sit down, Inspector. There's me chatting on and leaving you standing."

Finch sat down and Bland cocked his head inquiringly at him to remind him of Mrs. Bland's question.

"No," Finch replied. "She hasn't been identified yet."

He hesitated, wondering how to introduce Smith into the conversation. He was also curious about the Meyricks and would have liked Mrs. Bland's opinion of them. He knew a village shop is often the clearinghouse for gossip but he also knew how wary country people are of discussing each other with strangers.

"I've just been having a word with Mr. Meyrick," he said casually. "It was he who found the body but I'm afraid he couldn't tell me much."

Unexpectedly it was Bland who replied and not his wife.

"He wouldn't," he said with a little, dry laugh. "He's never been much of a talker."

Finch looked at Mrs. Bland, who said nothing, only smiled at her husband. Suddenly Finch understood the relationship. It was she who gathered the information and passed it on to her husband but it was he who cherished it, retained it, and turned it over in his mind as he sat, day after day, in that room beside the roaring fire. She was the mouthpiece; he the interpreter.

Finch turned his attention back to Bland.

"Neither of them had a lot to say," he remarked.

Bland looked knowing.

"Tight as a pair of closed fists, those two are."

Finch drew his chair nearer to Bland's with an air of mutual confiding.

"Mind you, I wouldn't like to cross her," he said.

Bland laughed again, a dry, rattling laugh that turned into a fit of coughing. Mrs. Bland jumped to her feet, but he waved her away impatiently. When the coughing fit was finished he wiped his lips carefully on a big, white handkerchief.

"Don't do for me to laugh too much," he explained. "It gets me on the chest. You're right about Mrs. Meyrick. She can be a tartar and no mistake. We've had sparks flying here in the shop before now, haven't we, Glad?"

"I don't like it," replied Mrs. Bland. "It's bad for trade. She's still not talking to Mrs. Bannister."

"Now that was a set-to," said Bland, his eyes shining at the memory of it. "I could hear them going at each other in here."

"What about Mr. Meyrick?" asked Finch. "Has he got a temper too?"

"Him?" Bland sniffed contemptuously. "He's too slow to catch a cold."

"I expect you were at school together," said Finch. "You'd know him well."

"Not me!" said Bland. "Me and Glad's from Edmonton. We set up here after the war with my army gratuity. But I know him. I may be sat here but there's not much I miss. She's the one with all the spark; he's the sullen type."

Finch reserved his judgment. Bland had not, after all, seen Meyrick earlier that evening, leaning forward in his chair, his face scarlet with rage.

There was silence for a moment. Finch wondered how he could introduce the subject of Smith. Bland was watching him with his head cocked on one side, inviting him to continue the conversation and yet there was a cautious glint in his eyes, like a wily bird's on the lookout for danger. Finch sensed he might flutter away out of reach if the wrong question were asked.

"Mrs. Meyrick said something about a man called Smith," he said in an offhand manner.

The husband and wife exchanged glances.

"Yes?" said Bland and waited.

"There's probably nothing at all in it, but Meyrick noticed a man with a dog near the wood last week," said Finch, deliberately keeping the information vague. "The Meyricks didn't seem to know much about him but I understand he comes into the shop sometimes. I wondered if you could help."

"Yes, he does come in," said Mrs. Bland slowly. She did not seem eager to speak, as if uncertain of the situation, and

35

kept looking at her husband to seek his guidance. But he had hopped out of reach and turned his eyes away from her to look at the fire, dissociating himself from the subject.

Finch relaxed into a conversational manner. It often amused his colleagues to see how his face and whole bearing could subtly change during an interview. Now, with his hands clasped loosely round one knee, his body bent slightly forward, his face interested, he became the listener and Mrs. Bland, naïve, flustered, was forced to assume the role of speaker. She felt herself impelled to continue talking.

"He comes in on a Friday morning mostly. Spends about a pound a week on groceries and the like. He's a bit odd to look at, long hair and a beard, like an artist, and he never says very much; but he's clean, I'll say that for him, and well-educated to judge by the way he speaks. He's been living in the village, well—I'd say eighteen months, wouldn't you, Harold?"

Two spots of bright color burned on her cheekbones. Bland, who had been slowly poking the fire and sending sparks spurting up the chimney, looked across at her.

"Tell him about the letters, Glad. He'll find out soon enough."

"I'm sure I've done nothing wrong!" she cried. "I only said I'd take them in here because he lives such a way down that lane and the postman'd never get down there in the winter. You have to put yourself out sometimes to oblige people."

"Of course," said Finch soothingly. "There's nothing wrong in that. When do the letters come?"

"Fridays, first post," said Bland promptly. Mrs. Bland retired from the conversation and sat, bright-eyed and trembling a little. Her husband wore the artless expression of a schoolboy who has decided to own up.

36

"Typewritten address," went on Bland. "Sent to J. Smith, care of the shop. It's one of them thin brown envelopes like they send from the Council."

This time it was Finch who cocked his head interrogatively.

"It's a London postmark," went on Bland. "SW 5. We don't know what's inside it . . ."

"We'd never dream of opening it," broke in his wife.

"But, well, we wouldn't be human if we weren't a bit nosy, would we, Inspector? I reckon it's money. It's too flat and thin for a letter."

"Does he ever open it in the shop?" asked Finch, turning to Mrs. Bland.

"No, sir. He puts them straight into his pocket. When he pays he has money on him already."

"Where does he live?"

"Taggett's Lane. That's a turning down the road, on the left, isn't it, Harold?" Mrs. Bland appealed to her husband.

He answered snappishly, as if the conversation had not gone well and he had lost the initiative.

"Always has been, as long as I've lived here. He's got Bedwell's old cottage, past Stokes' farm. It ain't much of a place. Bedwell was glad enough to get out of it and into a council house. It ought to be condemned if you ask me, but that old skinflint, Stokes, ain't likely to do anything except take the rent."

"What do you think of Smith?" asked Finch.

The question surprised Bland and then mollified him. It pleased him to think that the Inspector should ask for his opinion and he considered it carefully.

"Well, now," he said, with a knowing look, "they say it takes all sorts to make the world and I've seen a few sorts I can tell you, having been in the army. But don't it strike you as a bit odd that a man, and an educated man too, should come to a place like this and shut himself away in a cottage with no job, leastways not as far as we can tell?"

"As you said, it takes all sorts," said Finch noncommittally.

"I'll tell you something else," went on Bland, putting out his hand, for Finch had got to his feet as if to go. "He's not liked in the village. There's a good few won't come in the shop of a Friday morning when they know he's likely to be in. Isn't that so, Glad?"

Mrs. Bland nodded. She looked unhappy.

"But what can I do?" she said. "I can't refuse to serve him."

"And if he's mixed up in this girl's death . . ." began Bland, but Finch had had enough.

"There's no evidence at all against anybody at the moment," he said firmly. "I'm making routine inquiries, that's all. And I'm sure you'll do your best to stop any gossip spreading about my visit here this evening? Now I won't keep you any longer. You've both been a great help and I'm very grateful."

Mrs. Bland showed him out. At the door she hesitated and then said in a low voice, "You mustn't mind Harold too much, Inspector. He finds life a bit dull, just sitting all day long. He doesn't mean any harm, really."

Finch looked at her face, which was puckered up with distress, and smiled kindly.

"I understand."

But what he meant was that he understood her distress and her need for a few comforting words. He had no sympathy for Bland himself, although he made a mental note to talk to the man again. He could be a useful source of information, if the facts were sifted from the malicious gossip.

4

Finch walked back to the car and was unlocking the driver's door when there was the sound of bicycle wheels on the road and a man's voice called out, "Inspector Finch?"

"Yes?" he replied.

Russell, the local police constable, excited and out of breath, bumped his bicycle onto the grass verge.

"It's lucky I caught you, sir. Your sergeant sent me up to find you. A girl's just been reported missing from Framwell."

"Get in the car," said Finch. "I don't like talking police business in the open."

He opened his door, got in, and leaned across to push up the handle on the passenger's side. Russell climbed in beside him and sat, holding his helmet on his knees.

"Let me know it all. I want all the details," said Finch.

"Constable Leach, sir, came over from Framwell about three quarters of an hour ago to report this girl was missing."

"What girl?"

"He made his report to your sergeant," said Russell diffidently.

"Come on, Russell. Never mind the protocol. I know policemen gossip the same as everybody else and you know the area better than my sergeant does. Let's have the lowdown."

"She's Doreen Walker. I don't know her myself but Leach says the description fits: nearly sixteen, brown hair, average height. She works in Severall's, the drapers, in Wrexford. Her father reported her missing this evening."

"When did he see her last?"

"Yesterday, sir, Sunday, about half past two, after the midday meal."

"Yesterday!"

"Well, it seems she went to visit a friend in the village, a girl called Brenda Parsons. When she didn't come home her parents assumed she stayed there the night. She did sometimes, I understand. Then, this evening, about half past six, Brenda Parsons called at the Walker house to find out why Doreen hadn't been at work today. The two girls work in the same shop. The parents realized then that she was missing and the father called on Constable Leach to report it. As Leach had already had the report about the girl being found dead, he came straight up to Leverett's wood to find you, sir."

"Know anything about the girl?" asked Finch.

"Nothing of her, sir," replied Russell. "Leach did warn me once about the father, though. He's a bit of a local ruffian, I gather; heavy drinker, in and out of work, that type. He's had one fine for being drunk and disorderly and the Crown at Framwell had refused to serve him. So Leach rung me up to warn me, in case he turned up here, at the Wheatsheaf, but he didn't. Anyway, we had a bit of a chat about him. I think he's doing casual laboring at the moment. He's been suspected of larceny at a farm he was working at but nothing could be proved against him at the time. Anyway, they gave him the push. There's a big family, six or seven kids, and I gather Doreen was the eldest."

40

"What's Boyce done with him?" asked Finch.

"He told me to tell you that he'd sent Walker down to Wrexford police station to wait for you there, sir. He told Leach to go home."

"You cut off home too," said Finch. "Sergeant Boyce will manage without you and there's not much can be done at the wood until tomorrow."

Russell cycled off and Finch started the car and drove out of the village. He drove slowly down the hill, looking out for the turning on the left that led to Smith's cottage. What the Blands had told him about the man intrigued him. Tomorrow he would go and interview Smith. He was looking forward to it. But he had a more immediate task on hand which he was not looking forward to, the visit to the mortuary with Walker.

At the bottom of the hill he took the right-hand fork which led to the small market town of Wrexford, three miles away. It was not much of a town; a small shopping center, two garages, several pubs, a hideous brick chapel, and a fine Norman church that had been built when the place was a village and was now engulfed by houses. There was a small new building development on the outskirts of the town, little square bungalows with cherished gardens. A denser scattering of lights behind them showed where the council house estate had crept toward the fields.

It was still raining and the center of the town was almost empty of people. Nevertheless, there was a brief sparkle of animation from the street lamps and the lighted windows of the shops. As he drove through, Finch noticed Severall's, the shop where the dead girl, if it was Doreen Walker, had worked. It was a low building, obviously several small shops that had been turned into one, and the windows looked drab and unexciting, packed with merchandise which was arranged with little skill or artistry.

The police station was nearby in a side turning. It was a new building in white-painted concrete, with navy-blue tiles lining the entrance. It depressed Finch. It was too square, too new, too full of harsh white light and glossy surfaces. He pushed open the glass door and went in and the desk sergeant pointed out an interview room where Walker was waiting.

Walker was a thickset man, with a brutish, unintelligent face. He had obviously been drinking. As Finch entered the room he could smell the sour smell of beer. The floor near the chair where the man was sitting was littered with ash and cigarette stubs. Walker did not get up, and glared at Finch.

"If that's my girl Doreen they've found, I'll kill the bugger what did it with my own hands," he said as greeting. His speech was thickened.

Finch ignored the remark and said with deliberate politeness, "I'm sorry you've been kept waiting, Mr. Walker. If you'll come this way you may be able to help us with the identification."

The mortuary was down a corridor. It was a white, cold, glossy room. When the attendant turned down the sheet the dead girl's face was startlingly vivid among all that cold whiteness. Her thick, brown hair glistened; the lashes and eyebrows stood out clearly as if they had been penciled in. The livid marks on her throat had been covered with a white cloth but the bruise on her temple showed up purple against the skin.

Walker stared at her, then nodded in recognition and, turning away, began to cry. He wept awkwardly, like a young boy, his nose and eyes running, his fingers spread out across his face. The noise he made was horrible, a spluttering, retching cough. Finch was afraid he might at any moment vomit on the clean white tiles. He handed him his own handkerchief from his breast pocket, touched him on the arm, and led him back to the interview room. It was several minutes before Walker recovered sufficiently to tell a coherent story. Finch had sent out for tea for him. Brandy might have pulled him together sooner, but Finch thought brandy on top of the beer the man had already consumed was not a good idea. Walker wiped his face, blew his nose and, to Finch's relief, put the handkerchief into his own pocket. The shock of identifying his daughter had taken all the belligerency out of him. He was whining and self-pitying now, looking for sympathy.

The story he had to tell was simple and covered most of the facts that Finch had already learned from Russell. The girl left the house after the family meal on Sunday afternoon. She had gone on her bicycle to visit her friend, Brenda Parsons, in the village. When she did not come back he had not been unduly alarmed. He had gone up the road a little way on Sunday evening, looking for her, but as it was raining hard had thought she had probably stayed the night at Brenda's house and had gone to work with her on the bus in the morning. But when Brenda had called round to see why Doreen hadn't been at work that day he had realized something was wrong, and he'd gone to the village to report her missing.

Finch did not press him too far, although it seemed clear that Walker was by no means a responsible parent. He seemed vague about his daughter's friends, whom she met, what evenings she was out of the house or where she went. It was clear, too, that she stayed the night at her friend's house infrequently and Finch suspected that Walker had not been bothered to walk into the village to make inquiries about the exact whereabouts of his daughter.

"They're always gadding off, girls, these days," Walker said, by way of an excuse. "Although I'd've given her a bloody good hiding if I'd've known."

Known, presumably, Finch thought with weary contempt, that his daughter was being strangled.

He had Walker's statement drawn up and signed and arranged for a police car to take him home. He was glad to see the back of him. Tomorrow he would visit the Walker house and see the mother but he would be certain to go at a time when Walker would be away. The man left and Finch went into the office which had been assigned to him during the investigation. It was easier to make the police station at Wrexford a center of operations than to make the much longer journey to his headquarters at Chelmsford. Finch was making a tour of his new office, opening drawers, looking into the filing cabinet, finding paper and pencils preparatory to writing up a preliminary report on the case, when there was a tap at the door and the duty sergeant came in.

"I thought I'd let you know, sir, that the driver of the car that was supposed to take Mr. Walker home has radioed in. Walker asked to be dropped off at the Red Lion on the Wrexford road. Seems he hasn't finished boozing for the night."

Finch tossed the pencil and paper into the drawer of the desk.

"In that case," he said, "I'll go round to his house and see the girl's mother. I've got an hour before closing time. If Sergeant Boyce phones in, tell him where I've gone."

"I will, sir," said the sergeant.

"And I want to see a map of the area," said Finch.

The sergeant brought in an ordinance survey map and Finch spread it out on the desktop. It showed in good detail the countryside which, so far, he had seen only in the twilight. Leverett's wood was marked and the farm. So also was the turning where Smith lived. He followed the road down with his finger and took the left-hand fork, which led to Framwell, passing Leverett's wood on the left. A little farther on, a mile and a half, Finch judged, was another turning to the right, marked as Tye Lane, which was the address that Walker had given him. It was outside the village of Framwell. Finch also noticed, in his quick survey of the map, that a public footpath was marked, leading across the fields from Leverett's wood and joining the Framwell road just outside the village. The path cut a more direct route between the two places, the distance by road being, he guessed, about two miles, by the path only half a mile.

Finch folded the map up and slipped it into his raincoat pocket. "I'll keep this," he said. "I shall probably be needing it again."

Finch returned to the car and drove back through the town. His way led him past Leverett's wood and he slowed down and looked across at it. The lamps of the police cars remaining there showed up through the bare branches of the trees and hedges. Boyce was probably still there, supervising a night patrol, checking on the tarpaulin covers over the area where the girl's body had been found, searching the outbuildings of the farm. Finch could imagine him blundering about in the darkness and the rain, cursing with a monotonous regularity which took any invective out of the words. Boyce hated the countryside. He had been brought up in the back streets of Romford and he liked grass that grew in rectangles and trees that were spaced out neatly by the Council.

The dark hedges slipped past. Tree trunks stood out momentarily in the car's lights, their bark, in that flashing moment, deeply etched with shadow. Had Doreen Walker come along this road to meet her killer? It was a question to which he would have to try to find an answer although he doubted if there would be many witnesses. The road was lonely. Only now and again did a lighted square of a window shine through the darkness to indicate the presence of a house. There would not be many passersby either. People did not go out walking on a wet, cold evening.

It was just under two miles, he estimated, before he saw the turning to the right and the sign which read "Tye Lane." Slowing down, he turned the car into it. The lane was narrow but hard-surfaced. The hedges grew tall on either side so that, in the darkness, he seemed to be driving down a tunnel. Presently a lighted window appeared and he drew up outside a pair of small, brick-built cottages with slate roofs and two worn stone steps leading up to a single wooden gate that served both gardens. There was no way of telling which was the Walker house. When giving his address, Walker had simply said, "Tye Cottages, Tye Lane." Getting a torch from the car, Finch went up the steps and flashed the light over the gardens. On one side he could see, under the moving light, orderly ridges of well-dug earth. Swinging his torch in the other direction he saw an old enamel bucket lying on its side, an overflowing dustbin, trampled grass. Washing dangled in the rain on an improvised line slung between two trees.

"Walker's house," he said to himself and tramped up the path to the back door.

A woman opened it to him. She was a thin, hollow-faced woman, with a high, shiny forehead. There was a dark mark like a bruise on one cheek, and Finch wondered if Walker often knocked her about. She had the dulled, apathetic look of a woman who is under constant physical fear.

"Mrs. Walker?" said Finch pleasantly.

"Yes," she said flatly.

"I'm Inspector Finch. May I come in?"

She opened the door a fraction and he stepped into the kitchen.

"You've come about Doreen," she said. "It was her they found in the woods."

"I'm afraid so," said Finch. He moved his shoulders uncomfortably. He hated this part of his job, bringing news of a death to relatives. "Your husband identified her earlier this evening."

"I knew it must be her," Mrs. Walker went on. "I thought something must have happened to her yesterday. I wanted him to go out looking for her."

Her hand wandered up to the bruise and Finch guessed that was when she must have received it.

"Is he with you?" she asked, meaning her husband. She looked past Finch toward the door and he replied embarrassed:

"No, but he shouldn't be long."

"He's down the pub then," Mrs. Walker said, without any rancor. She seemed to accept this as a fact of her life, as she seemed to accept her daughter's death, unemotionally. Or perhaps she had already mourned for her in her own way. Her eyes were red-rimmed and her mouth trembled a little as she spoke.

"I'd like to ask you a few questions," said Finch, "but, if you would prefer it, I could come back another day."

"I don't mind," she replied. "You can come in now, if you want. I can't tell you much, though. Doreen was never a one for saying what she was up to."

She led him into the living room. It was untidy and squalid. Nappies were steaming on a string above the fire. There were clothes and newspapers on the chairs. At the table, still spread with a soiled cloth and dirty dishes, two small children were sitting eating bread and looking at him with round, unblinking eyes. An older boy was sprawled on

47

a shabby sofa under the window, reading a comic. A pram stood in the angle between the sideboard and the wall, with its back to the light, and a girl who sat beside it on a chair, her feet hooked over the bar, her knees spread out, was rocking it up and down negligently with her elbow. Out of the circle of faces, hers was the only one that showed any animation. Finch's gaze rested on it and registered it. It was a pert face, knowing, bold, and the girl had, in her thick brown hair and full lips, a marked resemblance to the dead girl, her sister. She gave him a grin and Finch looked quickly away, wondering if Doreen had smiled like that, with the same suggestive lowering of the eyelids. Death had refined Doreen. She had looked young, innocent. This girl, Finch guessed, was about thirteen and yet her smile was already full of sexual significance.

He cleared his throat and turned to the mother.

"Your husband has already made a statement about your daughter's movements yesterday. I gather she left home after lunch?"

"That's right." It was the girl who answered. "She went up the village to do Brenda's hair. Brenda said she'd give her four bob to do it, but she didn't go every week."

Mrs. Walker had sat down at the table and was looking down at the cloth, picking up the crumbs that the younger children had scattered. She collected them into the palm of her hand and seemed absorbed in the task. Finch turned back to the sister.

"Do you know what shoes she was wearing when she went out?"

"Her black 'uns I think," said the girl. "I'll have a look in the bedroom to make sure. You want to come?"

She stood up, pulling down her jumper so that her small breasts jutted out under the stretched wool.

Finch looked at Mrs. Walker.

48

"Would you mind if I look through Doreen's room? I might find something useful to the investigation, a letter or a photograph."

"All right," she said dully. She tipped the crumbs that she had collected onto a plate. "Pam'll show you."

"And how old are you, Pam?" asked Finch, as he followed her into a dark, narrow hallway.

"Thirteen, mister," she said, smiling obliquely at him over her shoulder. She took him, not upstairs, as Finch had expected, but into the downstairs room at the front of the house. It was dark and she switched on the light as they entered. The room had evidently been intended originally as a sitting room. There was a three-piece suite, covered in worn brown imitation leather, the armchairs of which were pushed into the fireplace alcoves while the settee, convertible into a bed, was let down and a child lay asleep at the foot. She stirred as the light went on and half raised her head.

"Pam?" she said sleepily.

"Shut up," said Pam, "else I'll tell Dad and he'll give you a hiding." The child huddled down again under the bedclothes and appeared to go back to sleep.

"Doreen, me, and Gracie sleep in here," said Pam huskily, giving Finch her special, slant-eyed smile.

Finch became brisk and official. "If you'll show me where Doreen kept her things, I'll be looking through them while you find out what shoes are missing."

"Top two drawers were hers," said Pam, pointing to a heavy, old-fashioned chest of drawers in brown varnished wood. A mirror hung on the wall behind and the top of the chest served as a dressing table. It was dusty with spilt powder and littered with an array of cheap cosmetics.

Finch jerked open the top drawer and looked at its contents with disfavor; then, with the tips of his fingers, began to sort over the confusion of underwear, stockings, hand-kerchiefs, jerseys, and other articles of clothing which were jumbled up inside. Some of the clothes were dirty; most of them were badly washed but mixed up with them he found several unopened plastic envelopes containing stockings and three cellophane packets of new underwear. There was a seductive silhouette of a naked woman on the front, printed in black, and the words "Venus See Thru Bra and Pants Set." A similar set of underwear, obviously worn, was in the drawer. The material was pink transparent nylon net and the edges of the brassiere and pants, too small Finch thought to have served much purpose, were edged with cheap lace.

The second drawer contained much the same confusion of clothes but thrust underneath it was a cardboard box which had once held chocolates and had a picture of poo-dles on the lid. He took the lid off and looked inside. It contained not, as he had hoped, any letters, only some pieces of cheap jewelry, a bottle of scent, and some photo-graphs. There were three and he looked at them quickly. All were of Doreen and only one seemed possible to en-large. It was a full-faced close-up, the kind of photograph that is taken at an automatic booth. While he was looking at it Pam, who had been rummaging about under the bed and chairs, finding shoes, came and looked over his shoul-der.

"She had that one took last summer in Southend."

"Is it like her?" asked Finch.

The girl nodded and her eyes filled with tears. She was suddenly a pathetic child.

"She were murdered, weren't she?" she asked.

"Yes, I'm afraid she was," Finch replied gently.

"Did he hurt her much, the man what did it?"

"No," lied Finch. "I don't think she felt any pain."

"I'm glad," said Pam. She scrubbed her hand across her eyes.

"Would you like to help me find the man?" asked Finch, and when she nodded, he continued, "Did Doreen ever tell you what she did in the evenings, whom she met or what she did?"

"She went out every Wednesday and Saturday," said Pam. "She had a 'alf-day from the shop on Wednesdays but she never come home. Mum thought she was out with Brenda and then went on to the Youth Club in the evening, but she never, not for a long time anyhow. I know 'cos I go to the club and she ain't been there for weeks and weeks. Brenda let slip that she'd not been out with her of a Wednesday afternoon either. I didn't tell Mum, though."

"Why not?"

"Because Doreen told me to keep my mouth shut or she'd give me a hiding," said Pam promptly. "She went out Saturday nights too. She used to go about half past seven. Said she was meeting Brenda but that ain't true neither."

"You don't know whom she was meeting?" asked Finch. Pam shook her head. "She never told me nothin'."

"Didn't you ask?"

"She said, 'Mind your own business.' "

Finch sighed. He had hoped for some definite information from the sister but perhaps the friend, Brenda Parsons, would be able to tell him more about the dead girl's friends.

He said, "Where does Brenda live?"

"Number eight, Oak Cottages. Them's the council houses in the village."

She had lost her pathetic look. The tears had dried and she was smiling at him again.

Finch closed the drawers and picked up the photograph that lay on the top of the chest.

"I'll ask your mother if I can keep this for the time

being," he said. "And if you think of anything that might be useful, you'll let me know, won't you? By the way, did you find out what shoes she was wearing?"

"It was her black 'uns," said Pam. "They're her best too. Black patent leather with high heels and a little bow on the front."

She took hold of his sleeve in a wheedling manner. "Can I 'ave her things, mister? If you ain't going to take her clothes away, can I 'ave them?"

Finch shook her off and said abruptly, "That's none of my business. You must ask your mother."

He went out into the hall and Pam came scuttling after him.

"And if you find her shoes, can I 'ave them as well?"

Finch did not answer but walked into the living room. His one desire now was to get out of the house as quickly as possible. Not only did he wish to avoid another encounter with Walker, who would soon be returning from the pub, but he felt suffocated by the atmosphere of poverty, fecklessness, and greed that surrounded him and which seemed to cling in his nostrils like an aroma; an aroma that had about it the sharp, bitter odor of human tragedy and despair.

Mrs. Walker was sitting at the table, rocking a baby, which was wailing with a tired, hoarse cry. She jogged it backwards and forwards, in an unceasing, unthinking rhythm, like someone sawing wood, and the baby's round, downy head lolled to and fro. The small children were still sitting at the table, their eyes glazed with sleep.

Finch made a few remarks of official sympathy, got her permission to keep the photograph, and left the house as soon as he decently could.

5

Outside, the Inspector took in great gulps of the cold, damp air. Then he shivered and, turning up his raincoat collar, fumbled his way down the path to the car. He unlocked it and got into the driver's seat. He turned on the head lamps and the windscreen wipers but could not bring himself to start the engine. A terrible feeling of depression swept over him. With his hand on the ignition key he sat staring out through the swath of dark glass, swept clean by the wipers, at the rain falling in long shafts past the headlights, the wet road beyond and a bedraggled portion of hedge and grass verge.

He wanted to go home. He wanted a bath and whiskey in front of the fire. He wanted the comfortable feeling of being the only one awake in a warm house, the pleasure of anonymity.

He passed a hand wearily across his eyes. It was a gesture familiar from his boyhood. Sitting at the round family table, with the pressure lamp hissing softly and giving off a hot white glare under its milky glass shade, he had often made this gesture, the momentary shielding of his eyes before he again bent his head to the book he was studying, the print of which had suddenly become too black and hard on the dazzling page.

"Tired, Son?" his mother would say. And he would stare

at her, bemused, partly pleased by her sympathetic notice, partly irritated that she could not leave him alone. She had had to seize on his brief lapse of attention from his books to make her presence known. "Here I am," she seemed to say, as she sat darning or knitting on the other side of the table, "notice me, smile at me, love me."

Had she ever realized that the books he so diligently studied were his means of escape? Finch had only come to terms with his guilt after her death. Of course he had wanted to escape. It was natural. He had been the clever one in the family. The life of a village was too cramped and confined. It was one of the reasons why he had joined the police, because it offered him a challenge, a chance to pit his wits against other people, and he had found satisfaction in his work, especially after his promotion, and promotion had been quick for him, and he had people like Boyce to take some of the routine off his shoulders.

Perhaps it was because the murder of Doreen Walker had taken place in a village so like his own boyhood surroundings that he felt depressed. It made him feel, in an obscure way, guilty, although why guilty he could not say. He shifted his shoulders uncomfortably. Perhaps he knew the type of people too well. He had shared a desk at school with a boy who might have grown up to be Meyrick, big-booted, clumsy, glowering. There had been a family like the Walkers. He remembered he had been forbidden to play with the boys, and the girl, they said, had nits. They had shouted "Nithead!" at her in the playground.

Or was he depressed because, having imagined he had left this background far behind, he had returned so many years later to find it so little changed? There was the same narrow-minded, parochial outlook and, in the case of Walker, the same fecklessness and brutality which a generation of education had failed to change.

And now, he supposed, he ought to drive into the village and interview Doreen Walker's friend, Brenda Parsons. He was not in the mood for it at all. He had seen too many people and their identities had begun to press in on him. He had, too, himself assumed too many identities so that now the effort of playing yet another was exhausting even to contemplate. But it would have to be done. He sighed deeply and, pressing the starter button, drove up the narrow road.

The village was a quarter of a mile from Tye Lane, scattered along each side of the road. There was a public house, the Crown, its steep gable picked out with colored lights, a school, a shop, a village hall, three or four brick cottages and a row of council houses identical in shape and design to those in Frayling. Finch slowed down the car. Number 8 was in darkness. He glanced at his watch. The time was nearly a quarter to eleven. Rather than risk getting the Parsons family out of bed at that time, he decided to postpone that interview with Brenda until the following day. The shop where she worked, Severall's, was only round the corner from the police station and, as Doreen had worked there as well, it seemed a good opportunity of killing two birds with one stone. If there was a manager, he would be able to interview him as well at the same time.

The last house in the row was the police house. Remembering what Russell had told him about Leach, and seeing there was a light still burning downstairs, Finch eased his official conscience by deciding that as he was in the village a talk with the local policeman would not be wasted. He parked the car and went to the back door, which was opened to his knock by Leach himself, a plump, unambitious, easygoing man, not many years off retirement and too used to police work to be intimidated by Finch's rank. He seemed genuinely pleased at the visit and showed Finch

55

into a warm, comfortable room where his wife, in a blue woolen dressing gown, her feet in slippers, was sitting knitting by the fire.

She was plump, like her husband, but she had shrewd eyes and she gave Finch a very level, bright look as he came into the room.

"You won't mind me being in my dressing gown," she said. It was a statement rather than a question and Finch immediately felt his spirits rise. He gave her an affable smile and sat down in the other armchair, which she indicated with a knitting needle and which had evidently only just been vacated by her husband as its soft, cushioned seat was still warm and creased from his ample backside.

"Wilf was just going to put the kettle on," she said. "He always makes the last cup of tea before we go to bed. You'll join us?"

"I will," said Finch.

He had taken off his raincoat and sat relaxed, with his feet extended to the fire. She looked at him with an indulgent, amused smile and then went on with her knitting. Wilf could be heard clattering about in the kitchen. Presently he stuck his head round the door.

"The tea's made," he announced.

He came in carrying a tray with the tea things.

"If it's an official visit," he said, "maybe you'd prefer to go into the office."

"No," said Finch. "What I want is more of a chat about Doreen Walker, what she was like, who her friends were, for instance."

"So it was Doreen," said Leach, pulling a long face, while his wife clicked her tongue in sympathy. "I thought it must be as soon as Mr. Walker came up here earlier this evening to report her missing. It's a bad affair."

Finch sipped his tea and waited. His face had assumed the

interested and sympathetic expression of a close friend of the family, ready to listen to the local gossip.

"Although I can't say I'm altogether surprised," said Mrs. Leach, readily accepting her part in the group as spokeswoman, which was what Finch had hoped for. "She was bound to be in trouble of some sort sooner or later, though, God knows, I didn't expect *that*. I thought she'd find herself in the family way. Didn't I say to you, Wilf, and not so very long ago either, that she was heading for trouble? Mind you, with a family background like hers, what else can you expect? Poor kid! She didn't stand much of a chance to be decent."

"Certainly the mother didn't seem to know what she was up to in the evenings," said Finch.

Mrs. Leach sighed. "She's too worn out to take much interest in anything. And Doreen wouldn't say more than she had to. You ask Mrs. Parsons. She was never very keen on Brenda chumming up with Doreen but still in a village you can't always pick and choose your friends. She said to me once, 'She's a sly girl.' She was too; kept things to herself. I know you shouldn't speak ill of the dead but there's no use pretending that Doreen was one of these open, honest girls because she wasn't."

"I wanted to call on the Parsons family," said Finch, "but it looked as if they'd gone to bed."

"They would be," said Mrs. Leach, glancing quickly at the clock. "They're early bedders. Mr. Parsons works at Cressett's dairy so he has to be up in the mornings."

"Tell me more about Doreen," said Finch.

Mrs. Leach gave him a shrewd look and smiled.

"You're getting what you want out of me, aren't you, Inspector? I bet the moment you came in that door, you said to yourself, 'There's a woman who likes a nice old gossip.' Well, you're right, I do. And being the wife of the local

57

bobby isn't much help. I listen but I have to watch what I say. All ears and no voice, that's me. So it's nice to be able to wag my tongue for a change and know what I'm saying is being taken notice of. Don't you shake your head at me, Wilf. The Inspector and me understand each other, don't we?"

Finch laughed out loud. He was enjoying himself.

"You're quite right, we do."

"Well, then," she went on, picking up her knitting and making the needles flash again, "you wanted to find out more about Doreen and you'll want the truth, so I'll tell you it. For one thing, she was a bit too fond of the boys. She was getting quite a reputation. That was another thing Mrs. Parsons didn't like about her. Brenda's a good girl but she's the type to be easily led. She only wanted to work at Severall's because Doreen had a job there."

"Could you give me any names of the boys Doreen went about with?"

Mrs. Leach nodded across to her husband.

"You write them down, Wilf, while I get on with my knitting."

While he fetched paper and pencil, she added to Finch, "I should think she's been out with every boy in the village that's around her age." She began to rattle off the names, which her husband wrote down.

When the list was complete, Finch asked, "Do you know who she's been going out with recently?"

"That I can't tell you," said Mrs. Leach. "Whoever he is, she's kept very quiet about him. But I know she hasn't been going to the Youth Club recently. I help with the refreshments there sometimes so that's how I know. And she hasn't been going to the Saturday night dances. They're not held every week; say once in three, depending what else's on, but she hasn't turned up for those for weeks and weeks and

58

she never used to miss a single one. Brenda might be able to tell you."

"I hope so," said Finch. "Her sister, Pam, couldn't tell me much."

Mrs. Leach clicked her tongue again, this time unsympathetically.

"There's another one who's going to be just like Doreen, given another couple of years. She's already started hanging about the boys. In fact, I'm not sure she isn't worse now than Doreen was at her age."

The clock struck eleven and Finch got up.

"I'm keeping you from your bed and we can't have that," he said. "There's only one more point I'd like to clear up. Walker said he thought Doreen was spending the night, Sunday night, that is, at Brenda's house. Was this likely?"

Mrs. Leach shook her head decisively.

"I don't think Doreen's stayed at Brenda's for over a year. Mrs. Parsons didn't like encouraging her. It wasn't so bad when Doreen was younger. She felt a bit sorry for the girl, but since there's been more and more gossip about her she's put her foot down. So if Mr. Walker told you that it means he couldn't be bothered to go out looking for her."

"I thought so," said Finch. "And I suppose you didn't see anything of her yourself on Sunday evening?"

"No, I'm afraid not. We were in by the fire with the telly on."

Finch turned to Leach. "Have you seen anything of her around the village in the evenings? I gather she was out every Wednesday and Saturday night."

But Leach shook his head. "No, but the village isn't lit, except for the one lamp by the bus stop, and if she was doing a bit of courting on the quiet, she wouldn't want to be seen."

"True enough," said Finch, although he suspected that

Leach was too easygoing and too near to retirement to bother to go looking for anything that wasn't under his nose.

He held out his hand to Mrs. Leach.

"Thank you," he said. "You've been a great help."

"You probably think me a sharp-tongued old busybody," said Mrs. Leach as they shook hands. Her face was suddenly sad. "I'm not. I've stuck up for Doreen many a time when the other women have been running her down. But whitewashing her won't find the man who did it and it's a man you're looking for, you can depend on it. You had to know the worst to understand."

"I realize that," said Finch.

Leach saw him to the door and Finch turned the car and drove back along the Wrexford road.

Boyce was waiting for him when he got back to the police station. The sergeant looked gloomy and tired.

"I thought I'd better wait and give you my report," he said, "although it's about as much as would go on the back of a postcard. There's still no sign of the shoes but what was found I've had packed up." He indicated two large plastic bags that stood on the floor. "It's all stuff found in the vicinity. Surprising what does get left in woods. Most of it's rubbish though. By the way, what happened about that man Walker? Did he identify the body?"

"Yes. The girl's Doreen Walker. Lived at Framwell, that's the village about three miles down the road from where she was found. I'll write the report up later and you can read it. She was a bit of a tart, if half what I've heard is true."

He produced the photograph and the list of boys that Mrs. Leach had given him.

"I'll get copies of the photograph for circulation tomorrow and I want you to go and see everyone on this list and find out what they were doing Sunday evening. I'll want a house-to-house inquiry set up in the village too. I'll get a questionnaire drawn up, but basically it will be, 'Have you ever seen Doreen Walker in a man's company, if so who was it?' She went out regularly on Wednesday and Saturday evenings. You'll need two or three constables to help you on that."

Boyce, who had been looking over the list, said, "Looks like she had a fair old number of boy friends." He picked up the photograph. "Not bad-looking but I can see what you mean about 'tart.' "

He covered over the lower part of the face. "It's the eyes that give it away."

"You should see the sister," said Finch, crushing out his cigarette. The old depression returned. "Not fourteen and she was giving me the come-on."

But Boyce only saw the funny side and laughed.

"That I should like to have seen."

Finch got up impatiently.

"I'm tired, Tom. I want to get home to a bath and bed and I've got this questionnaire and report to write up yet, so let's cut the chat and make it snappy. Tomorrow I shall want to have a good look at the wood where she was found and get some idea of the locality in daylight. Then I've got two people to interview: a man called Smith, who was seen going into the wood a couple of days ago, and the dead girl's friend, Brenda Parsons. Doreen spent Sunday afternoon with her. By the way, she left home on a bike. She may have left it at the friend's house and I'll check on that tomorrow but let me know if a bike's found."

"That reminds me of something," said Boyce. "We've been concentrating on the missing shoes but it did cross my mind that there was no handbag near the body. Of course, she may not have had one with her."

"I'll check on that too," said Finch. "Anything else?"

"Nothing that I can think of at the moment."

"Right then," said Finch. "To get back to tomorrow's plan. I want you to come with me to get a search of the wood and the surrounding area properly organized. We'll need at least five men on that. Then we'll split up. I'll go to see Smith and you go into Framwell and have a talk with the people on this list. Meanwhile the copies of the photograph should be ready. I'll pick them up here in the afternoon and then interview the Parsons girl. She works round the corner at Severall's, the drapers. Doreen Walker worked there as well so I may pick up some useful information. If both of us draw a blank, we'll get the house-to-house inquiry started on Wednesday. But if you do turn up anything important, you'd better ring through here and leave a message, otherwise I'll see you here at six o'clock tomorrow evening. The path report should be ready by then."

"Right," said Boyce. He took another look at the photograph before handing it back to Finch. "Would you say she was the perfect murder victim?"

"What do you mean?" asked Finch snappishly.

"Nothing much," replied Boyce. "Only isn't there supposed to be a type that's more likely to get murdered? Almost asks for it, in a way?"

Finch looked at the photograph as Boyce had done, covering up the face so that only the eyes showed. They smiled at him under lowered lids. He studied it for a moment and then put it into his pocket.

"I don't know, Tom," he said more kindly. "Murder cases don't often come my way, and when they do they're usually domestic and straightforward. There's not much mystery to homicide except in detective stories. She may have asked for it; I don't know. All I know is she's got a father who's too bloody idle to walk up the road in the rain to look for her; a mother who's too stupid or too apathetic or both, to stop herself from getting pregnant and can't keep the kids she has got properly clean; and a kid sister with a roving eye—oh, God, it's enough to make you give up."

"What? Police work?"

"No. Hope."

"Oh, that," said Boyce cheerfully. "You've got to look on the bright side. You think too much, that's your trouble."

"I don't know," said Finch, moving his shoulders restlessly. "Perhaps you're right. I do know I've got that report to write up before morning. Come on, Tom. Let's shut up shop."

They left the office, Finch pausing at the desk to leave his home telephone number with the duty sergeant in case he was needed, and they parted company on the steps of the police station.

It was still raining and the streets were empty. The pubs were closed and the lights in the shop windows had gone out. Finch shivered and, pulling his raincoat firmly round himself, made a quick dash for his car.

On the drive home the sentences that he would write in his report began to form in his mind.

"At 3:10 P.M. on Monday, March 14, in answer to a request from Detective Sergeant Baker stationed at Wrexford police station, I proceeded to Leverett's wood, near the village of Frayling, accompanied by Detective Sergeant Boyce, to investigate a reported discovery of a dead body, since identified as Doreen Walker, aged 15 years 7 months, of Tye Cottages, Tye Lane, Framwell . . ."

6

Smith, meanwhile, knew nothing of all this. On the Monday, the day that the girl's body was found, he had been working in his garden. It was a long, triangular-shaped piece of ground to the side of the cottage and enclosed on the one side by the high hawthorn hedge that bounded the lane and on the other by a low bank surmounted by a three-stranded fence of sagging barbed wire supported on poles, with a ditch on the near side and the open fields beyond. The hedge and the fence ran together in a point at the farther end where stood a clump of elder bushes.

The garden pleased Smith. He had never owned a piece of land before and he had planned its cultivation with great care. When he had first taken the cottage the garden had been a tangled wilderness of brambles and nettles, thrusting up between the accumulation of years of rubbish: tin cans, rusty iron, broken bottles, and the rotting remains of a cotton mattress. In the first months he had slashed and dug, hacked and burned a way through the wilderness, reducing it, at last, to four orderly plots, intersected by paths constructed from the stones and broken bricks he had found lying about the garden.

It had taken time, physical effort and, moreover, planning, for in order to buy the tools he needed he had had to save for many weeks, cutting down his expenditure to the minimum and then walking the three miles to Wrexford to purchase them. But it had been achieved. The soil had been cleared of weeds, the earth dug, the seeds bought; only the weather had been against him, too wet and cold, the ground too heavy.

That Monday morning, however, was fine. A clear, pale sun shone in a sky of unimaginably fragile blue. Every blade of grass and twig seemed to be outlined by a line of light. The warmth of the sun drew the moisture from the wet earth and Smith, as he worked, fancied he could feel the soil exhaling.

He began work early in the morning, breaking up the soil first with the hoe and then reducing it to a fine tilth with the rake. Cairn lay on the path lazily watching the man as he drew the rake backwards and forwards with long easy sweeps. The seed packets lay on the path beside the dog and its ears twitched whenever the wind, which was light but blew from time to time in stronger gusts, rattled the packets together.

Smith began to mark out the rows with a line, pegging one end and rolling out the string to the far side of the plot. He was breathing deeply, not through effort but because soon he would be planting the first seeds and this excited him strangely. He had read the instructions on the packets, he had planned exactly where the seeds should be planted. They had grown in his imagination through many dark winter afternoons and evenings; runner bean plants like dark, green tents; round, close-hearted lettuces and cabbages; formal rows of onions and leeks; the light, feathery foliage of carrots.

He made the first shallow trench and, stooping, walked backwards along the row, dropping between his fingers one by one the hard, dry, shriveled peas. They lay against the dark earth like pale beads. It seemed impossible that they would ever grow. Carefully he raked the soil over them and speared the empty packet on a sharp stick at the end of the row. It fluttered in the wind and reminded him of the photographs that are placed over graves in Italy, only these pictures were reminders of the living seeds down there in the earth.

He worked steadily throughout the morning, aware of nothing outside this triangular world, bounded by hedge, sky, and earth. The storm, when it came, surprised him by its suddenness. The hawthorn hedge protected him from the rising wind which was driving the clouds from the northwest. He was aware first of a change of quality in the light, a stirring of grass and branches, Cairn's uneasiness. Looking up, he saw the sky beyond the lane was a boiling confusion of dark clouds. The thin sunlight had gone and the taller trees began to thrash about. Cairn sat up and started whining. The first rain drops fell, as hard and direct as bullets.

Smith ran to retrieve his tools and the packets of seeds which he thrust inside his shirt to protect them from the rain. Calling to the dog, he ran up the path toward the back door. As he opened it, the wind took it from his hand and banged it back against the outer wall. He had to throw the tools down on the floor and pull at the door with both hands to get it closed. Its inner surface was darkened by the rain before he could fasten it and his head and shoulders were wet. Cairn, who had bolted between his legs, had gone under the camp bed in the living room and would not be coaxed out. He lay there trembling and Smith left him there. It seemed the kindest thing to do. He went to the window, slowly rubbing his hair dry with a towel, and watched the rain. He was anxious about the newly planted seeds but, all the same, he found the storm exhilarating. He had rarely seen rain unleashed with such force. The window

66

streamed with it and, blurred by the falling cascade, he could see the hawthorn hedge writhe and twist. The garden path was lost to sight as the rain lashed back, inches high, in its own spray.

The following morning he went out to the garden again to inspect the damage. The weather was calm but the sky was lead colored and oppressively low. It seemed to be slung just above his head like a sagging, gray canvas. Smith was afraid that most of the seeds had been washed into the earth or washed away completely by the surface water that had run off the topsoil and now lay gathered in great lead puddles in every declivity of the ground. There was nothing to be done but replant and he thought himself lucky that the storm had interrupted his work before more than a quarter of the seeds had been put into the ground.

He was raking the soil level again when the dog at Stokes's farm began barking. Smith stopped working and Cairn sat up. Both listened intently. The dog barked only when someone went to the farm or passed by in the lane. Cairn shifted his front paws uneasily and a low growling noise came from his throat, but Smith, walking across the garden toward him, silenced him with a gesture. They stood together on the path, Smith's hand on the back of the dog's neck. The farm dog was silent now but Smith could feel his own dog's body vibrating excitedly under his hand, the hair on his neck bristling upward. The dog had sensed the approach of someone.

Soon a darker shape passed behind the massed, dark twigs of the hawthorn hedge, a hand fumbled at the gate, which was shoved open, and a man came up the path toward the cottage.

The kitchen garden was shielded from the front path by a tangled hedge of roses that had run wild. Apart from cutting a gap in the center to give him access to the front door Smith had not troubled to prune them, preferring their small, fragile flowers to the heavier blooms of well-tamed bushes. Through this gap he observed the man; a stocky figure in a beige-colored raincoat, the collar of it turned up. The man knocked on the door in an authoritative manner and, as no one came, stepped back to examine the front of the cottage. He had the professional air of a surveyor or valuer in his stance, the cock of his head, the foursquare position he took up in the center of the path, his hands rammed well down into the pockets of his raincoat.

Smith's mouth flickered upward. He gestured to the dog to come to heel and walked toward the gap in the hedge. Although he walked as silently as he could, the man heard him. He turned quickly, taking his hands out of his pockets.

"Mr. Smith?" he asked. His voice was pleasant, with a slight country accent that was detectable more in the intonation than in the actual sounds. It had also, Smith noticed, an official ring about it.

Smith did not reply until he reached the gap. He stopped there, not passing through it, so that the two men confronted each other over the barrier of intertwined rose brambles.

"Yes?" said Smith.

"Inspector Finch of the Essex Constabulary," replied the man. "I wonder if I might have a talk with you?"

"Yes?" said Smith again.

Finch made a slight movement with his shoulders that suggested a complex of emotions: irritation, discomfort, the sense of being, momentarily, at a loss. But his face betrayed nothing only the pleasant, official half-smile above which the eyes, cool and intelligent, were taking in and retaining everything.

"If we could go inside, sir?" Finch suggested. "It's a bit chilly for standing about."

Smith walked through the gap in the hedge to the front door and opened it. The dog went in first, Smith pausing to unlace and remove his boots, which were heavy with mud, and carrying them inside in his hand. Finch followed his example, stooping down to pull off the Wellington boots he was wearing, steadying himself with one hand on the lintel post. Smith stood inside the room waiting for him. He noticed how, while Finch was taking off his boots, he kept glancing up to observe the interior and Smith had the feeling that each time he did this he had taken a swift, mental photograph of the room. Click! He had taken the far wall with the camp bed against it, the folded blankets lying on it, the leather suitcase pushed underneath. Click! Now the fireplace with the fire laid in the hearth with paper and twigs, the stack of logs beside it, the pile of books on the mantelshelf above and the deck chair drawn up to one side. Another darting glance had taken in the table under the window with the oil lamp on it, the wooden chair, the book left lying open where Smith had been reading as he ate his breakfast. He had already photographed Smith himself as he turned to face him in the garden.

The second boot was eased off. Finch stood them neatly side by side on the doorstep and padded into the room in stockinged feet.

"There!" he said. "It's a muddy old walk up the lane."

Smith stepped swiftly across the room and put his hand on the back of the upright, wooden chair, laying claim to it.

"Sit down," he said.

There was nowhere else to sit except the camp bed or the deck chair and neither was the right sort of seat from which to conduct an interview. Finch moved his shoulders restlessly again. He felt the other man had outmaneuvered him. He lowered himself gingerly into the deck chair which was set on the lowest rung thrusting his knees uncomfortably upward. There was a sardonic look on Smith's face as he too sat down with one elbow on the table and his legs crossed, comfortable and at home.

Then Finch nearly laughed. Here, at last, was someone to reckon with, someone who would not easily be led or coaxed or bullied into speaking. He settled himself back in the deck chair and prepared to enjoy himself.

"It's a nice little cottage you have here," he said, looking about him. "A bit cut off, for my taste; too far from the village, but pleasant all the same, if you like a quiet life."

He paused but as Smith made no reply Finch, not at all put out, resumed the conversation in a pleasant, easy style.

"Sort of place I've often thought of retiring to; in the country, with a bit of garden, plenty of time for reading and pottering about," he added, cheerfully lying. Finch had a modern house on the outskirts of Chelmsford where he was comfortably looked after by his widowed sister, a good, plain cook like his mother, who knew when to keep her mouth shut, and he had no intention of changing his way of life.

"No electricity, I notice. Now, that's a drawback. I like the modern conveniences."

He heaved himself out of the deck chair and walked about the room, looking at the books on the mantelpiece, the view from the back window across the fields. He reminded Smith of Cairn the first day they came to the cottage, walking about, getting to know the place.

"Kitchen through there?" asked Finch, stopping at the door and when Smith nodded, he went on, "Mind if I take a look? It's interesting to see how other people live."

He went through into the kitchen and then Smith heard him climbing the stairs, walking about the bedroom floors which creaked under his weight. There was a rattle as he moved one of the buckets.

Presently he came back into the room and Smith could not resist asking, with a curl of his lips, "Have you seen it all?"

"I think so," replied the Inspector, unabashed. "Your roof leaks. You ought to get that fixed."

He did not sit down again but stood leaning against the fireplace. Neither man spoke and Finch, whose nerve, despite his smiling expression, was beginning to get rattled by the other man's silence and composure, took out a packet of cigarettes and offered one to Smith. He refused it, looking away quickly from the proffered packet and Finch guessed that he wanted one; had probably smoked at one time and had given it up unwillingly. The Inspector felt a thrill of exultation. He had found a weakness in the man at last.

"Mind if I smoke?" he asked and before Smith had time to reply he lit a cigarette. Never had one tasted so good. As he drew in the smoke he watched Smith's averted face and saw his long hands clasp convulsively together.

Suddenly Smith jumped up from his chair and, taking a box of matches from the mantelshelf, knelt down on the sacking rug and lit the fire.

Finch looked down on his bent head. The brown hair was thinning on top. Long pieces fell forward to show glimpses of the scalp. Thin flames crept up between the twigs, illuminating part of his cheekbone.

"Why have you come here?" asked Smith, without looking up. "What are the questions you want to ask?"

"Did I say anything about asking questions?" said the Inspector.

"You implied it," said Smith sharply. He stood up, facing Finch. "I want to know why you have come."

"Just a routine inquiry," replied the Inspector. "Do you know Leverett's wood?"

Smith looked puzzled and Finch pointed out the window.

"The big wood two fields away with a bridle path going through it?"

"Oh, yes, that wood. I didn't know the name. Yes, I know it."

"Were you there at any time last Sunday?"

Smith thought for a moment and then replied:

"No, not on Sunday."

"When were you there last?"

"A few days ago."

"Which day exactly?"

"Friday, I think."

"Can you be more exact?"

"Is it important? I suppose it must be. Very well, let me think. Yes, it was Friday. I'm quite sure. I had been to the village and I went to the wood in the afternoon."

"Do you go there often?"

"Usually once or twice a week. I collect wood, fallen branches and logs, for the fire."

"And you weren't there on Sunday?"

"I have already said I wasn't."

"Why are you so sure?"

Smith shrugged. "I just am sure."

"But you weren't sure which day you *had* been there last, until you thought about it," persisted the Inspector.

Smith smiled. "You obviously don't understand my way of life, Inspector. The passing of time has very little interest for me. What happened last week is no longer important. What happened yesterday is usually not important either. But over the past three days I have been planting the garden. I began it yesterday. The day before, Sunday, I got the ground ready, measured it out and burned the last of the rubbish. I remember hearing the church bells as I was working. In the afternoon it rained a little. I sat in here, at the table, and drew up a plan of the seedbeds. I did not leave the cottage all day."

"I see," said the Inspector and he did see, too, in a strange way, how this man, living alone, might forget certain days and yet remember quite clearly the events of three successive days because they followed a pattern of interconnected actions. All the same, he knew this man to be intelligent and self-composed. If he wished to lie or withhold information he would do it with assurance.

The Inspector moved his shoulders restlessly.

"Ever seen this girl?" he asked abruptly, holding out the photograph of Doreen Walker. It was the snapshot he had found at the house. Smith examined it.

"No," he said, after a moment.

The Inspector returned it to his wallet.

"She came from Framwell. Ever been there?"

"That's the next village, isn't it?" asked Smith. "No, I don't know it. I've walked by the footpath across the fields. There's a stile at the end, just before you get to the village. I haven't been any farther than that. Is that all you wanted to know?"

"Aren't you curious to know why I'm asking these questions?" asked the Inspector, suddenly irritated by Smith's calmness.

"Not really," replied Smith. "Other people's lives don't interest me."

"It's her death I'm concerned with," said Finch sharply. "She was found strangled in Leverett's wood."

"I see," said Smith. "I'm sorry I can't help you. As I told you before, I don't know the girl. I never saw her before."

"I may have to ask you to come down to the police station to sign a statement to that effect," said Finch, using his official manner.

There was a hesitation so small that if he had not been watching Smith closely Finch might have missed it altogether. Then Smith quickly regained his composure.

"Certainly, Inspector."

73

"I'll let you know when," said Finch, walking to the door.

He can stew over that, he thought to himself as he picked his way down the rutted lane. I don't know why he hesitated but there's something he's not sure about. I'll keep him dangling for a bit and then have him in.

7

The pathologist's report was waiting for him when he returned to the police station at Wrexford. He took it into the office that had been assigned to him during the investigation and read it through. It confirmed that death was due to strangulation and placed the time of death between 9 P.M. and midnight on the Sunday evening. The report also mentioned the bruising round the lips and chin and the large contusion on the temple which Finch had noticed when he first examined the body. Both had been inflicted before death and the wound on the temple, caused by a blunt instrument or possibly a heavy blow with a fist, had been severe enough to cause probable unconsciousness. There were no other marks of violence on the body, except for another bruise, on the right shin, but that was a week to ten days old and was fading.

The report went on to list other facts that the Inspector had not known. As he read them he considered carefully what they signified. The girl was six weeks pregnant. She had had sexual intercourse shortly before her death. Her stomach contained, besides the partly digested remains of a meal of fish and chips, a quantity of alcohol. There were minute fragments of fiber under her fingernails. These had been sent for microscopic examination and a more detailed report on them would be sent later.

Finch sat back in his chair. The pieces were falling into place and they were beginning to add up to a picture. Doreen Walker was pregnant. She had been drinking. She had permitted sexual intercourse to take place; there was no indication of rape. She had then been attacked. Somebody, some man, had put his hand over her mouth, hit her on the side of the head and then strangled her. She was not quite sixteen.

Mrs. Leach had been right when she had said, "It's a man you're looking for." The problem was, which man? Meyrick? Smith? There was no evidence to point to either of them and yet a question mark remained over both. Meyrick's outburst and Smith's hesitation could not be overlooked. Or the man could be someone entirely different, someone who had not yet entered the investigation and in that case Brenda Parsons, the dead girl's friend, seemed the only possible lead left to the identity of this man.

He put the report away in the file he was using for the case. It was already beginning to fill up with paper: Walker's statement, Finch's own report on the interview with Meyrick and the Blands, Boyce's report on the interview with Collins, who kept the farm at the end of the lane. Finch had seen the farmer again that morning, hoping that the man might have remembered something that could be of help in the investigation, but he had learned nothing more than Boyce had done on that first afternoon. Collins and his wife had heard nothing, seen nothing. They had spent Sunday evening watching television. The dog had not barked, but never did unless someone actually entered the farmyard. Yes, courting couples did use the lane and the wood, but he'd seen nobody there for months. It was too wet and cold, in his opinion, for anyone to be out; certainly he didn't stick his nose outside the door after dark if he could help it. Cars often used the lane, sometimes just to turn round, sometimes they were parked there, but as long as they kept clear of his gate, it didn't bother him. He hadn't noticed or heard a car on Sunday night.

The search of the wood had revealed nothing new either. Boyce and five constables were still searching it when Finch had left for his interview with Smith. He had found out one useful piece of information, though. The footpath that led directly across the fields to Framwell was hard-surfaced, probably followed the site of a Roman road. It was quite feasible that Doreen could have arrived at the wood by that path. It was only a few minutes by bicycle, a quarter of an hour by foot; a much quicker route than by road. She might not, however, have met the man at the wood at all. Their rendezvous could have been almost anywhere, in any secluded spot that lovers find for themselves on a wet Sunday evening in March. If they had met elsewhere, then the man had brought the body to the wood to dump it, not expecting it to be discovered so soon. This line of thinking, however, would rule out Meyrick as a suspect. He would hardly pretend to discover the body so soon after he had hidden it.

Finch rubbed his chin thoughtfully. Unless Brenda Parsons was able to give him a name or at least some definite information on the identity of the man that would lead to a quick arrest, he could see the case dragging on and on. And until he interviewed her, speculation was useless. He put the file away and, putting on his coat, walked round the corner to Severall's.

He had been right in thinking, when he first drove past it the night before, that the shop had been converted out of several smaller premises. Only the door to the central shop was usable, the others being nailed up and used as extra display space, and he pushed it open and went in. This part of the premises was the haberdashery and children's

77

section and was crammed with merchandise: spools of sewing cotton and ribbon, hanks of wool, trays of knitting needles and thimbles, table mats, bias binding. Two wooden counters occupied much of the space and the free area in the middle was covered with worn lino that showed the regular grooves of the floorboards underneath.

An elderly man stood behind one counter talking to another man, obviously a traveler, who was scribbling down an order in a notebook. The elderly man looked up when Finch entered and said, taking him to be a customer:

"I shan't keep you long, sir."

"That's all right," said Finch pleasantly and walked about, looking at things.

Two open doorways led out of the haberdashery department and Finch glanced with seeming casualness through them. On the left was the men's department. No one was in there. The doorway to the right led to the ladies' department where a middle-aged woman with a long-suffering expression was unfolding Celanese nightdresses for the inspection of a customer, who felt the material and looked doubtful. Finch turned away before they noticed his presence.

The traveler snapped the elastic band round his order book and made for the door. Finch moved forward toward the counter, glancing back to make sure the man had gone, and saw him walking to a green van that was parked by the curbside.

"Mr. Severall?" asked Finch and introduced himself. "I expect you realize why I am here. I'm making inquiries into the death of Doreen Walker who I understand was employed here. I should like to have a talk with your assistant, Brenda Parsons."

"Oh, deary me, she's out at the moment," said Mr. Severall. He was a little dried-up man with a nervous cough. "I sent her out a few minutes ago to buy some aspirin for my wife. Mrs. Severall has come to help out in the shop and she's finding it a bit of a strain."

He spoke hurriedly, anxious to give Finch a full explanation.

"But Miss Parsons shouldn't be long. The chemist's only down the road. Perhaps you would like to wait in here for her? I'll send her in to you the very moment she comes back."

He opened a door at the rear of the shop and showed Finch into a room, part office, part store. It was small and dark with a dirty window overlooking a yard. Cardboard boxes were piled everywhere. Finch glanced at some of the labels. "Gents' Hose. Assorted Colors." "Ladies' Knickers. W.X." "Children's Socks. Beige." On the wall above a large roll-top desk hung an advertisement with a colored photograph of a nude girl. She was kneeling on a fur rug, pouting provocatively. A wing of blond hair fell over one eye. Her breasts, tipped with round, pink nipples, tilted upward. "There's a Zing in Perriman's Fruit Cocktail" read the slogan.

Mr. Severall coughed behind his hand. "We are all very deeply shocked about Miss Walker. It's a terrible, terrible business."

"What was Miss Walker like?" asked Finch.

"Like?"

"What was your opinion of her?"

Mr. Severall looked unhappy. "I'm afraid I don't understand the young people of today, Inspector. Their attitude seems so very different to what I'm used to."

"You had trouble with her?"

"Not exactly. She was—well, really not the type of girl we would choose to employ but I'm afraid we have to take what we can get. There aren't many young girls these days

interested in working in a small family business like ours."
He coughed again. "I believe I heard the shop bell. If you'll
excuse me, it may be Miss Parsons." Finch let him go. He
could always question him again on another occasion. At
the moment he was more interested in the dead girl's
friend.

But when Brenda Parsons came in he felt gloomy about
a satisfactory outcome to the interview. She was a big, awkward girl, with fat legs and a frightened expression. Finch
smiled at her in a fatherly manner, hoping to put her at her
ease, and seated her in the only chair in the office. Above
her head, her hair frizzed out and deadened with too many
cheap perms, the sleek blonde winked and postured.
Brenda sat, heavy and cowlike, her short skirt showing her
big knees straining the stockings. Finch tried to lounge
comfortably against the wall but felt he loomed too large.

"Now, Brenda," he said in a voice that held a nice balance between the pleasantly avuncular and the seriously
official, "I'm sure you want to do everything you can to help
us find the person who killed Doreen, don't you?"

"Yes," she said uncertainly.

"Then perhaps you would answer a few questions. There's
no need to be shy." Finch smiled his cheery uncle smile.
"Now I believe Doreen called to see you on Sunday afternoon?"

"Yes."

"What time did she arrive?"

" 'Bout a quarter to three."

"And what did you do?"

"I washed me 'air and Doreen put it up on rollers."

"Anything else?"

"We listened to some pop records in my bedroom."

"Did she stay for tea?"

"No. She 'ad a cup of tea and a biscuit. She said she

80

wasn't 'ungry and perhaps she'd be 'aving fish and chips later."

"What time did she leave?"

" 'Bout 'alf past seven."

"Did she say where she was going?"

"No. She just said she'd 'ave to go 'cos she was meeting someone."

"Who?"

"A fella."

Finch suppressed a sigh of exasperation. He was already finding the interview heavy going.

"What fellow? Did she mention his name?"

"No."

"Did she say where she was meeting him?"

"No."

"Brenda, would you think very carefully and tell me what she did say?"

"She looked at the clock and she said, ' 'Ere is that the time? I've got to be off 'cos I've got a date.' And I said, 'What, on a Sunday?' And she said, 'Yes, 'e's got tonight off as well.' "

Finch gave this a moment's thought and then asked, "As well as what?"

"As well as other evenings, I suppose," said Brenda, shrugging her fat shoulders.

"So she gave you the impression that she was meeting a man she met on other evenings of the week, but not usually on a Sunday?"

This time it was Brenda who needed time to think. She frowned and then said simply, "Yes."

Finch pursued it further.

"Her sister told me that she went out Wednesday afternoon, her half-day at the shop, and was also out on Wednesday evening. She was supposed to be at the Youth Club, or so her mother thought."

"She ain't been at the club for weeks."

This confirmed what Pam and Mrs. Leach had told him and Finch pressed for more information.

"How long is it since she went to the club?"

"Nearly three months."

"Do you know where she went instead of coming to the club?"

"No, but she told me if I met her mum or dad, though, to tell them she'd been at the club."

"Why did she do that?"

" 'Cos her dad've given her a hiding, I suppose," said Brenda, shrugging.

"Why should he do that?" asked Finch, thinking if she shrugs again I'll take her by her thick neck and shake the information out of her.

" 'E's like that," said Brenda.

"Do you know where she went on Wednesday evenings?"

Brenda shook her head.

"Or Wednesday afternoons?"

"Not always. Sometimes she'd say 'I'm going on the bus' or 'I've got to catch the train,' but she never said where to. She did say once she'd been to the pictures in Southend and it was ever such a good film." She paused and looked at Finch warily. "She used to pick up boys sometimes."

Ah, thought Finch, we're getting somewhere at last.

"Where did she do this?"

"Pictures, sometimes, or in a caff. Last year I went with her once to Brentwood on a Wednesday 'alf-day and Doreen picked up a couple of fellas in a snack bar, one for her and one for me, and we went to the pictures, but I didn't like it much so I didn't go again."

"Why?" asked Finch fascinated. She went red and wriggled on the chair.

"My fella got too fresh and anyway my mum didn't like me going out with Doreen 'cos she says she's fast, so I used to come straight home on the bus after that."

"So as far as you know she used to go to different places on a Wednesday afternoon and sometimes she used to pick up boys?"

"That's right," said Brenda. "Or she might have been meeting this other fella."

Finch rubbed a hand wearily across his eyes.

"Which fellow do you mean?"

"The one she met on Sunday, of course," said Brenda. She looked at him pityingly from under her frizzed-out bangs. "She's been going out with a fella for weeks now."

"So she had a regular boyfriend?"

"Well, she ain't been to the club or the dances of a Saturday night, so she must 'ave met someone, mustn't she?"

"Let's get this clear," said Finch. "You think, but you are not sure, that she had met someone about three months ago whom she had been meeting regularly since every Wednesday and Saturday, and you think, but again you are not sure, that she met him last Sunday evening, although this was not a usual time for them to meet?"

Brenda had fixed her eyes unblinkingly on Finch's face during this recital and seemed to have difficulty in following the reasoning behind it. However, she finally said, "Yes," and Finch sighed. He felt he might be getting somewhere at last through the labyrinth of vague half-fact and supposition on which Brenda based her knowledge of Doreen's private life.

"Now," said Finch, "do you know who this person was? His name, for instance?"

"No," said Brenda.

"Did she ever tell you anything about him?"

"Not much."

It seemed to dawn on the girl that the Inspector was finding the interview difficult. She made a helpless gesture with her hands.

"Doreen never said much about anything. She was . . ."

"Secretive?" suggested Finch, as the word seemed to be beyond Brenda's limited vocabulary.

"That's it. I used to ask her things and she'd just say, 'Wouldn't you like to know?' But I know this fella she'd been meeting wasn't one of the boys from the village 'cos they go to the club and they asked me several times where Doreen was. And I think he was older than the boys she used to go around with 'cos I mentioned Stan Baker to her once at the shop. He's ever so keen on her and she just laughed and said, 'I ain't interested in kids like him anymore.' "

It was a long speech for Brenda and she stopped a little out of breath.

Finch beamed at her. "Now that's the sort of information I'm looking for," he said encouragingly. "Can you tell me any more?"

"Well, I think he might have been married but I ain't sure about that. It was something Doreen said straight out, but she was joking, larking about on the bus going to work one morning with the conductor, just 'aving a bit of a laugh, and he said, 'If I wasn't married with six kids, I'd fancy you,' joking like, and she said, 'What's being married got to do with it?' "

"Is there anything else you can tell me, even if it's only an impression?"

"Well, one Saturday after work she stopped at the

chemist's to buy a new lipstick and she said, 'I hope he likes the taste,' and I said, 'Who?' and she said, 'You wouldn't 'alf laugh if I told you.' "

Finch mulled over this piece of information, then he asked, "Did you get the impression that you'd laugh *because* you knew him or *if* you knew him?"

But this was too subtle for Brenda. She looked bewildered and shook her head. "I couldn't say."

The girl was visibly tiring. She sat drooping on the chair, her fat shoulders sagging. Her legs fidgeted and she kept looking longingly toward the door.

"I won't keep you much longer," said Finch kindly. "Just tell me this. When she left you Sunday evening, did she go on her bicycle?"

"Yes," said Brenda.

"Can you describe it?"

"It's just a bike. It has a basket on the front. She used to put her bag in it."

"Her handbag? Did she have a bag with her when she left your house?"

"Course she did," said Brenda. She seemed amazed that Finch should think a girl would go out without a handbag. "I saw her put it into her basket myself when I went to the door to see her off."

She stopped and the memory of that occasion seemed to affect her. She blinked her eyes.

"She said, 'Ta-ta. See you Monday,' " said Brenda and her voice trembled.

"You run along now," said Finch, patting her shoulder. "You've been very helpful and I can see that talking about Doreen has upset you."

She blundered to her feet and went out. Finch, left alone, gazed for a moment at the naked girl in the photograph and then, crossing the room, flicked a finger against her buttocks.

"You're not the type to let yourself get pregnant," he said.

8

No other topic but the murder was discussed in the village
for the next few days. Now that the girl's body had been
identified and the case had been given a local slant, interest
in it deepened. After all, she had come from Framwell, only
five miles down the road, and some of the people knew the
family; the mother was a second cousin to the Thrales and
everyone agreed that the father was no good. There had
been talk about him before, when he had been fined for
being drunk and disorderly; the case had been reported in
the local newspaper. Members of the darts team, too,
remembered seeing him in the Crown at Framwell when
they had played an away match, and quite a few of the
women were sure they had been served by Doreen when
they had been to Severall's for buttons or stockings or
children's socks.

While the gossip in the shop remained on that level, Mrs.
Bland did not object. She darted about the shop, fetching
pots of jam and half-pound packets of biscuits, nodding and
agreeing and storing up the details to report to her husband, who sat by the fire, straining to hear, trying not to
cough, impatiently waiting for her to come through to the
living room to repeat what each customer had had to say on
the subject.

It was when the talk shifted to a more serious level that

she began to get alarmed. But the question was bound to be asked, sooner or later, "Who had killed the girl?" And, as soon as that question was asked, the talk always turned to Smith. Mrs. Bland did not like it. It frightened her. In vain she tried to draw the women off with suggestions of tramps, or patients escaped from the mental hospital at Roxleigh, or passing motorists. The women would not be drawn. Smith seemed to them strange and outlandish enough without bringing tramps or mental patients into the picture. After all, hadn't he been seen near the wood and what was a grown man doing walking about in a wood anyway? Woods were for courting couples in summer or children out bird's-nesting or primrosing. Added to that, the police had been to see him, asking questions. Why should they bother to do that if they did not have their suspicions? "No smoke without fire," the women said darkly. "And he looks the type who might."

Mrs. Meyrick was often in the shop in the days immediately following the discovery of the crime. She was the most vocal in the condemnation of Smith. Still inwardly frightened by her husband's outburst in Finch's presence, and of the Inspector's possible reaction to it, she was fighting for her own in the only way she knew: to attack somewhere else and lay the blame at another's door. She had, moreover, a strong personal dislike of Smith whom she saw as an outsider and sharper than herself. She was afraid of him, without knowing why, and wanted, obscurely but passionately, to do him harm.

Mrs. Bland began to dread the sight of her, coming up the road toward the shop, her gaunt figure tightly buttoned up in her old black overcoat, her jaw working. The other women stopped their chat when she entered, allowing her to take over the conversation, nodding and agreeing in deference.

"You can't tell me he's any good. Not a soul comes to visit him, for one thing. Eighteen months he's been here and not a sign of anyone asking after him. If you ask me, he's hiding from something."

The women nodded and muttered.

"He does get a letter once a week," pointed out poor Mrs. Bland.

"And there's something fishy there too," snapped back Mrs. Meyrick, her eyes quite fierce. "Typewritten they are. And addressed here. You want to watch yourself over them letters. The police'll have something to say about that, I'll lay."

"Do you think I ought to stop taking them?" Mrs. Bland asked her husband later. The shop was empty at last and she had made a pot of tea because she felt all of a tremble. She sat drinking it in quick little sips.

"You bide your time," advised her husband. "The Inspector didn't say nothing about you not taking them. Just carry on normal. He'll. tip the wink if he wants anything done different."

"I only did it to oblige," cried Mrs. Bland. "But I don't want any trouble, Harold."

"What trouble?" asked her husband. "Is it Smith you're worried about or old Ma Meyrick?"

"I don't know," wailed Mrs. Bland. "I just feel there's going to be trouble.

She could feel it looming up somewhere inside her, like a cloud threatening rain. It took all the pleasure out of everything. Even the little room, usually so bright and cheerful with its twinkling brasses and gay cretonne covers, looked drab. The fire had sunk in on itself. Sniffing, she got up to poke it into a blaze.

"Here, here," protested her husband. "You'll have the bottom out of the grate in a minute. Cheer up,

Glad. You mustn't take it to heart. There's bound to be ill feeling."

She wished she could accept it as cheerfully as he did. Indeed, he seemed to thrive on it. His cheeks were flushed pink and his eyes were very bright and lively. For a moment she almost hated him.

"It's all right for you, sat there. You're not in the shop, listening to it," she flashed out.

The tinkle of the shop bell severed the conversation and she went through to serve. He began coughing again almost immediately. She could hear it through the closed door and knew it was because she had upset him and she felt sorry for her outburst.

To make up for it she made toasted cheese for supper when she closed the shop and they sat round the fire, with the curtains drawn close, watching a variety program on the television. The cloud receded but did not entirely go away. It remained somewhere behind her shoulder. If she turned her head suddenly she felt she might see it; no bigger than a man's hand but dark and ominous.

The first indication that Smith had of the growing feeling against him in the village occurred the following Thursday morning. It had been arranged by Mrs. Bland, in another effort to oblige, that the oil van which called at the village should stop specially at the end of the lane so that Smith could fill his two cans and save himself the long walk up to the village and back.

The van driver, Colin Edge, a youth from the village, had agreed to this arrangement. He did not care much for Smith, whose beard, long hair, educated voice, and aloof behavior Edge had equated in his own mind with every quality of class, politics, and beliefs which he did not understand and consequently disagreed with. Commie, crank, snob, hippie, lay-about, Londoner were all words which

Edge used in talking about Smith and all of them were condemnatory. However, as he worked on a sales-commission basis he saw nothing against stopping at the road's edge and selling him four gallons of oil once a week, although by the way he banged the tins about he liked to think he was expressing what he really felt about the man.

On the Thursday following the murder Smith took the two cans as usual and walked up the lane. It was a fine day, a day of flying cloud and sudden sunshine. Cloud shadows chased across the fields. The leaves were opening, uncurling like green hands, and the landscape was losing the etched severity of winter.

Smith, with Cairn sitting at his side, stood waiting on the grass verge. He had a long vista down the hill to the crossroads. Presently the van turned the corner from Wrexford direction and came grinding up the hill toward them. Smith picked up the cans which he had stood in the grass by his feet.

The van did not stop. It went past him, gathering speed as the hill flattened out, with Colin Edge at the wheel staring purposefully straight ahead.

Smith made no sign. He watched it go up the road toward the village, then he said to Cairn, "We'll walk to the shop."

Mrs. Bland was quite flustered to see him in the shop on a Thursday. As it was, she was dreading his usual appearance on Friday morning to collect his letter and the week's shopping, after all the talk there had been. Luckily, as she told her husband, the shop was empty.

He simply said, "The oil van did not stop this morning. If I leave the cans here, could you get them filled before tomorrow?"

Mrs. Bland did not know what to answer. She guessed why the van had not stopped and she wanted to be pleasant to him on this account and yet at the same time to get him out of the shop before anyone came. Words tumbled out.

"What a pity—all that walk—and you've missed the van again. Just this minute gone. Tomorrow? Well, I'd like to oblige but . . ."

"It doesn't matter," said Smith. "I'll go into Wrexford."

"All that way? Dear, dear me. I wish I could help but the van won't be back till next Thursday. What a shame! It's a fair old drag into Wrexford."

"I'll enjoy the walk," said Smith with a faint smile and, picking up the cans again, he walked out of the shop.

Mrs. Bland had not heard him say so much at once since he had first come to the village, as she told her husband afterwards. But she hadn't cared for the smile. It had a bitten-off look about it, sort of sarcastic, not really amused.

Smith was not amused. He had planned to work in the garden as the day was fine. He avoided going into Wrexford as much as possible because he disliked the shops and the people, and he was not looking forward to the three-mile walk home, carrying the full cans. The oil, however, was a necessity. He needed it for the lamp and the cooking stove. With Cairn at his heels he set off down the hill.

The Inspector noticed him crossing the road toward the hardware shop. Finch himself was standing in Severall's talking to the owner. Mr. Severall had coughed and spluttered and waved his hands about but, at last, Finch had got him talking about Doreen Walker. What he had to say seemed to have little significance. He had had to warn her several times about her offhand attitude to customers and there had been an occasion when he had threatened her with dismissal when he had found her being overfriendly with one of the travelers. After that he had moved her out of the Ladies' Department to the haberdashery counter where he could keep more of an eye on her and there had been no further trouble.

Finch sighed. The information did not add very much to what he already knew, or could guess, about the girl; a "bit too fond of the boys," as Mrs. Leach had put it. He was just about to leave the shop and he and Mr. Severall, who had accompanied him from the office, were standing at the door, when Finch caught sight of Smith through the glass panel.

He noticed him first of all for the reason that other people were noticing him, some even turning round in the street for a second look, because, with his beard and hair and thin stoop-shouldered figure in the long, brown plastic raincoat, he presented such an odd appearance among the house-wives out shopping in that small market town.

A moment later he realised it was Smith, but before he, on a sudden impulse, had time to call Severall's attention to him, he had gone into the hardware shop, leaving the dog sitting outside on the pavement. Finch had Mr. Severall send for Brenda Parsons. He did not really think either of them would recognize Smith in connection with Doreen Walker but he could not afford, in a murder investigation, to let slide even the faintest possibility. The three of them waited, pressed together at the glass, for Smith to leave the shop opposite. Brenda Parsons smelled of cheap scent and armpits. Mr. Severall kept coughing nervously behind his hand.

"Tell me if you recognize anyone who leaves the shop," Finch told them.

After a few minutes Smith came out and the dog got up, wagging his tail, and took his place at Smith's heels.

"That man," said Finch.

"Ooh he looks ever so queer, like a beatnik," said Brenda. But she could not recognize him, nor could Mr. Severall.

Finch was disappointed. Although the evidence against

Smith was thin, and he had no particular wish that the man might be guilty, he would nevertheless have been glad of an identification. It would have been something positive to work on. So far the inquiries into the case were leading nowhere. There had been several days of boring, back-breaking, routine investigation that had produced nothing. It was in a gloomy mood that Finch returned to the police station.

Smith walked back to the cottage. The cans were heavy and awkward to carry. Quite often he had to put them down and ease his aching hands. The handles had cut into the skin, leaving deep marks across his palms and fingers. Each time he stopped, Cairn sat down patiently and waited.

They left Wrexford behind. The trim bungalows on the outskirts gave way to fields, green with young corn. Smith walked faster, with a sense of freedom. In the town he had been aware of the looks the passersby had given him and, although they had shown no sign, he had felt taut inside all the time he had been walking the streets among the other people. He had not noticed the Inspector, with Brenda Parsons and the shopkeeper, watching him through the door of Severall's because he had got into the habit, whenever he had to go to Wrexford or the village, of keeping his eyes fixed on the middle distance so that the curiosity of the passersby should not be too oppressive. This way his immediate surroundings became blurred and softened.

When they got back to the cottage he was very tired. He lay down on the camp bed for a time, flexing and unflexing his fingers until the circulation returned to them. When he was rested he got up and prepared a meal for himself and something for the dog. He ate and, having washed up the dishes, went outside to work in the garden.

He had spent the evening before making bird-scarers for the seedbeds. They were curious objects, constructed from

94

wood and wire, like skeleton trees, with pieces of paper and bright tin dangling from the branches on strings. When he fixed them in the ground they had, with the spinning disks and fluttering shapes, the appearance of small pieces of modern sculpture and he watched them amused and a little proud too. He got enormous satisfaction in making even an ordinary object with skill and care.

When he had set up the bird-scarers he finished raking a seedbed for a later sowing of lettuce and carrots, cleared the ditch where the heavy rain had brought down part of the bank, and cut up logs for the fire.

It was getting dusk when he carried them into the house and stacked them by the hearth. He felt tired, but it was a pleasant fatigue this time. Kneeling on the sack he struck a match and put it to the neat little tent of paper and twigs that he had already made. With the same match he lit the oil lamp that stood on the table under the window. Soon the fire was burning up and he put some logs on it. As the flames licked up round the wood the resin oozed out and fell, hissing and spitting, onto the fire. The room was bright with the light of the leaping flames and the steady glow of the lamp. Cairn stretched himself out in front of the fire, his belly exposed to the warmth. When Smith came to sit down in the deck chair, he merely half lifted his head and let it drop again. A contented grunt and a wagging of his tail acknowledged the man's presence.

Smith sat reading while the dog slept. The only sounds in the room were the spluttering of the fire and the light rustle as the man turned the pages of the book.

Suddenly Cairn woke up, instantly alert. With ears pricked he lifted his head to listen. Smith listened too and could hear the dog barking at Stokes's farm. Then the hair on Cairn's scruff stiffened and he made low, growling noises in his throat. Smith silenced him. There were other noises now, outside in the lane; voices shouting and whooping and derisive laughter. Something thudded against the outside wall of the cottage.

Cairn barked and Smith let him go. The dog bounded to the front door and leapt up against it. The shouting intensified and more missiles struck the cottage. Something slapped against the window.

Smith ran across the room and opened the door and Cairn went leaping out into the dark garden, barking hysterically. The lights of torches in the lane wobbled and bobbed uncertainly. A group of dark figures at the gate broke from a cluster and began running away up the lane, shouting as they went. Smith could not distinguish what they were shouting.

He quieted the dog and went into the cottage to fetch the matches. When he struck one he was surprised and angry with himself to see his hands were shaking. Shielding the match, he examined the walls of the cottage. They were spattered with lumps of soft mud. The one that had struck the window had made a mark like a dirty star across the glass. Smith pulled a handful of grass and wiped the pane; then he called to Cairn, who was still at the gate, bristling and snarling, with his nose thrust between the bars.

He went inside and for the first time since he had occupied the cottage bolted the back and front doors.

9

The Inspector was still in a gloomy mood when he returned to the police station, after seeing Smith in Wrexford. He walked back with his hands thrust deep into his raincoat pockets, his shoulders hunched, and shut himself up in his office.

The sight of the reports piled up on his desk did little to mitigate his gloom. Much of the information so painstakingly gathered had added little of significance to the solution of the case. Boyce, whom Finch had put in charge of the more routine investigation at Framwell, had found out nothing. All the boys on the list supplied by Mrs. Leach had alibis for the Sunday evening when Doreen had been murdered. The house-to-house inquiry had been completely negative. Nobody had seen Doreen Walker in the company of a man on the evening in question, although several of the people interviewed, mostly the women, had commented on Doreen's behavior which had borne out Mrs. Leach's statement about the girl's reputation in the village. Nor had Boyce any more luck with his inquiries at the public houses, off-licenses or fish-and-chip shops in the neighborhood. Acting on Finch's instructions, he had visited them all within a three-mile radius of the village, an area which Finch thought reasonable, considering the girl had a bicycle. Nobody could recognize the girl from the photograph. He was now extending his investigation to a six-mile radius, but it would take time. As Boyce said, the number of pubs and fish-and-chip shops that could be found in an area as large as that, which included several villages and a couple of small towns, could not be visited in an afternoon.

Finch had taken the Wrexford end of the case and had at first appeared more successful. Doreen Walker's photograph had been identified by the proprietor of a snack bar in a side turning near Severall's, by the booking-office clerk at the railway station, and by two conductors who worked regularly on the buses that went through Wrexford. The information they gave added substantially to the over-all picture of what she did on Wednesday afternoons, the half-day in the town.

It seems she was in the habit of having a sandwich and a cup of tea at the snack bar, but the proprietor said she always left on her own, although once or twice customers had offered her a date. She gave the impression of being in a hurry to meet someone.

The booking-office clerk, who was nineteen and had acne, remembered her at once because, as he said, she looked as if she might enjoy "a bit of fun." He was able to give Finch the information that on several Wednesday afternoons over the past three months she had booked day return tickets to Shenfield, Romford, and Ilford. He was uncertain of the dates but thought it was earlier in the year, in late January or February. More recently, certainly within the past three weeks, she had twice booked single tickets to London. Inquiries at all these stations had proved negative. None of the staff could remember her getting out at those stations.

The two bus conductors remembered her for much the same reason as the clerk, although the older of the two had remarked, "She was a bit too much of the come-hither type." They could only remember her on two occasions, once when she had gone all the way to Southend. The younger conductor was quite positive about this.

"She sat upstairs and we had a bit of a chat every time I came up for a fare. She said she was going to Southend to meet her boyfriend."

When the bus reached the terminus, he had gone straight into the office, because he wanted time for a cup of tea before the return journey. He had seen her walking away but had soon lost sight of her in the crowd of people at the bus station, so he could not say if anyone had met her. This had been several weeks ago, in February, he thought.

The older conductor remembered her getting off his bus at Bell Green, five miles outside Wrexford. He had thought this strange at the time, because there was nothing there except the crossroads and a couple of cottages. She had started walking up the road, in the same direction that the bus was traveling, away from the only habitation. This had been in late January. He was certain of this because he'd been transferred to another route in February.

"I stood on the platform and watched her until she was out of sight," the conductor said, when Finch interviewed him. "I thought it a bit odd at the time. She was wearing a red coat and high-heeled shoes. I know about the shoes because she stumbled a bit coming down the stairs and I remember thinking at the time, 'It's a wonder these girls don't break their necks wearing heels that high.' She was all dolled up, as if she was meeting someone. No, there wasn't anything in sight, not a person, not a car, nothing."

It was all written down in statement form and it added up to very little. Nobody had seen her in the company of a man. The diversity of the meeting places puzzled Finch too. The places were miles apart: Southend, Shenfield, Romford, Ilford, London, and Bell Green.

Inquiries into how the girl spent the evenings on which she was known to be meeting someone met with the same lack of success. Boyce's inquiries had turned up nothing and Finch, in an effort to pick up information, however trivial, had interviewed the sister, Pamela, again. Pamela, wearing makeup and a short black skirt and tight jumper which Finch suspected belonged to her dead sister, could tell him nothing new. Doreen went out every Wednesday and Saturday evening at seven o'clock, on her bicycle. She usually returned before eleven, before her father came back from the pub, because there were rows if she was late home. Pamela had no idea whom she met or where she went. Her likeness in that second interview to her dead sister was striking and Finch found himself staring in fascination at her neck.

Finch had had extensive searches made for the missing bicycle, shoes, and handbag but these had also been negative. Groups of constables under Boyce's direction had been combing woods and hedgerows. Appeals in the local newspapers had brought in an assortment of old shoes and bicycles, long abandoned, from places as far as ten miles away, but none of them were Doreen's. There had also been the usual crop of reports of girls in red coats, resembling Doreen, being seen in many different places, all of which had to be painstakingly investigated. The latest one, of a girl with brown hair and a red coat, seen in Colchester, had arrived only that morning.

There was another report waiting for him when he returned from interviewing Mr. Severall. It was the report on the forensic analysis of the threads found under the girl's fingernails. Finch saw it lying on his desk and tore the envelope open eagerly. The report read:

"The threads are of artificial silk, dark red in color and of a cheap quality. They are short in length and show evidence of having been broken at a time previous to being caught up by the deceased's fingernails, as the ends of several of those in the fingernails of the left hand are frayed by wear and show discoloration by dirt.''

When he had read through the report, Finch examined the photograph of the fibers which was enclosed in the envelope. The silk threads had been photographed under magnification and showed quite clearly the teased-out ends of the individual fibers that came from a long process of fraying rather than from the sudden snapping of the threads.

With the photograph in his hand Finch walked up and down the office, thinking deeply about the significance of this information. The color, dark red, would suggest a man's tie but would a man wear a tie that was frayed? It would be likely if the man was careless of his appearance, a man like Smith or even Meyrick. Finch summoned up mental images of the two men. When he had interviewed them, Meyrick was wearing a shirt, with the neck open; Smith, a navy-blue roll-neck sweater, with no shirt visible. Either of them might wear a frayed, red tie, unless. . . . A sudden idea came to the Inspector and he strode quickly to the door and threw it open.

"Spencer!"

The duty sergeant at the desk looked up startled.

"Yes, sir?"

"Have the Walker girl's clothes come back from forensic yet?"

Finch had sent them off the day before, with a sense of clutching at straws, to be submitted to a detailed laboratory examination, although he held out little hope of anything useful being found on them. The mud clinging to the coat was almost certainly from the wood where the body had been found and there was small chance of fingerprints being discovered as the shoes, the most likely surface for prints, were still missing.

"They've just come in, sir, with a report," replied the sergeant.

"Then send them in here at once," said Finch.

A young constable brought in the clothing, neatly wrapped in plastic sheeting. A report lay on the top and Finch put it to one side as he ripped open the tape that bound the parcel together. The coat lay at the bottom with the lighter clothes, her skirt and jumper, the thin, cheap nylon underwear and stockings, on the top. He slid these off the pile and, grim-faced, turned the coat inside out. The dark red silk lining was obvious. He ran his hands quickly over it. There was no sign of a tear or a broken place. He paused for a moment, thinking this over, and then, with a sudden inspiration, turned the lining of the pockets inside out. The plucked silk showed only too clearly where the girl's nails had clutched at the linings, especially in the left-hand pocket where the lining was already frayed at the seam and several threads had been clearly drawn out and snapped off. She had been attacked, therefore, while her hands were in her pockets, before she had time to defend herself.

Boyce entered the office at this moment and found Finch bent over the coat, thoughtfully rubbing the silk between finger and thumb as if testing its quality. Boyce raised his eyebrows.

"Why do you put your hands in your pockets, Tom?" asked Finch.

"Me?" said Boyce, taken aback by the question.

"Yes, you. Or anybody, come to that."

"Because you're cold," suggested Boyce. "Or leaning up against a lamppost with nothing better to do."

Finch whistled gently and went on rubbing the silk.

"And where would you go on a wet, cold Saturday evening, if you were fifteen and liked a bit of the you-know-what and didn't want to be disturbed?"

"Haystack? Shed? Back seat of a car? Could be anywhere," replied Boyce. "When I was on the beat I once found a couple at it in a telephone box."

"There isn't a phone box within a mile of the wood," said Finch. "Could be a barn, though. Or a car. If he's an older man, he could have a car. What would she do with the bike, though?"

"Stick it behind a hedge," suggested Boyce.

"No, we'd've found it by now," said Finch. "Or someone else would have done. Then there's her bag and shoes. I can understand the bag; that could easily have been dropped somewhere. But not the shoes."

"Perhaps they fell off during the struggle," said Boyce.

"There wasn't a struggle. She had her hands in her pockets."

"Well, then, while he was carrying the body into the wood to dump it."

"Then they'd still be there. It was dark, remember. If you were carrying a dead body, would you notice if the shoes fell off?"

"Perhaps he noticed they were missing and went back to find them."

"Oh, I don't know," said Finch, going to stand hump-shouldered at the window. "He could have done, I suppose. It doesn't seem to add up, though. If I'd just killed a girl I wouldn't go hunting around in a wood in the dark for a pair of shoes. And anyway, aren't we assuming too much in thinking the body was dumped there? Supposing they met in the wood and he killed her there?"

"It could be," agreed Boyce, "although, as you said yourself, it was a cold, wet March evening, For my money, they'd find somewhere sheltered."

"If it was the back seat of a car," mused Finch, picking up Boyce's earlier suggestion, "then he could have killed her anywhere and brought the body to the wood in the car. But doesn't that assume the man had a local knowledge? I'm beginning to think it does. The Framwell road is unlit and you can't see the wood from the road, if you're just driving past in the dark. If she'd picked up with someone outside the district, a Southend man, for example, the chances are he wouldn't know the wood and he'd have dumped the body nearer the road's edge; just tumbled the body out into a ditch. No, I feel she was killed somewhere near the wood by a man she was in the habit of meeting locally on a Saturday and Wednesday evening. The fact that she was killed on a Sunday doesn't radically alter the pattern. She leaves home on her bike, in this case in the afternoon because she's made an arrangement to set Brenda Parsons' hair. She leaves the Parsons home at the usual time of seven o'clock, saying that she's going to meet someone. Now, I think that was the same man she met on the Wednesday and Saturday evenings and for some reason he was free on Sunday evening as well. We have Brenda's evidence to support that. They met somewhere near the village. I don't think Doreen Walker would want to cycle far for a date. She could have gone across the footpath to the wood, or by the road. Anyway, they meet. They make love. He kills her. She's not expecting the attack. She has her hands in her pockets. But I don't think it happened in the wood. She was wearing her best coat and a pair of high-heeled patent-leather shoes, not the outfit for a bit of rustic lovemaking in the wet undergrowth. Look, Boyce, I want you to go over the route and examine any shed, haystack, barn, anywhere where they might have gone for shelter, but near enough to the wood for him to know about it and to have got the body there without too much trouble. Examine the outbuildings at Collins' farm again. I know you've been over them once and the barn was locked anyway, but try again."

Boyce said, "I'll get that organized. I agree that a man with local knowledge sounds plausible, but what about the Wednesday afternoon dates? He doesn't fit in with her going off to Southend and London."

"I know that," said Finch. "And I'm beginning to wonder if the Wednesday afternoons weren't spent with somebody entirely different, or indeed with several different men. We know from what Brenda Parsons told us that she wasn't past picking up boys. She may have gone on the off chance of meeting someone in a pub or a café. I want to work on the local angle first. If nothing comes of that—and God knows we've drawn enough blanks so far—we'll have to try further afield and start going round the pubs and cinemas in the places she was known to visit. I hope it doesn't come to that, though. It's going to be one hell of a sweat."

He crossed the room and looked at the map which hung on the wall.

"London, Ilford, Romford, Shenfield, Southend. And Bell Green. Why the hell that place? And why only single tickets to London? She took day returns everywhere else she went to on the train."

"It suggests she was getting a lift home," said Boyce, "which wouldn't tie in with the local angle."

"Possibly," agreed Finch. "But I'm not abandoning the local angle until I've exhausted it. Have you thought, Tom," he added, suddenly turning from the map, "how lucky this man has been? Nobody's seen him. Nobody's heard of him. Doreen Walker was the sly type who liked keeping a secret. There's not even a fingerprint to go on. The three things that might show a print, her bike, shoes, and bag, are missing."

"Could be very clever as well as very lucky," commented Boyce.

Unbidden, the thought of Smith rose in the Inspector's mind. Smith would be clever enough to cover all traces of himself if he wanted to, although there was one loophole that remained open, the letters that came every Friday and which led—where?

Abruptly Finch went to the desk and began wrapping up the girl's clothes in the plastic sheeting. The report that had accompanied them from the forensic laboratory caught his attention and he picked it up and began to open it.

"See if the canteen's open and rustle up some tea, if you can," he said to Boyce, "while I have a clear-up in here."

Boyce came back a few minutes later with a tray of tea things to find Finch jubilant.

"Something's turned up at last!" he cried. "It was a long shot but it came off. It's a print of an index finger, found on the middle button on the girl's coat and it's not one of her prints. They've checked that." He pushed the coat and the photograph of the print at Boyce.

"Only part of a print because the button's only partly smooth. See, it's got a broad, smooth rim and the center of it is etched across, but it's enough to make an identification possible. Tom, I want you off fingerprinting tomorrow."

"Who?" said Boyce, putting down the tray. The prospect seemed to fill him with gloom.

"Well, we'd better have the Walker family done, for elimination, and anyone the girl could have come into contact with. The Parsons family too. One of them might have handled the coat. Also the boys she was known to have gone out with."

"They've already been checked," said Boyce. "They all had alibis for the Sunday evening."

"I want them printed," persisted Finch. "We'll do the whole bloody village if necessary."

"Anyone else?" asked Boyce.

"Meyrick; he found the body. And Smith."

Finch added the last name after a small hesitation.

"There's not much on him," said Boyce. "You haven't even got a statement from him yet."

"I have my reasons for that," said Finch. "I'm keeping him dangling on purpose. Just put it down to a hunch, if you like."

"All right," said Boyce, shrugging. "One more to print won't make all that amount of difference."

"And now we'll have tea," said Finch, looking pleased with himself and walking spring-heeled across the office. "We'll have a nice cup of tea by way of a small celebration because I feel it in my bones that this case is beginning to move at last."

It was the next day that Boyce, taking a constable with him, went to Leverett's farm to fingerprint Meyrick. Meyrick was clearing up the yard when the police car drew up in the lane and he regarded them with a surly face as they walked toward him.

"What do you want?" he said. "I told the Inspector all I know. He wrote it down and I signed it. You was there."

"Just another routine inquiry," said Boyce cheerfully. "We want to take your fingerprints, Mr. Meyrick. It's a question of elimination."

Meyrick put his hands in his pockets and looked sullen.

The constable, who was country bred and understood Meyrick's type of temperament, said, "It's all right. They've found a fingerprint, see? We'll take your fingerprints and then we'll know it isn't yours. You go and wash your hands and we'll go into the barn."

Meyrick gave him a look and then walked over to an outside tap by the barn wall, turned it on and began washing his hands with a bar of yellow soap that stood on a slate on the window-sill. Boyce and the constable went into the barn where the constable began unpacking his ink pad and paper onto the inner ledge of the window, which he first spread with his handkerchief.

"Better in here than the farmhouse," he commented. "He'll feel more at home."

"Proper little psychiatrist, aren't you?" said Boyce with a laugh, and the constable, who was looking for promotion, tried to look busy and unself-conscious.

Meyrick allowed himself to be fingerprinted but gave no cooperation. The constable had to lift the man's great heavy hand and spread the inert fingers out while he pressed each one on the ink pad and then rolled it across the paper.

"It'll wash off," he assured Meyrick who, when the operation was completed, stared at his outspread, ink-stained fingers as though they were diseased. He made a sort of hawking noise in his throat and then hurriedly wiped his hands down the sides of his trousers. The constable began to pack up his apparatus and Boyce said pleasantly:

"I hope that's the last time we shall have to worry you, Mr. Meyrick."

Meyrick did not answer but slouched out of the barn and across the yard. The two policemen shrugged to show their indifference to his attitude and walked off in the other direction to the police car.

In order to get to Smith's cottage they had to leave the car in the lane opening and walk. Smith was scrubbing the floor of the living room and had left the front door open so that the wet flagstones would dry more quickly. Cairn had been shut up in the kitchen because he had kept running in and out, bringing in mud from the garden. Because of the noise of the scrubbing Smith had not heard the dog barking at the farm and so had not been warned of their approach. He was only aware of their presence when they appeared at the gate and blocked out the light from the doorway. Both men were embarrassed at finding him on his hands and knees. They explained their business, standing on the doorstep, while Smith, his hands red and wet from the hot, soapy water, listened with an impassive face. The dog, hearing the voices, began to whine and scratch at the kitchen door.

"Wait a minute," said Smith, and he went through to the kitchen to quiet the dog and to fetch newspapers, which he spread across the patch of wet floor between the door and the table.

Boyce and the constable went in, first scraping their feet elaborately on the iron scraper near the door, despite the spread paper. Smith lifted down the wooden chair and the deck chair which he had placed on top of the table while he was washing the floor. The room smelled of damp earth from the garden and soap.

"Sit down," said Smith, but neither of the policemen accepted and remained obstinately standing. Boyce, with a heavy curiosity, quite unlike the Inspector's darting appraisal, was staring about him. The constable, who had gone red in the face for some reason, began hurriedly to get out his apparatus.

"Nice little cottage," said Boyce. Smith did not bother to answer but went over to the table and spread out his hands for his fingerprints to be taken.

"Is that all?" he asked when the operation was finished.

"Yes," said Boyce and could not resist adding, "for the moment."

He had taken an immediate dislike to Smith. The burly sergeant was sensitive to other people's attitude to himself and he felt Smith had snubbed him in some subtle way that he could not quite define. He brooded over it as he walked down the lane to the car.

"Funny customer," remarked the constable. He had not much cared for Smith either but, being subordinate to Boyce, had not been so personally disturbed by the man.

"I suppose so," growled Boyce, and would not speak again all the way back to Wrexford. The constable, who was driving, wondered what he had said or done to offend him.

Without holding out much hope for a positive identification, Finch dispatched the prints, including Smith's and Meyrick's, to the fingerprint department and got on with the routine investigation of the case. Later that afternoon he and Boyce were talking over the day's inquiries, which had still produced nothing definite, when the report came back.

Finch was astounded when he read it.

"We've clicked on the fingerprint!" he cried jubilantly.

"Smith's?" asked Boyce, leaning forward excitedly to take the piece of paper.

"No, Meyrick's," said the Inspector. "On your feet, Tom. I want him down here at the station."

10

Mrs. Meyrick was straining potatoes at the kitchen sink when Boyce arrived. She heard his feet on the concrete path and glared up fiercely over the half-curtain of net that covered the lower panes of the window. With the saucepan still in her hand she opened the back door.

"You're the police," she said accusingly. "What do you want now?"

"I'd like a word with your husband," replied Boyce, who, although Finch had warned him of Mrs. Meyrick's temper, was nonetheless a little taken aback by her fierceness.

"I'm just dishing up his supper," she said, showing no inclination to ask the sergeant inside. Indeed, she half closed the door and Boyce had to lean his big frame against it to stop her from shutting it in his face.

"It's important," he said firmly.

She looked at him for a moment, her jaw working, and then with an ungracious jerk of the head, told him to come in.

On the sideboard the wireless, a large, old-fashioned set with tarnished gold fabric behind a fretwork panel, was blaring out "The Archers." Meyrick was sitting in his usual place by the fire and was staring through the bars at the glowing coals behind, with his hands hanging loosely between his open knees. He merely looked up when Boyce entered the room.

"I shall have to ask you to accompany me to the police station," said Boyce, raising his voice against Mrs. Archer, who was telling Dan Archer about the Women's Institute meeting in tones of Amazonian tête-à-tête.

Meyrick's reply was inaudible and then Mrs. Meyrick stalked over to the wireless and turned it off with a sharp click. The sudden silence was startling.

"What did you say?" asked Boyce.

"What for?" repeated Meyrick. He seemed to have acquired some of his wife's belligerence and glared at the sergeant.

Boyce, however, had no intention of being intimidated by Meyrick and he answered in a firm, official manner.

"For further inquiries."

His tone of voice and large bulk quickly deflated Meyrick, who got up from his chair, mumbling vaguely that he'd fetch his coat. But Mrs. Meyrick's spirit was not so easily broken.

"I'm coming too," she said, and stalked over to get her own coat which was hanging on a hook on the back of the kitchen door. Thrusting her arms into the sleeves, buttoning it up briskly, she defied the two men to refuse her.

Boyce put the pair of them into the back of the police car and got in beside the driver. They were silent throughout the drive and Boyce, glancing from time to time into the rear mirror, caught glimpses of them from an oblique angle, Meyrick, hands dangling, staring apathetically in front of him, Mrs. Meyrick, rigid and clutching her handbag fiercely with both hands as if she expected at any moment to have it snatched away.

The sergeant on desk duty at the station looked up in surprise when Boyce ushered them both in. He seemed about to say something but after one look at Mrs. Meyrick's formidable jaw he quickly dissociated himself from the situation and began writing busily in the duty book. Boyce tried to ignore her.

"The Inspector will see you in the interview room, Mr. Meyrick," he said, addressing himself directly to the man. He added, because he felt sorry for him, "There's no need to worry. It's only a routine matter."

Meyrick, who was staring about him and blinking in the bright light, looked pathetically lost and bewildered. He fumbled with his hands, not knowing whether to put them in his pockets. In that bare, bright, official room it seemed too casual a thing to do.

"I thought you said it was important," snapped Mrs. Meyrick. She had crowded up close to her husband as though she had every intention of accompanying him to the interview. The sergeant cleared his throat and turned over a page of the book.

Boyce said firmly, "If you'll sit down over there, Mrs. Meyrick, your husband won't be long."

She looked mutinous, and the sergeant, treading heavily, came from behind the desk and pulled forward a chair. Between them both, Boyce's bulk and the uniformed chest of the sergeant thrust forward, she subsided into the chair and sat with her knees close together and her bag held upright on her lap like a shield. She had given in but it was easy to see that it was only a temporary truce. She was ready at any moment to come back fighting. The sergeant, returning to his place behind the desk, noticed for the first time that she was wearing felt bedroom slippers.

Boyce took Meyrick along the passage to the interview room where Finch was waiting for him. Two straight-backed chairs were drawn up, one on each side of a wooden table. The Inspector was sitting in the one facing the door

113

with Meyrick's statement, typed out and looking official, open in front of him.

Finch had set the scene deliberately but, in case Meyrick should be too cowed by the display of formality, he had lit a cigarette just before the man entered. A lopsided circle of smoke, hanging above his head like a jaunty halo, was just beginning to disperse.

"Sit down, Mr. Meyrick," said Finch. Boyce, who had been asked to be present at the interview, drew up another chair on Finch's right.

Meyrick sat down and looked from one to the other, wiping the palms of his hands slowly up the knees of his trousers.

He said, "What do you want?"

The Inspector did not immediately reply. He sat with bent head and appeared to be engrossed in reading over the typewritten pages that lay in their folder on the table in front of him. Boyce put up a hand to his mouth to hide a grin. He knew this old ploy, worked by headmasters, bank managers, and police inspectors the world over. It had its effect on Meyrick, who swallowed uneasily and began shifting about his feet in their heavy, working boots.

Suddenly Finch looked up.

"I've asked you here, Mr. Meyrick, because I am not too happy about the statement you gave us."

He waited, fixing Meyrick with his eyes.

"No?" said Meyrick, forced by the silence into speaking. "What's wrong then?"

"That's for you to tell me," said Finch suavely. "I shall read the statement over to you, Mr. Meyrick. I want you to listen to it carefully. If there is any sentence, word, or phrase in it that you wish to alter, will you please tell me?"

Again he waited for Meyrick to answer.

"All right," said Meyrick uneasily.

In a flat, monotonous voice Finch read over the statement. It had been translated from Meyrick's original verbal statement into official terms. The Inspector's colorless voice took from it any life that it might have had.

" 'My name is Reginald Arthur Meyrick and I am employed by Mr. James Collins of Leverett's Farm, Westham Road, Frayling, Essex. On Monday, March 14, I was plowing the field adjacent to Leverett's Wood. Because of a storm I had occasion to seek shelter in the wood. I noticed what I thought to be a bundle of clothes lying in the bushes near where I was sheltering. On closer investigation I found it to be the body of a girl. I did not touch the body but returned immediately to the farm, where, obtaining my bicycle, I rode into the village, a distance of approximately three quarters of a mile, and reported my discovery to Police Constable Russell. The time of my discovery of the body was approximately 12:40 P.M.' "

When he had finished reading the statement Finch sat back in his chair and looked at Meyrick, who shifted about, clasping and unclasping his hands.

"Well, Mr. Meyrick," said Finch at last, "is there anything you wish to add to or change in your original statement?"

"I dunno," said Meyrick. His face had taken on a stubborn expression. "That's what I said, or leastways that's the way you writ it down. And that's the way it happened. I don't know what you're getting at. There ain't anything wrong as I can see."

Finch said, "I think I must warn you, Mr. Meyrick, that fresh evidence has come to light which suggests that part of your statement is incorrect. I am not," he added quickly, waving away Meyrick, who had half risen from his chair, "suggesting for a moment that you have deliberately lied. I think that your memory of what happened is faulty. Now

I want you to think back again very carefully to that Monday afternoon and try to remember if there is anything, however small, that you have forgotten and may now wish to change."

Finch knew he was being pompous and official. Boyce, who understood him, knew he was trying his best to be absolutely fair to the man. In a murder investigation, where evidence might point to the guilt of a person, Finch in his interview of that person assumed this impersonal and official attitude, cutting himself off from any emotional contact.

But to Meyrick, with his limited intelligence, it seemed he was being trapped. Dumbly he turned between the two men, utterly bewildered.

"I dunno what you mean," he said.

Finch glanced at Boyce, who leaned forward and took over the questioning.

"Mr. Meyrick, we'd like you to think back to the time you discovered the body. Would you please tell us again, in your own words, exactly what happened. Try to remember everything. It may be important."

"Well," said Meyrick slowly, "I was stood under this tree. It were raining. I see this bundle. It's red. When the rain eased, I went over to have a look. I saw . . ."

He stopped.

"Go on," said Boyce. "Tell us everything you did or saw."

Meyrick swallowed heavily.

"I saw it was a girl. She had brown hair and a red coat on. Her face was all puffy and a funny color, sort of blue. There was marks on her throat. For a minute I couldn't take it in, like. Then it dawned. It turned me up. I started running and I fetched my bike and went up to the village."

Finch got up, pushing back his chair impatiently. There seemed no way out of the situation except by means of a direct question.

116

"Did you touch the body at all?" he asked. "Think carefully. This could be very important."

The puzzled way the man swung his head to and fro to look at both of them suggested that he had not made the connection between the taking of his fingerprints that afternoon and this inquiry. The movement was heavy, confused, like that of an animal that has been backed into a corner and does not know what is expected of it. There was no outburst as there had been the first time the question was asked.

"I can't remember," he said finally. "I might 'ave done. It turned me up, seeing her there. She was lying under the bushes. I had to part them to get a proper look."

He made a gesture with his arm as he spoke, as if thrusting aside branches and ducked his head at the same time.

"Can you be positive you did not touch the body?" insisted the Inspector. Meyrick did not understand, and Finch rephrased it. "Are you sure you didn't touch her?"

"No," he said, "I ain't sure. I bent down, you see. I couldn't make it out at first. Like a bundle it was and all wet. It'd been raining . . ."

Now that he had started to talk, he wanted to go on and on, explaining, telling over and over what he had seen. The sweat stood out on his forehead.

"All right," said Finch. "You can go, Mr. Meyrick. I shall have your statement rewritten, bearing in mind that you may have touched the body, but you are not sure. Perhaps you will be kind enough to call in at the station tomorrow to sign it?"

Boyce held the door open but Meyrick did not understand that the interview was over. He still sat facing the Inspector. Finch got up.

"You can go home, Mr. Meyrick," he said. His voice was tired. The man blundered over to the door, with Boyce and Finch following.

Mrs. Meyrick jumped to her feet when she saw her husband coming back. She had been sitting, clutching her handbag, chewing over and over the injustice of it all. When she saw her husband's face she boiled over.

"What have you been doing to him?" she shouted. "What do you want with him anyway? Dragging him down here at this time of an evening! Bloody police! He hasn't even had his supper!"

"I'm sorry, Mrs. Meyrick," said Finch soothingly. She swung round to face him. All of them, the sergeant behind the desk, Meyrick, Boyce, and a fresh-faced constable who had come in to see what all the noise was about, held themselves suspended, watching and waiting for the explosion.

"You! Don't you bloody speak to me! You want to get off your backside and get out and find the man who did it. That bleeding man Smith. Bring *him* in and leave my bloody man alone!"

The constable, snorting with uncontrollable nervous laughter, had to go away. The sergeant glared. Boyce stepped forward.

"Come on now, Mrs. Meyrick. The car's outside to take you home. You go before you say something you might be sorry for afterwards."

The veiled threat was enough. She stalked off, Meyrick trailing behind her. The group of policemen relaxed. Boyce laughed and touched the Inspector on the shoulder and Finch let out a great comic sigh of relief. The sergeant walked off to find the constable and tell him what he thought of him.

"She's a tartar and no mistake," said Boyce.

"I wonder if she meant what she said about Smith," said Finch, suddenly sobering. "It could be unpleasant for him if the people in the village believe he's guilty."

"Oh, I don't know," replied Boyce laconically. He had

not Finch's imaginative capacity for putting himself in another person's place. "From what you've said about him he sounds a cool enough customer. I can't see a bit of gossip bothering him."

But Finch reserved his judgment. He knew what village gossip was like, insidious, spreading, and sometimes vicious, and he made a mental note to ask Russell, the next time he had occasion to speak to him on the telephone, to let him know if he heard any threats uttered against Smith.

The Inspector thought a great deal about Smith during that afternoon. What kind of man was he to wish to live alone in that isolated cottage? Was there some mystery or unhappiness in his past that he was trying to escape from? A tragedy perhaps? Or a scandal? Had the man not become involved in the Walker case, Finch would have found him intriguing, worth investigating for himself alone. He wanted to understand him, to take him to pieces, as he had taken to pieces other people in the course of police investigations, gently probing, during long hours of questioning in interview rooms, the secret and sensitive places in their hearts and minds. Smith, the Inspector realized, would not be an easy subject for such an investigation. Indeed, he would be something of a challenge, for he was better equipped than most people; he was more intelligent, had more poise and self-assurance. He would not be easily tricked or bullied or cajoled into revealing himself. Like a fox, he would be adept at self-concealment, quick to see a trap and to avoid it.

Thinking about Smith the Inspector began to want to see him again, but there was no excuse either for visiting the man in the cottage or for asking him to present himself at the police station, except to make the statement about his presence in Leverett's wood which Finch was reluctant still to demand of him. He still felt that this was a trump card

119

which he must hold on to and not squander. He wanted to wait until the right opportunity for playing it came along.

An opportunity came sooner than he had expected. The investigation of the case continued but it had become a routine matter. Despite inquiries there seemed no further evidence to connect the murder with Meyrick or Smith or, indeed, with anybody else. Boyce was sent off to Southend with the dead girl's photograph to make a tour of the cafés, dance halls, cinemas, and snack bars that she might have visited on the Wednesday afternoon she was known to have spent in the town. Finch himself went to Brentwood. In neither town was she positively identified, although the proprietor of a snack bar in Brentwood and the girl in the ticket office of a Southend cinema thought they might have seen her. Neither of them could be positive about the date and in both cases the girl was alone so that, even if it was Doreen Walker, the police were no further in their investigations. The man in the case remained as faceless and nameless as ever.

It was on his return from Brentwood, tired and out of temper, that Finch received some information that seemed to put Smith back into the case.

As he entered the station, the sergeant on duty stopped him and, nodding over to a man who was sitting on a chair by the wall, said:

"Someone to see you, sir, about the Walker case."

Finch walked over to the man. He was reading an evening paper which he nervously folded up as Finch approached. He was a short, slight man, with full eyes, a little mustache stuck perilously to his upper lip, and greased-back hair. He had a shabby-smart appearance, like a seedy dandy. There was dandruff on his collar and nicotine stains on his fingers.

"I believe you wanted to see me," said Finch.

120

"Are you Inspector Finch?" asked the man. His voice was higher than it would normally be because of nervousness. When Finch nodded, he continued in a quick rush of words an explanation that had obviously been rehearsed.

"It's about that girl's death, Inspector. I believe I may have some information about it. I'm not sure, mind you, but, after talking it over with my wife, I decided I ought to come along and tell you."

"You were quite right to do so," said Finch "And if you'll come this way, sir, I shall be only too pleased to listen."

The old-fashioned courtesy and the use of the word "sir" set the little man at his ease. It was with almost a swagger that he preceded Finch into one of the interviewing rooms. Finch made him comfortable in a chair, gave him a cigarette, and asked his name.

"Lamport. George Lamport."

"Well, now, Mr. Lamport, and what have you to tell us?" asked Finch.

Lamport licked his lips and plunged into his story.

"The other Saturday evening I was driving my mother-in-law home. We live in Wrexford, by the way, and my wife's mother had come over for the day to give a hand with the children as my wife was down with flu. The wife's mother lives in Romford, that's several miles from here, just off the main Chelmsford road. Well, it was pouring with rain and she's not a bad old sort, so after tea I said to her, 'If you'll hang on till we've got Sally (that's the youngest) settled down, I'll run you home.' Anyway, to cut a long story short, I took her back, stopped there for a cup of tea she insisted on making, although I was anxious to get back to the wife, and then I started for home. The traffic was very busy on the main road, going quite slowly because of the rain, so I thought to myself, If I turn up some of the side roads, I'll probably be home just as quick. I'd meant to come back via Harbury but I must have missed the turning. I was driving quite slowly, looking out for signposts. Besides that, it was still raining, though not quite so heavy."

Finch shifted in his chair but said nothing. He knew he would have to let Lamport tell the story in his own way.

"Well, eventually I came to this village. I didn't know it. Never been there in my life before. But I did notice the pub, the Crown. It had fairy lights all round the roof and that made me notice it. Well, last Friday, when we got the local paper, what should there be on the front page but a photo of that very pub! And then it dawned that it was the village where that girl had been murdered. They were asking for any information that might be useful so I said to my wife, 'I wonder if I ought to say anything about seeing that couple?'"

"What couple?" asked Finch sharply.

"I was coming to them," said Lamport. "You see, as I was driving out of the village I noticed this couple standing in a gateway. I thought to myself at the time, Fancy going courting in this weather."

"Just a minute," said Finch. He left the room and returned soon with a large-scale map of the district and a photograph of Doreen Walker. He showed the photograph to Lamport.

"Was this the girl?"

Lamport examined the photograph with great interest.

"Is this the girl that was murdered?" Then he shook his head. "I'm sorry, Inspector. I didn't really get much of a look at the girl. She had her back to me. All I can tell you is she seemed young and she either had long dark hair or a dark scarf tied over her head."

"Did you notice the color of her coat?" asked Finch.

Lamport thought for a moment and then shook his head.

122

"No, I'm afraid I didn't."

"Or a bicycle?"

"I didn't see one."

"All right," said Finch. "Now what about the man? Can you tell me anything about him?"

Lamport frowned with the effort of thinking back. He was at ease now enjoying the situation and the feeling of importance it gave him. Nevertheless, Finch felt he was a reliable witness, a truthful man at heart.

"I can't tell you much about him," Lamport said. "He was tall and was wearing a long, dark coat or it might have been a mackintosh. He wasn't wearing a hat and he had the collar of his coat turned up. I got the impression he had a beard, but I wouldn't be positive. It could have been the shadow of his coat collar. He was standing facing the girl and when I drove up he turned his head away as if the headlights had dazzled him so I only caught a glimpse of his face."

"Would you recognize him again?" asked Finch.

Lamport sucked in his lower lip doubtfully.

"I might," he replied.

His confidence seemed to be waning, because he added, "I'm sorry I can't be more help, Inspector. But I only caught a glimpse and I didn't take all that much notice of them."

"You've been a great help," said Finch, and indeed he meant it. Lamport was the only independent witness to come forward with anything like useful information. Finch felt Lamport had brought him luck. He was at the turning point in the investigation. Lamport had seen Doreen Walker, of that Finch was certain, and in the company of a man who was most probably her killer.

It was in a cheerful, optimistic mood that Finch got Lamport to verify the exact date, which Lamport, after careful

123

consultation with his diary, confirmed as Saturday, March 12, the day before Doreen Walker's murder. The exact time he was not so sure about. He thought it was about ten past seven, as he reached home soon after half-past. The exact place Lamport and Finch worked out together from the map and Lamport was able to put a cross on the map at the spot where he thought he had seen the couple.

Using all this information, Finch drew up a statement which Lamport signed before he left.

When Boyce returned to the station later Finch was still in his cheerful, optimistic mood. Boyce read through Lamport's statement but did not share the Inspector's enthusiasm.

"It's a bit vague," he said.

"But it's something to go on at last," said Finch, who refused to have his spirits dampened. "We know Doreen Walker was out meeting someone on that Saturday evening. The times coincide. And I'll wager anything that the man she met on the Wednesdays and Saturdays was the same man she met on the Sunday."

Boyce sat down heavily on a chair and loosened his overcoat. His feet hurt him and he was tired.

"I still don't see it need be her. It could have been any courting couple."

"I don't think so," said Finch. "It must have been a local couple. It's several miles to the next village and it's likely that a courting couple from further away would have been in a car. Well, you don't get out of a car on a wet evening to stand in a gateway. You park the car somewhere quiet and do your courting on the back seat. Leastways, that's what I'd do. So that's out. Now, I've checked with Leach and there was a twenty-first birthday party going on at the hall that evening. Most of the young people from Framwell had been invited. I grant you, a couple could have slipped

124

out of the hall for a quiet cuddle, but look at the map! The hall's here," Finch stabbed at the map with a finger, "the gateway's roughly here. That's nearly quarter of a mile away. A courting couple from the party would have kept nearer the village. No, I'm convinced it was Doreen Walker. She was meeting someone secretly so she'd arrange a meeting place outside the village, where she wouldn't be likely to be seen."

"Where was her bike then?" asked Boyce, stubbornly unconvinced.

"Lamport didn't positively say there wasn't one. He just said he hadn't noticed one. It could have been propped up in the hedge."

"I suppose so," admitted Boyce.

"But do you see the implications?" said Finch excitedly. "She meets a man outside the village and he's *on foot!* If there had been a car, you can bet your life she'd have dumped the bike and got into it double quick and been driven off. She wouldn't have hung about a gateway in the rain. So, it follows the man hadn't got a car and lived within walking distance of that gateway. Now, look at the map again."

Finch put one finger on the place on the map where Lamport had seen the couple.

"Lamport couldn't be absolutely sure but it's somewhere along this piece of road. He remembers seeing a road sign for an S bend shortly before he saw them and slowed down considerably to take the corner. So he reckoned it was along this stretch of road. Now, there are two fields marked here, presumably with gates to them. We'll have to check on that. *But*," and Finch's voice rose in excitement, "what is marked on the map, higher up the road I admit, is the stile and leading from that stile there's the footpath to Leverett's wood. Let's assume then that the man comes by that foot-

125

path, climbs the stile, finds he's a few minutes early and walks down the road a short way toward the village. He meets Doreen, coming up the road and they stop in the nearest gateway."

"Smith?" asked Boyce.

They exchanged glances.

"It could very well be," said Finch quietly. He folded up the map. The mentioning of Smith's name seemed to have sobered him. The excitement went out of his voice and he became quiet and serious.

"That's what I'm beginning to think, Tom. Let's look at Lamport's statement again. He says a tall man in a long, dark overcoat or mackintosh. That would fit Smith. A man who possibly had a beard. Only possible. We must remember that. He could not be positive on that point. Smith has a beard. He must be a man, moreover, if my assumptions are correct, who could have walked across the fields to meet Doreen Walker. Now, we know Smith is familiar with Leverett's wood. He also admitted to me he has walked across the footpath as far as the stile."

"It could have been someone who walked along the road," Boyce pointed out. "Or it needn't have been Doreen Walker at all but some other girl."

"That's what we're going to find out," said Finch. "I want a house-to-house checkup in Framwell. I want the name of every person who was away from home that Saturday evening. I want to know whom they were with, where they went, what they were doing, and if any of them stopped, even for a couple of minutes in a gateway. And I want that stretch of road and every gate opening thoroughly searched for any scrap of evidence that might be useful. Take as many men as you think you'll need, Tom, and impress on them how important it is. I want this end of it sewn up as tight as it can be before I make the next move."

The next move was decided on late the next evening, when Boyce, heavy with fatigue, had gone home and Finch, alone in the office, sat down at his desk to go over the reports. They were all negative.

He got up, stretched, and went to stand at the dark window.

"Right," he said aloud. "We'll get Lamport over for an identification parade and we'll have Smith up. And Meyrick too. Why not?"

11

Smith was working in the garden when Russell came to fetch him. The policeman had ridden down from the village after receiving a telephone call from Finch, telling him to bring Smith to the end of the lane, where a police car would be waiting to take him to Wrexford police station. Russell was not informed of the reason.

It was a lowering day. Low clouds threatened rain. Smith had cut back the elder trees in the corner of the garden and had made a bonfire, but the wood was too green and damp to burn. It smoldered fitfully, sending out loose coils of smoke which, because of the lack of wind, hung about the garden, spreading and flattening out just above ground level.

Smith made no comment when Russell told him he was wanted at the police station. Holding out his dirty hands to indicate that he would wash them, he gathered up his tools and went into the house with Cairn following. Russell walked up and down the garden paths, looking at the seedbeds while he waited. From time to time he squatted down to look more closely at the empty packet at the head of each row. They were stained and faded by the rain. Russell was himself a keen gardener and he found himself admiring the neatness and order of Smith's efforts. The soil had been raked to a fine tilth and he had planted a very comprehensive selection of seeds. Russell was surprised and felt a fellow sympathy for the man. He had not imagined Smith, with his beard and untidy clothes, to have bothered with a garden at all.

Presently Smith reappeared, locked the front door, and put the key in his pocket. He had already bolted the back door from the inside, precautions he had got into the habit of taking since the evening the youths from the village had thrown mud at the cottage. Cairn was with him.

Russell eyed the dog doubtfully. "I don't know that you can bring the dog with you," he said.

"The dog comes," said Smith, "or I stay."

Russell shrugged. He had no orders regarding the dog and if that was to be Smith's attitude, he preferred to let the police driver argue it out.

They walked up the lane together, Russell wheeling his bike. He tried once or twice to get Smith into conversation on the subject of gardening but the man would not be drawn. In the end the policeman fell silent, thinking, Let him stew in his own juice, then.

The police car was already drawn up at the end of the lane. Russell, excusing himself, hurried forward to have a quick, whispered consultation with the driver about Smith's dog before Smith himself came up. The driver shared Russell's opinion. He had no instructions about it and had no intention of wasting time in an argument. He opened the rear door and Smith and the dog got in, the dog lying down on the floor, close to Smith's feet. Russell mounted his bicycle and rode off up the road.

The drive to the police station was completed in silence. Smith stared out the window and Cairn, who was lulled by the movement of the car, slept with his inert body heavy on Smith's feet. At the station the driver said briefly:

"If you'll go inside, sir, the Inspector would like to see you."

Smith went in. Finch was waiting by the desk, talking to the sergeant. They both looked up and Finch said pleasantly:

"I see you've brought your dog, Mr. Smith. Perhaps you could leave him here with the sergeant at the desk."

Smith said, "Do you want me to sign a statement?"

There was a sharp note in his voice and Finch wondered again why the question of the statement should cause him such apparent anxiety.

He said smoothly, "Not at the moment, sir. If you have no objections, we would like you to take part in an identification parade. It's simply a matter of elimination."

"Like the fingerprints?" asked Smith.

Finch ignored the irony in his voice and replied, "Just so, sir. You may, of course, refuse to take part in the parade . . ."

"I have no objections," said Smith, "apart from it being a total waste of time. What do I do?"

"The sergeant will show you," said Finch. "And may I thank you for your cooperation?"

There was a note of irony, too, under the official courtesy. The two men looked at each other and both suddenly smiled, Smith with that odd, lopsided quirk of his mouth, Finch with a broader grin. The sergeant sensed an understanding and feeling of camaraderie between the two men which he could not understand and was surprised.

"If you'll come this way, sir," he said noncommittally and, while Finch walked off with a jaunty step down the corridor, he indicated one of the interview rooms to Smith.

"Stay," Smith ordered the dog. Cairn looked up, flickering the white of his eyes in appeal, but he knew by the tone of Smith's voice that the command had to be obeyed and he lay down on the floor by the desk, sighing heavily.

In the interview room a collection of raincoats was spread out on the table. The sergeant sorted them over and selected one.

"If you wouldn't mind putting this on, sir, and turning the collar up," he said.

It was the correct length but much too broad across the shoulders and it accentuated Smith's stoop. The sergeant watched him put it on without a flicker of expression on his face.

"This way, sir," he said when Smith was ready and led the way back to the entrance hall.

Cairn wagged his tail hopefully as Smith came out of the room and sat up, but lay down again disappointed when the two men, the sergeant in front and Smith following, passed him and continued on down the corridor.

"He won't be long," said the constable who had taken over duty at the desk. He had a dog himself and was sympathetic. All the same, his eyes were speculative as he watched Smith's retreating back in the borrowed raincoat. He had seen the photographs of the dead girl, taken before the removal of the body from the wood, and he had been revolted and yet at the same time horribly fascinated by them.

At the end of the corridor the sergeant turned left and then opened a door with a frosted-glass panel which led onto a short flight of concrete steps. Below was a small, square asphalt yard, enclosed on three sides by buildings in a new, raw-looking yellow brick and on the fourth side by a high fence of creosoted wood. It was not raining but the low, gray clouds and damp air gave everything a wet, dull gleam. A group of men, all wearing raincoats like Smith's, were standing about the yard in a desultory way, as if waiting for a train.

The sergeant, whose territory clearly ended at the door, was careful not to step outside.

"If you'll go down the steps, sir," he said, "Detective Sergeant Boyce will tell you what to do."

Smith walked down the steps, slipping his hands into the raincoat pockets as he went and feeling, in one, a half-smoked cigarette, and, in the other, a soiled handkerchief. He removed his hands quickly from the pockets and brushed his fingertips down the front of the coat. Boyce came up to speak to him, his manner officially polite.

"The men will be forming up into a line soon, Mr. Smith. You may stand where you wish in the line."

Smith ran his eye quickly over the group of men. Two, like him, had beards. The others were clean-shaven. He saw but did not recognize Meyrick, who was standing, awkward and glum, by himself. Several men, plainclothes policemen, Smith guessed, were talking together. There were about a dozen of them in all.

Meyrick, who had seen Smith glance at him, turned away. He had been at work when the police car came to fetch him and he was very conscious of his dirty boots. He had tried to clean the mud off, surreptitiously pulling lumps away with his fingers in the back of the police car, and then had not known what to do with them, and had put them, at last, in his jacket pocket. Remembering, too, the humiliation of the previous visit to the police station, when his wife had caused the scene in the hall, he had avoided meeting anybody's eye and had walked with bent head into the yard, wearing the borrowed raincoat.

When Smith's glance fell on him, and he had turned away, it had been because of this humiliation. He felt everyone, including Smith, must know about it. All the same, even in this cowed mood, he felt a surge of envy and dislike for Smith who had, despite his shabby appearance, shabbier even than Meyrick's, nevertheless walked into the yard with an air of assurance. Meyrick wondered if what his wife said

132

about Smith was true; that he had killed the girl. He tried not to listen to what his wife said. It was easier to let her talk on, but the murder had deeply disturbed him. Finding the body had been bad enough but now the police would not let him alone. He was frightened by this and he was frightened, too, by the fierceness of his wife's anger toward Smith. When it became too savage, he would get up and leave the room and then she would shout after him, "That's right! Walk out! You'd turn your bloody back on anything."

He would go out to feed his ferrets. The sight of their sharp snouts poking through the wire netting in the front of the cage and their white, vicious teeth was soothing. He pushed pieces of food high up through the wire so that they had to stand on their hind legs to reach it, exposing their long, creamy bellies.

He had walked out the evening before when she had been going on about Smith but, this time, the ferrets had given him no comfort. Her words which she had shouted after him kept repeating in his ears:

"He'd see you swing for it before he'd open his trap!"

They did not hang people for murder these days, he knew. There had been something in the newspapers about it sometime before and his wife had grumbled when she read it; she believed in hanging. But still they put you in prison. He watched the ferrets scuttling up and down the cage, rearing up to sniff for food, their tiny, pink paws clutching at the netting like hands. He stood watching them and thinking about the dead girl. Supposing the police thought he had killed her? Supposing he couldn't make them understand?

His thoughts were running on the same lines now as he stood in the yard waiting for the identification parade to begin. Presently Boyce came up and began shepherding the men into line, walking along it to satisfy himself that all the collars of the raincoats were turned up at the same angle so their lower faces were in shadow. As he reached the end of the line the door into the main building opened and Finch came down the steps accompanied by Lamport. Boyce immediately joined them and they held a whispered consultation at the foot of the steps.

"Now," Finch was saying to Lamport, "I want you to walk along the line of men; take your time, there's no need to hurry. If you recognize anybody, don't speak to him, just touch him on the arm. Is that quite clear?"

"Yes," said Lamport nervously. The fact that he was a key witness in the Walker case and was to assist the police at an identification parade had excited a lot of interest both at work and in his family circle. There had been talk of nothing much else for the past two days. But now that the time had actually come he was very uncertain of himself. He felt he could not remember a single detail of that face, glimpsed so briefly in his car headlights on that wet Saturday evening. Very self-consciously he crossed the yard and began slowly to walk along the line of men, stopping in front of each one to look into his face.

Smith kept his eyes fixed firmly on the middle distance. At first he had regarded the identification parade with a kind of sardonic amusement but when the man began to walk down the line he was suddenly aware of the seriousness of it and felt curiously violated by the thought that a total stranger should be allowed to scrutinize his features so closely. The man drew level with him. Smith tried to concentrate on a point beyond the man's left shoulder but his face, with its protuberant eyes and stupid little bit of a mustache, remained in focus. He could smell the man too; a mixture of cheap hair oil and cigarettes. Smith suddenly yearned for a cigarette and remembered the half-smoked end in the pocket of the raincoat. It would be easy to take it. The owner of the coat would probably never know it was missing.

After what seemed like an eternity, while the man's eyes crawled over his face, taking it in feature by feature, he moved on to the next man in the line and Smith was able to relax.

Lamport came to the end of the line. He was embarrassed at having to stare into their faces. As he said to his wife afterwards, "It didn't seem decent, staring at them like that."

He had not been able to identify anybody either and he was not sure what he ought to do next. He walked back to where the Inspector was standing.

"Any luck?" asked Finch.

Lamport said, "I'm not sure. It could be the fourth man along from this end. But it was dark that night, you see, Inspector, and I only caught a glimpse of his face. He was turned more away from me, so I caught him on the side view, if you know what I mean."

Finch glanced across to the line of men. Smith was the fourth man. Turning back to Lamport he asked:

"Left or right profile, sir?"

Lamport was flustered. "Right, I think. Yes, it would be. I'd be driving on the left and he was facing me, but had turned away as if my headlights dazzled him."

Finch exchanged a look with Boyce, who stumped back to the line of men and, raising his voice, said:

"We shan't keep you much longer. If you'll all turn your heads and look to the left, the witness will come down the line again."

The man standing next to Smith said softly, "Oh, Christ," and shifted his weight to his other foot. He was one of the group of men who had been talking together before the parade and who Smith had guessed were plainclothes policemen. By the tone of his voice he was plainly unimpressed both by the witness and by the way the parade was being organized by his superiors.

Smith, with the other men, faced to the left. The collar of the raincoat grazed his chin and felt uncomfortable. Lamport began to walk along the line again. When he stopped in front of Smith this time, Smith could not see him but he was aware of the man's eyes on his face. He seemed to stand there for a long time and the muscles in Smith's neck ached with the effort of holding his head at that unaccustomed angle. Then the man moved on and Smith relaxed again. He wondered if he was being oversensitive but it seemed to him that the man did not linger nearly so long over his scrutiny of the other men's profiles.

Finch watched Lamport's progress and noticed the time he spent looking at Smith. He cursed him under his breath for lacking in tact and common sense. The Inspector also noticed that Lamport hardly stopped at all by Meyrick, simply giving the man's profile a cursory glance before moving on again. It was certainly Smith and only Smith that Lamport was interested in. Finch wondered what would be his next move if Lamport made a positive identification. He did not believe for a moment that Smith would readily confess to the murder and one man's identification would not be enough evidence for a court of law. It would have to be followed up by all kinds of inquiries; a thorough search would have to be made of the cottage and a detailed investigation into Smith's movements over the past three months, which would not be easy as the man lived alone and appeared to have no friends. There were always the letters that came every Friday. They might throw valuable light on the man's background and family. From his voice and manners he was obviously educated. Perhaps there was something in his past that he wished to hide or forget.

Mrs. Meyrick, mused the Inspector, seems convinced of his guilt but that's probably malice and a misguided attempt to protect her husband. Which reminds me, I must get Meyrick to sign his amended statement while he's here.

He wondered, then, if he ought to get Smith to make a statement also, about his movements on the day of the murder and about his reason for his visit to Leverett's wood on the Friday afternoon but, remembering Smith's hesitation, he decided to postpone it a little longer. It would be a good excuse to get Smith back to the station on another occasion.

Lamport had finished and was walking across the yard toward him. Finch could tell by his face that he still could not positively identify Smith. The Inspector, as he spoke to him, was careful to keep his own face empty of expression.

"Any good now, sir?"

Lamport shook his head.

"The fourth man along is the most like him, but I couldn't be certain, not absolutely, one hundred percent."

"That's quite all right," said Finch noncommittally. "Thank you for coming, Mr. Lamport, and for being so cooperative."

"I only wish I could have picked him out for sure," said Lamport, and then added, in confusion, "I mean, I don't like the thought of anyone being found guilty on my say-so, but in a murder case . . ."

"Of course," said Finch, and led the way back into the station, while Boyce dismissed the men.

A few minutes later Smith followed them into the building. When he reached the front office Finch and the man had gone. Cairn jumped up eagerly, placing his forepaws on the front of the raincoat and making ineffectual leaps on his back legs in an attempt to reach Smith's face. Smith patted him and tumbled his ears about.

"He missed you," said the constable. He knew the outcome of the identification parade had been negative. All the same, the fascination of guilt still hung about Smith and his reputation of being odd, different from everybody else, had a certain glamour. The constable longed to draw him into conversation but all that Smith said was "Yes."

The sergeant's glance, heavy with official warning, fell on the constable, who became silent.

"Here's your coat, sir," said the sergeant. He had Smith's brown plastic mackintosh over his arm. Smith changed coats while Cairn, still excited, milled round him, wagging his tail and nudging Smith's feet. It was a signal to go.

"There's a car available if you want to be driven home," said the sergeant.

"I'll walk," said Smith and, with the dog running ahead a little way and then bounding back, he left the station.

The clouds had turned to rain but it was a fine rain. Smith's hair and beard were soon misted with it. He could see it gathering on his lashes. Cairn's fur was sprinkled with fine drops and his whiskers and bushy eyebrows were hung with them. It gave him a comical, clownish look. He bounded along the road in front of Smith, happy to be free after the long incarceration, happy that Smith had returned to him, happy that they were going home together at last. Every so often he would stop and wait for Smith to catch up with him, turning round to face him and wagging his tail. And each time that Smith caught up with him, he rubbed his hand affectionately over the dog's head and Cairn thrust his muzzle, the nose cold, the breath warm, into the palm of his hand.

The warm breath made Smith remember the cigarette

end in the pocket and how he had yearned so much for a cigarette that he had thought of stealing it. That was the last time anything like that would happen, he was sure. Never again would he feel that yearning to smoke, and this realization added to his sense of freedom.

He was throwing sticks for the dog as they went up the lane to the cottage. Cairn ran joyously to retrieve them, splashing through the dun-colored puddles which lay between the ruts. Once he startled a blackbird, which scrambled away through the hedge and fled, scolding loudly, across the field.

The sticks he threw for Cairn reminded Smith of his own fire. He would light it, he thought, as soon as he got in. Then he would dry Cairn and change out of his own wet clothes. Later, when the room was warm, he would take a bath in front of the fire, in the big zinc tub that hung on the wall outside the back door. If he lit the fire under the boiler as soon as he got in, the water would be hot in an hour. Afterwards he would read. These thoughts made the anticipation of his return to the cottage even more pleasant than usual and he broke into a run, in pursuit of Cairn, who had picked up the last stick that Smith had thrown for him and was playing a game with it, worrying it as it lay on the ground, tossing it up into the air and then dashing off with it in his mouth, growling in pretended anger at Smith's pursuit of him.

"Come here, sir!" shouted Smith, in mock command.

Breathless they arrived at the cottage, Smith laughing, the dog laughing, too, in his own peculiar way, wrinkling back his lips over the stick which he still held clenched between his teeth, while the whole of his rump swayed with the vigorous beating of his tail.

Then, suddenly, the game was over. Smith stopped

laughing and stepped forward, frowning, to stand in the open gateway.

He was certain he had closed the gate when he left the cottage earlier that afternoon with Russell. He remembered he had pulled it hard shut with a bang and, as the gate was warped and needed a good shove to open it, it was unlikely that the wind could have blown it open and, anyway, there was hardly any wind that afternoon.

"Heel!" said Smith, Cairn obeyed instantly, dropping the stick and slinking into place behind him. The authority in the man's voice was real this time.

Smith stood listening. The house was quiet. The door was shut and there seemed no sign of entry or disturbance. He was about to get the key from his pocket and unlock the door when he noticed that the gap in the tall hedge of wild roses that ran along the path and gave access to the kitchen garden looked freshly used. Two or three long brambles were bent down and awry, as if someone, unused to the narrow gap, had pulled them to one side.

Smith stepped into the opening. The garden beyond had been completely destroyed. Everything movable in it, the sticks with the seed packets speared on them, the bird-scarers of wood and metal, even the bricks in the paths between the beds, had been pulled up and either broken or flung about the garden. The seedbeds themselves had been trampled and the soil kicked up into heaps.

With his hands jammed tight in his pockets, Smith picked his way down the garden on what remained of the central path. A seed packet, caught against a brick, fluttered like a trapped bird and he stooped down to look at it. Bent down to a level with the garden, he saw scattered among the churned-up earth some runner beans that had begun to germinate. A single root, like a greenish-white hook, had split the wrinkled side of each bean. He picked one up and then, with a sudden flexing of his fingers, squashed it hard so that the green inner portion of the bean broke through the outer skin. The white root snapped and fell off. For a moment Smith looked at the clean inner portion of the bean, sticking out like pale flesh through the stained skin, and then he flung it away across the garden and walked back to the cottage.

12

Finch was disappointed with the outcome of the identification parade. It had taken up several hours of his time and had added very little to the solution of the Walker case. Although Lamport had said the man could have been Smith, his evidence was too inconclusive to be of any real value, except to keep Smith in the forefront as a possible suspect. But it was real evidence the Inspector was looking for; indisputable facts; positive identification which would bring Smith, or whoever was guilty, into a court of law to be tried for the girl's murder.

This element of inconclusiveness seemed to bedevil the case. There had been many promising openings which on investigation had led nowhere, or not far enough to carry the case beyond a certain limit. Boyce, with the help of several detective constables, had visited every public house, off-license, and fish-and-chip shop within a ten-mile radius of the girl's home, and had come back with very little. Three publicans and the proprietor of a fish-and-chip shop said they thought they recognized the girl, but could not be sure. Neither could they be certain if the girl, who might or might not be Doreen Walker, had been accompanied by a man.

Boyce, acting on Finch's instructions, was carrying the investigation farther afield, following the report of a girl answering Doreen's description having been seen in Colchester, and was taking the girl's photograph to snack bars, public houses, cinemas, and dance halls in the town, but so far these inquiries had produced no positive identification either.

The publication of the girl's photograph and an appeal for information, in both the local and the national newspapers, had brought in a good response, as they always did, although Finch knew from previous experience that much of the information, if not all of it, would prove useless. There remained a chance, however, that just one of the public-spirited people who telephoned or wrote in might have indeed seen Doreen Walker and while that chance remained every piece of information had to be followed up.

In the meanwhile, as the dossier grew in size and the number of people involved and the hours spent increased in number, the only definite facts that remained, high and dry like islands in a sea of possibilities, were two: Meyrick's fingerprint had been found on the button of the girl's coat and Smith had been seen in the vicinity of the crime two days before it was committed.

Of these two facts Finch favored following up the second. Meyrick, although he had acted suspiciously at the first interview, when he had denied touching the body, had later admitted that he was not certain of this. Smith, on the other hand, while giving a plausible enough excuse for his presence in the wood, had been chosen by Lamport as the man most resembling the man he had seen talking to a girl who might have been Doreen Walker.

Finch sighed. Once again this line of reasoning came up against the barrier of inconclusiveness. *If* the girl was Doreen Walker. *If* the man was Smith. The case had the "Now you see it, now you don't" quality of a Find the Lady game. But in this case, it was the identity of the murderer which remained hidden, shuffled about under a whole series of what seemed promising inquiries, which, when tapped, proved empty after all.

But, even so, Smith always remained; Meyrick, too, but to a lesser extent; and in the need for something positive to be done, some definite action to be taken, Finch's money was on Smith.

He thought about him a lot after Lamport, still embarrassed, still apologizing, had signed his statement and left. Sitting quietly in his office, Finch ruminated on the man and when Boyce returned later that afternoon he had developed a plan of action.

Boyce was not too happy with it. It involved officials high up in the police hierarchy and Boyce's instinct was to stick to the routine, door-to-door investigation. If Finch was going to investigate Smith's background, his attitude was that Finch would learn far more by questioning the people in the village.

"Won't do," said Finch. "There's too much gossip about him already. We've had a taste of it ourselves, with Mrs. Meyrick baying for his blood right here in the station the other evening. Besides, he's a mystery in the village. Nobody seems to know where he comes from or what he was doing before he came to the village. No, this needs a subtle touch. I'm going to put down a little ground bait and see if he makes a nibble. I want him to come out into the open. He's got something hidden, I feel it in my bones, but whether it's murder remains to be seen. But what I do know is, you won't get anything on him by knocking on doors."

He rubbed his hands together in pleasurable anticipation. Now that he had come to a decision regarding Smith, a decision which he had been working up to for some time, Finch was already feeling better. It was like a nagging pain finally assuaged. With a springy step he went over to the telephone to make the necessary arrangements for his plan to be put into action.

Delay was inevitable and Finch fretted for the next two days while his superiors discussed his demand. At last, on the following Wednesday, the telephone rang. It was his superintendent, who passed on permission from those above him, with a coda that he, the Superintendent, was relying personally on Finch's good judgment and tact in the matter.

"I shall be as careful as a cat with a mouse," replied Finch, smiling at the aptness of the simile. For he intended playing Smith gently. And for the moment the question of whether or not he would catch him seemed irrelevant. The hunt was up, the quarry chosen, and Smith would, Finch felt sure, prove better game than Meyrick.

It was, then, in a very good humor that he drove to Frayling to see Mrs. Bland. She was serving a customer and was both pleased and flustered to see him.

"Oh, Inspector," she began but Finch smiled and said, "I'll wait," and walked about the shop, with his hands in his trouser pockets, studying with apparent interest the tins of meat and vegetables and the packets of breakfast cereals on the shelves.

The woman Mrs. Bland was serving watched him avidly. She kept turning round, with the excuse, "I'll just see if there's anything else I want while I'm here."

Mrs. Bland tried to keep her mind on the bill as she added it up, but her thoughts kept wandering to her husband. He had been complaining only the evening before that nothing much had been happening about the case recently. There had been two exciting climaxes, the aftermaths of which, still highly charged, had been played out in the shop: Meyrick's visit to the police station to amend his statement and his subsequent visit, with Smith, to attend the identification parade. In each aftermath Mrs. Meyrick had played a central role. Indeed, in the first instance Mr. Bland had been able to overhear most of the action himself without gathering it secondhand from his wife. Mrs. Meyrick had been like a fury, calling down wrath on Smith, Finch, and the whole of the police force.

"I told them!" she had shouted. "Dragging him off like that! Didn't even give him time to have his tea. The meat dried up in the oven and the vegetables ruined. You go after Smith, I told them. He's the one you ought to have in."

On the second occasion, the identification parade, at which she had not been present and for which she had only her husband's inadequate account to rely on, her role had been more subdued. Nevertheless, it had been interesting. Twice the man had gone back along the line and each time he had stopped the longest in front of Smith. She had dragged this information from Meyrick, driving him into a corner at last. He had slunk out of the room soon afterwards, to feed his ferrets, and had stood brooding for half an hour in front of their cage before he could bring himself to return to the house. But she had said no more. Appeased, her lips folded in quiet triumph, she had riddled out the fire and bolted the back door, without referring to the matter again.

All the same, in the shop the next morning she had used this information to good effect. Mr. Bland, who knew she was in there, strained and strained to hear what she was saying, but she had kept her voice low. It had been quiet innuendo this time, not righteous fury. Finally, he had given up trying to hear and had poked the fire irritably and was only restored to good humor when Mrs. Bland found time, between customers, to come through to the living room and recount all that had been said.

146

So, remembering her husband, Mrs. Bland cast about in her mind, as she totted up the bill, how she could get the Inspector into the living room where her husband would be able to hear everything that was said for himself.

"You'll come through for a cup of tea," she said, when the customer had gone. But Finch was not going to be drawn. He had no intention of saying what he had to say in front of Bland, who was far too sharp and knowing and would seek out all kinds of hidden meanings in what the Inspector wished to say. So Finch said cheerfully, "Thank you for the offer, Mrs. Bland, but I can't stop now. I just called in to ask if you'd heard anything said in the shop that might be useful to the case. You know how people talk and they don't often realize that what they say could be important in this kind of investigation."

"What kind of things?" asked Mrs. Bland, a little fearful that she might be expected to repeat all the gossip that had taken place in her hearing, some of which was slander, as she very well knew.

"Gossip about Doreen Walker," said Finch. "If anyone has mentioned seeing her over the past few weeks. We're trying to trace her movements, find out her friends, that sort of thing."

Mrs. Bland relaxed. "I've heard nothing," she said, "and I don't expect I shall. I mean, she wasn't from this village and people tend not to mix. But if I do hear anything I'll certainly let you know."

"Thank you," said the Inspector, moving toward the door. With it half open he paused as if he had suddenly remembered something else.

"Oh, there's one other little matter I'd better clear up while I'm here. It is Friday, isn't it, that Mr. Smith collects his letter?"

"That's right," said Mrs. Bland, in a fluster again because she still did not feel too happy about this subject.

"I suppose you've never noticed him posting any letters at any time, have you? I see the pillar box is just across the road."

"No," said Mrs. Bland. "Not to my knowledge, that is."

"Well, perhaps you'd let me know if anything turns up," said the Inspector. He deliberately made the last remark vague, leaving it to Mrs. Bland, or her husband, to interpret it in whichever way they pleased, but certain that they would take it to refer both to information about Doreen Walker and Smith, without Finch having to express his intention openly.

He was right. Mrs. Bland, hurrying through to the little living room with the news of the Inspector's visit, repeated word for word what he had said, including his final remark. They puzzled over it together, Bland asking innumerable questions in an effort to discover the Inspector's true meaning.

"What did he look like when he said it, Glad? Could you tell by his face if he meant Smith?" he asked.

"I don't know," replied Mrs. Bland. "He just looked ordinary, casual, as if he wanted to check up when the letter arrived and if Mr. Smith wrote any letter in reply. Then he said about me letting him know and he didn't seem any different."

Peck about as much as he could, Bland could get no further. He thought about the problem for several minutes, staring into the flames of the fire. Finally, he made up his mind.

"You let him know on both counts, Glad," he advised her. "It won't come amiss."

"Do you think so?" asked Mrs. Bland, who was already trembling at the thought of Smith coming into the shop on Friday morning.

"Stands to reason," her husband replied. "He had him up for identification, didn't he? There's something in the wind. You keep a sharp eye on that pillar box and if you see Smith posting a letter, you get on the phone to the Inspector double quick."

For the next two days Mrs. Bland fretted continuously over the letter and Smith's arrival on Friday morning to collect it. She slept badly and could not keep her mind on serving in the shop. It would have been no good confiding her fears to her husband, who was looking forward to the coming excitement with delighted anticipation. It came as a great disappointment, therefore, when on the Friday morning the postman came but did not bring the customary letter for Smith. Mrs. Bland ran through to the living room with the news. Bland was astounded.

"No letter?" he cried. "That's odd. That's very odd. They've come regular every Friday up till now."

"I said to the postman, 'Is that all?' " said Mrs. Bland. "He only left the one, a receipt, and I could see straightaway it wasn't for him. The postman said, 'No. That's the lot.' "

Bland pinched his lower lip between his fingers and shook his head. It was beyond him.

"Do you think I ought to ring the Inspector and tell him?" asked Mrs. Bland. She felt she had been placed unwillingly in a situation which she did not understand and which was growing more and more complicated. Bland thought it over.

"You could," he said slowly, at last. "It wouldn't do no harm. See what Smith says first, though, and then you can tell the Inspector what happens."

"Oh dear!" cried poor Mrs. Bland. "I don't know how I'm going to face him when he comes in. I'm all of a tremble just thinking about it. What shall I say to him, Harold?"

As it happened, there was no time for her husband to give

149

his advice. The bell over the shop door rang at this point and, when Mrs. Bland went through to serve, Smith was standing in the shop.

He seemed taller and more peculiar-looking than ever. Every hair in his beard had a glistening life of its own. His eyes, a pale gray-blue, dominated his face and Mrs. Bland found it impossible to avoid them.

"Your letter hasn't come," she said, all of a rush. "The postman's been, but there wasn't one for you. I can't understand it. I did ask."

She felt, in an obscure way, that Smith would blame her for the nonarrival of the letter. He certainly seemed surprised, although as his face was expressionless at the best of times it was difficult to tell what he was thinking or feeling. There was a long and uncomfortable pause and then he said:

"I see. I'll take the shopping."

He gave her the usual written list but this time she fetched the items in silence. She could not bring herself to think of anything to say. In silence, too, he paid, put the shopping into the plastic bag and left. She waited long enough to see him walk away up the road with the dog at his heels and then hurried back to tell her husband. On his advice, she telephoned the police station but the Inspector was out and she had to leave a message.

"Tell the Inspector it's Mrs. Bland and the letter hasn't come."

The words were her husband's and she repeated them after a flurried consultation with him, one hand over the telephone receiver. Whoever was taking down the message read it back to her. It sounded flat and inane. Indeed, the whole episode, so talked about and worried over, had gone stale. Nothing much seemed to have happened, after all.

It put Mr. Bland in a bad temper for the rest of the day.

He had been looking forward to Smith's arrival ever since the Inspector's visit. Now he was like a child deprived of a long-awaited treat. He sulked and complained and had several bad coughing fits. Mrs. Bland was at her wit's end to know what to do with him.

It would have cheered him up to know that Smith had been deeply affected by the news that the letter had not arrived, although he had not shown it. He had become so accustomed to its arrival every Friday morning that it had never occurred to him to doubt it. He had come to rely on it. The whole of his financial arrangements, the shopping, the rent, saving toward additional expenses, rested on the weekly sum of five pounds.

When he got back to the cottage he went immediately to the place where he kept his savings. Since the mud-throwing episode and the spoliation of the garden he had stopped keeping it in the tin on the mantelpiece, although on neither occasion had there been an attempt to break into the cottage. But he had got into the habit of keeping any paper money hidden inside a book and the silver and copper money on a dark ledge above the head of the stairs. He hated this procedure of hiding the money away. It seemed such a mean and despicable thing to do. But without the money his present way of life would be impossible and he no longer trusted the inviolability of the cottage.

He collected the money and counted it. There were two pounds, six shillings and sevenpence, fifteen shillings of which he would need immediately for paying the rent. The only other large item of expense would be oil, which he would fetch from Wrexford on Tuesday and probably by then the letter would have arrived. Meanwhile he had no envelope in which to put the rent money and he had to use one of the paper bags in which his groceries had been placed. After writing his name on it and the amount that it contained, he walked up the lane to put it through Stokes's letter box.

After that he did not know what to do. He was feeling restless and disquieted. Normally he would have read or gone for a walk but the uncertainty over the letter had disturbed him and he could settle down to nothing. The feeling persisted throughout Saturday but he hesitated to go back to the shop, which he guessed would be full of customers. Late in the afternoon, however, he made up his mind and set out for the village, accompanied by Cairn.

Mrs. Bland had just closed the shop and was sweeping up the floor before switching off the light and going into the house to prepare tea for herself and her husband when she was startled by the sudden appearance of a face in the glass panel of the shop door. It was Smith. He stood with his face close to the glass, looking into the lighted interior end trying to attract her attention. The sight of his bearded face pressed up against the dark glass gave her quite a turn, as she told her husband later.

He indicated that he did not want to come in and mouthed the word, "Letter?" She could read the word quite easily by his lip movements. His breath clouded the glass. She shook her head vigorously. For a moment his head, cut off, it seemed, from the rest of his body in the dark, remained at the window. Then he turned and went away.

He was back again on Monday morning. This time she was serving a customer and he waited outside, sheltering in the porch from a downpour of rain. When the woman left he entered. She spoke before he had time to ask the question.

"It still hasn't come, Mr. Smith."

He hesitated and, for a while, he seemed nonplused. Then he said, "I'd like to buy some writing paper and envelopes."

He chose the cheapest brand out of the selection she put on the counter in front of him.

"Do you sell stamps?" he asked next.

"I don't, I'm afraid," said Mrs. Bland. "But if it's only one you want, I always keep a few by me for my own use and I could sell you one of those."

He bought a stamp, felt in his pocket as if looking for something, and then asked for a pen, a cheap one.

All the time she was serving him Mrs. Bland was in a flutter; not only because he was there but because she wanted to run through to the living room to tell her husband what was happening. Smith was obviously going to write a letter. The news would please Harold. Things seemed to be moving at last.

She did not wait long enough in the shop to see that when Smith left he turned up the road, not in the direction of the cottage. The rain was falling fast and he did not want the long walk back to the cottage to write the letter and then the return journey to the village to post it. He went toward the church, where he would be out of the rain and not likely to be disturbed.

The church stood on a corner, cut off from the village by a line of trees. A long gravel path wound up from the gate to the porch, through the graveyard, neglected and overgrown, with clumps of young, vigorous nettles pushing up between the graves, the headstones leaning awry.

Smith sat in the porch on a wooden bench that ran along one wall and wrote his letter. He addressed the envelope, sealed it, and stuck on the stamp. Beyond the porchway the rain fell heavily. Puddles formed in the worn gravel path. He sat for a while watching the rain until Cairn whined and stirred uneasily. The dog wanted to be on the move again, but Smith could not bring himself to leave the shelter of the porch. He patted the dog and then got up to read the church notices pinned on the board above the bench.

Still the rain continued to fall, and on a sudden impulse Smith took hold of the big, round, iron ring in the door, turned it and stepped inside the church. Cairn, left outside, scratched unhappily at the door and then lay down with his nose close to the crack along the bottom, waiting for Smith's return.

Inside it was gloomy. The air smelled of damp plaster and wood and the must on old hymnbooks. Whitewashed arches rose toward the beamed roof, which was lost in shadows. There was a suspended silence which the noise of the rain, drumming on the windows, did not dispel. Smith sat for a time in a pew at the back of the church, then getting to his feet he walked about, his footsteps sounding loud and hollow on the tiled floor. Presently his feet touched a strip of coconut matting and, stooping down to roll it back, he saw a brass effigy set in a stone slab. It was of a woman with a coifed headdress, her hands placed together, the tips of her shoes showing beneath the long, sculptured folds of her dress. Her face, a perfect oval, smiled sweetly up at him. The eyes were long, full-lidded with round pupils that gave her an innocent and gentle look. Smith rolled the carpet carefully back to cover her.

Cairn had begun scratching at the door again and was uttering little yelping cries. The disappearance of the man inside the unknown building disturbed him, so did the smell of the interior which seeped out along the bottom of the door. There was nothing about the smell that he could recognize, except a sense of loneliness and loss. Smith, hearing in the dog's cries its anxiety and uneasiness, returned to the porch.

It was due to Mr. Bland's insistence that his wife return immediately to the shop that Mrs. Bland was able to witness the posting of the letter.

"You get back in there, Glad," he warned her, when she had hurried in to tell him of Smith's arrival and his purchase of writing materials. "You never know, he may have stopped up the road to write it instead of going home."

"In all this rain?" she asked derisively. She had hoped for time to make a cup of tea and to sit down in comfort to drink it.

"There's the bus shelter," he had pointed out.

So, very unwillingly and a little irritated by her husband's insistence, she had gone back to stand guard in the shop. But her annoyance was forgotten when Smith came trudging past the shop, not from the direction she expected, and stopped at the pillar box across the road. She saw him slip an envelope inside the box, bend down to read the collection time on the front, and then walk on down the road.

"What did I tell you?" cried Mr. Bland triumphantly when she told him this news. "Now where would he have gone to write it? I know! The church. I bet you he went in the church to write it. Save himself walking home in the rain and back. Now you get on the phone to the Inspector, Glad, and tell him."

She spoke to the Inspector this time. He sounded cheerful but a bit offhand.

"Did he, now?" he said. "Well, thank you for letting me know, Mrs. Bland." He than rang off. The incident appeared to be finished. No police car arrived to collect the letter. Finch put in no appearance. Instead, everything seemed as usual. The red post-office van drew up at the customary time, the box was cleared of mail, the van drove off again. It was all very disappointing.

But to Finch the episode had been most satisfactory. Later, at the sorting office, certain instructions were given. The address on the letter Smith had written was copied down and then it was returned to the batch of mail awaiting dispatch for London. Another letter, in a buff-colored envelope, its address typed, was placed in the pile of mail due for local distribution the following morning. The bait had been taken and the fish could now be played.

13

The following morning Finch went to London. He traveled by train to Liverpool Street Station and then made his way by underground to Sloane Square.

It was a clear, sunny morning. Spring seemed to have come at last. Even London, which Finch usually disliked intensely, had a certain charm. The sky was clear blue above the rooftops. The pavements shone and the shop windows sparkled. A woman was selling long-stemmed pink roses from a basket outside the underground station. The fragile blooms lay close together among white tissue paper.

Finch sauntered up the King's Road. He was in an excellent mood. The subterfuge with the letters had paid off. He had played a subtle game both with the Blands and with Smith and all of them had responded in just the way he had wanted. The Blands had watched Smith and Smith had written the letter.

Abercorn Terrace was a turning off the King's Road. Finch paused at the corner to look about him. There were shops on each side of the road; a discreet chemist's, with old-fashioned curly gilt lettering on dark glass above the door, tins of baby food neatly pyramided in one window and in the other bottles of perfume standing on pools of pink silk; on the other side, a boutique, with models made of wickerwork, artificial marguerites instead of eyes, displaying the latest fashions. Long feather boas in yellow, green, and purple hung round their necks and trailed to the ground. Next door was an Italian restaurant, artfully simple, with its red-and-white checked curtains and Chianti bottles strung up in the window. The menu was pinned up in a glass box beside the door, beautifully written in an elaborate foreign hand.

The houses began after this, a double row of small period houses, each with a first-floor balcony, a semibasement with railings and four steps up to the front door. They were all painted white with black railings and, seeing the long vista of them in the bright spring sunshine Finch was reminded of a row of neat dolls' houses, belonging to some well-behaved little girl. Somewhere along that façade of identical sash windows, each with its windowbox and brightly painted front door, would be hidden a hook to unfasten it and open it back to reveal miniature staircases and rooms, peopled with little, jointed dolls.

Number 14 had a dark-blue front door with a brass knocker in the shape of a dolphin. Two clipped bay trees, lollipop-shaped like a child's drawing, stood in white china tubs at the top of the steps. White hyacinths and variegated ivy filled the window box. Finch knocked on the door. There was a shrill barking inside the house and a voice raised to quiet it. A moment later the door was opened by a woman. She was small-boned, dark-haired, and of the type that Finch always mentally classified as "posh." Under one arm, like a parcel, she was carrying a white miniature poodle with a curly topknot. It barked again on seeing Finch and she slapped it across the nose to silence it.

"Yes?" she said sharply, taking in at a glance Finch's shabby raincoat and crumpled tie.

"May I speak to Mr. Michael Elliot?" asked Finch.

"My husband is not at home," she replied and seemed about to close the door.

158

"I am Inspector Finch, of the Essex Constabulary," said Finch, raising his voice, and it amused him to see how quickly her attitude changed.

"You had better come inside," she said.

Finch followed her into a narrow hall. He looked about him, perfectly at ease, taking in the gray-and-white striped wallpaper, the pale gray fitted carpet, and the gilt wall lamps with their deep pink shades.

"Did you say Essex?" Mrs. Elliott asked.

"That's right," said Finch.

She hesitated for a moment, frowning and hitching up the dog under her arm. Then she said:

"I think it would be better if I telephoned my husband to come here to see you, rather than you going to his office."

"It would certainly be more private," replied Finch, putting a faint emphasis on the last word. He was deliberately provoking her. He knew her type. She was too well-bred to ask him directly what his business was with her husband and, in his present jaunty mood, he wanted to play her as subtly as he had played Smith and the Blands. She obviously had her suspicions as to why he was there. She had pounced on the word "Essex" quickly enough. But he had no intention of enlightening her. He would take a small revenge for the hard, cold stare she had given him on the doorstep.

"You may wait in here," she said abruptly, opening a door.

The room, like the hall, was decorated in pink, gray, and gilt. It was like an elegant trinket box, full of small, glittering treasures: white porcelain figures on the mantelpiece below a huge, gilt-framed mirror, bowls of hyacinths, and silk-shaded lamps. A silver tray, set with a cut-glass decanter and six wineglasses, caught the sun and splintered it. It was all too fragile and too perfect.

Finch, catching sight of himself in the mirror, a homely

figure in his raincoat behind the white china shepherdesses, grinned mockingly. He wondered if Smith had known this room.

He'd be as much out of place in it as I am, thought Finch. It seemed to bring the man suddenly very close and to create a bond between them which the Inspector had been uneasily aware of on other occasions and had never wished to acknowledge before.

Walking about the room, looking at the objects it contained, Finch tried to analyze this feeling of fellow sympathy but could find no articulate expression for it. He had realized Smith's intelligence on their first meeting and something of the complexity of the man's character, a trickiness about him that was intriguing; this Finch knew. The mystery of who he was and why he had chosen his present way of living Finch also acknowledged as being part of the man's appeal. But these elements were not enough to explain why, suddenly, in this room, catching sight of his own image in the glass, he should be so powerfully aware of the other man; and why he felt that the mere discovery of the man's identity was no longer important; and that he was searching for something deeper, which had, in a curious way, significance for himself as well. It was as if he had begun to identify himself with Smith and, in the search for Smith's identity, he was looking for something hidden in himself.

Finch stopped pacing about the room and stood staring out the window at the façade of houses opposite. His mood of self-satisfaction had vanished. He realized he had come to this place for the wrong motive; not to search for the man who had murdered Doreen Walker but for reasons that were so complicated, so deep, so personal that he could himself only partly understand them.

He was interrupted from these thoughts by the sight of

a black Humber drawing up outside the house. The car door slammed, a man came quickly up the steps, the front door opened. There were voices in the hall; Mrs. Elliot's clear, well-bred accent, a man's deeper tone. Finch turned from the window as the drawing-room door opened and a man entered.

Despite the dark city suit, the clean-shaven chin, the well-brushed hair, Finch could see an immediate resemblance to Smith. Michael Elliot was heavier built, broader in the shoulders and fuller-faced, but he had Smith's slightly stooping figure, light gray eyes, and well-defined mouth. He entered quickly as if he had hurried from the office and had not yet slowed down his pace, one hand already extended to shake Finch's hand, the other indicating a chair.

"I'm sorry you've been kept waiting, Inspector. Sit down. My wife is making coffee for us. Cigarette?"

In several quick movements he had Finch seated on one of the elegant, little, silk-covered chairs, had snapped open a silver cigarette case and flicked his lighter to offer Finch a light. They were the movements of a man well-rehearsed in social behavior and yet a little flustered, as if he were anxious about the interview.

He sat down opposite Finch, his legs crossed, his cigarette held at a nonchalant angle, but it was all a pose. His eyes were strained and the other hand, clasping the arm of the chair, was tense.

"Now, what can I do to help you, Inspector?" he asked.

Finch began warily, watching Elliot's face closely for any reaction.

"I'm making a few routine inquiries, Mr. Elliot, concerning a Mr. John Smith of Frayling, Essex. We have reason to believe you may know him."

Elliot did not seem surprised. Like his wife, the word "Essex" had probably prewarned him of the subject of the interview. He looked the Inspector in the face and said in a voice of overelaborate heartiness:

"Don't tell me my young brother's been getting into trouble with your chaps!"

"Your brother?"

Elliot recrossed his legs and leaned over to tap cigarette ash into a little painted dish that stood on the table beside him. It was obvious he was giving himself time to think. When he leaned back in his chair he had made up his mind what attitude he ought to take.

"May I ask exactly what inquiries you are making?"

Finch eyed him thoughtfully and decided to be brutal.

"Certainly, Mr. Elliot. We are checking up on your brother's identity and movements in the course of a murder investigation."

"Murder!"

The word fell like a stone in that room, shattering its aura of delicate and fragile beauty.

"Murder!" repeated Elliot. "I really cannot believe that Francis . . . It's ridiculous. Surely, Inspector . . ."

He was almost gobbling with shocked surprise.

"We are simply checking on your brother, in a process of elimination," said Finch smoothly.

He had forgotten now his feeling of special identity with Smith as his old delight in the skill of interviewing returned. He would land Elliot quite easily now. The man had been gaffed. He only needed drawing to the bank.

"However, you can appreciate," Finch continued, "how important it is, in an inquiry of this kind, that we have absolute frankness. A girl has died. Your brother is something of a mystery to us. We need some information on him."

"Of course, of course," Elliot agreed hastily. He got up and stood by the fireplace, fiddled for a moment with a china figure, moved it an inch along the shelf, turned it slightly. Then, thrusting his elbow up on the ledge, he began to speak rapidly, avoiding Finch's eyes.

"My brother is rather a strange person; solitary; prefers his own company; that sort of thing. We were in business together; a small, family business started by my grandfather. It's reasonably successful and the idea was that both Francis and I should go into the firm. After my father's death, I took over the general sales side and works management; Francis, the office management and personnel. I am afraid there were disagreements. While my father was alive things weren't too bad; but it seemed to me, after his death, that Francis wasn't pulling enough weight. He's not a business-man, Inspector, and more and more of the running of the firm got left to me. There were other matters, more personal, trivial even, that we disagreed about. They seemed important at the time, however, and it became obvious to both of us that we could not continue running the business together. It was decided that Francis should leave and I should appoint a manager in his place. He seemed quite happy with this arrangement; relieved, in fact. I understand he found a cottage in the country and has gone there to live. He likes the country. He often went away at weekends in the summer and stayed at little, out-of-the-way country pubs."

"And you wrote to him every week?" prompted Finch, for Elliot appeared to have concluded his explanation. "Under the name of John Smith?"

"Oh, yes, that!" said Elliot, laughing as if it were a minor but amusing detail. "Francis has always been very—how shall I put it?—reserved. He dislikes people knowing too much about him. He said that as it was a small village and people were certain to gossip he wanted to preserve his anonymity, as he called it. As for the letters, well, it was an arrangement we made before he left the business. My father had left it equally divided between us, a joint partnership. It was agreed that I should pay Francis so much a week out of his share of the profits and send it to him, care of the local shop. It seemed a small enough amount to ask for, but he said it was all he wanted. Of course, had he asked, I should have been perfectly happy to have doubled or even trebled the amount."

He took a spotless white handkerchief from his pocket and wiped his lips.

Guilty conscience, thought Finch. I bet you were pleased to have got rid of him so cheaply.

"So you parted on friendly terms?" asked Finch, probing deeper. A tightening of the facial muscles, almost a wince, twisted up Elliot's features. He looked deeply unhappy.

"No, Inspector, I'm afraid I can't say that. There was a quarrel. It all seems so very petty now, but at the time . . . Really, is all this necessary? Surely this raking over of past family differences can hardly interest you?"

"As you wish, sir," said Finch, half rising in his chair as if to go. "We try not to press witnesses to give information unwillingly."

Elliot was immediately all apologies.

"Oh, Inspector, I don't want you to think I am holding back information. I realize you have your duty to do. It was —well, there was a stupid quarrel about a dog."

"Cairn?"

"Is that its name? I forget now. Yes, I believe Francis did call it that. It was a stray that started hanging about the yard. Some of the men encouraged it by giving it food. It became rather a nuisance and I arranged for the R.S.P.C.A. to come and collect it to have it put down. Francis heard about it and became very angry. Really, I had no idea he was fond of it; although I heard afterwards that he had been buying food for it and taking it for walks and so on. He had also given instructions that it should be allowed to sleep in the store. I couldn't agree to that. I mean, we have stocks of quite expensive paper and card. Anyway, there was a quarrel and Francis walked out with the dog. I went round to his flat later that evening. I imagined that the whole business would have blown over and that he'd see sense, but he was quite adamant. He said he was leaving. We talked it over and came to the financial arrangement I have told you about. He left the next morning and a few days later I received a letter, just giving the address and the name he wished to use. I wrote letters to him and enclosed them with the first few lots of money I sent him, but he never answered them. I'm afraid now I only send the money."

"I see," said Finch. "By the way, you will be receiving a letter from him, probably by this afternoon's post. The last lot of money you sent was delayed, I understand, but he has since received it."

"Oh," said Elliot. He seemed bewildered by this piece of information, not sure how to take it.

"Well," said Finch, cocking his head and regarding Elliot speculatively, wondering if he had any more to tell, "you have been very frank with me, sir. This kind of information can be very useful in understanding the people involved in a police investigation. It's not just a question of fingerprints, you know, and analyzing the dust in trouser turnups. We have to use a bit of psychology, too, from time to time."

"Yes, I see," said Elliot. He looked down at the toe caps of his beautifully polished black shoes, seemed about to say something, and then changed his mind.

"You were going to say . . . ?" prompted Finch, but he would not be drawn. Avoiding Finch's eyes, he merely said:

"I think perhaps I ought to give my wife a hand with the coffee things, if you'll excuse me for a moment."

He left the room, carefully closing the door behind him. Finch listened intently but he could hear nothing, only the faint vibration of Elliot's voice talking to his wife. It went on and on.

Giving her a full account of what's been said so far, thought Finch. I wonder what he was going to say in here, just now? He had something on the tip of his tongue but he couldn't quite bring himself to spit it out. Perhaps that's what they're discussing.

The kitchen door must have opened at this point, because Finch distinctly heard Mrs. Elliot say sharply, "Very well, then," and the next moment Elliot came back, carrying a tray of coffee things and preceded by his wife.

He put the tray down on a low table, fidgeted for a moment with the lid of the coffeepot, and then said:

"I had better make that phone call, darling, while I think of it. It is rather important."

It was so patently a lie and he behaved so uncomfortably as he told it that Finch suspected it was of his wife's arranging. While Elliot went out of the room, Finch watched Mrs. Elliot's face as she set out the coffee cups. There was a firmness about the lips which suggested determination of action and a rigidity about the nostrils which hinted that she was not going to find that action pleasant. She looked up but Finch had anticipated her glance and was examining his hands noncommitally.

"With milk, Inspector?"

"Please."

She passed him a cup of coffee and the sugar bowl, watched while he added sugar and passed the bowl back, and then said:

"Michael has been telling me about your inquiries. I understand it is a murder case."

"Yes," said Finch, and waited.

"A young girl, I believe?"

"Yes," said Finch again.

"I cannot understand why my brother-in-law should be implicated."

"Just routine inquiries," said Finch.

"I see."

She paused and the rigidity about her nostrils became more pronounced.

"Tell me one thing, Inspector. Was this girl assaulted before she was killed?"

"Sexually, do you mean?" asked Finch.

She tightened her mouth to show her dislike of the word and the blatant way in which he had uttered it.

"Yes. Was she?"

"No," said Finch. "But . . ." and he paused deliberately to take a sip of coffee, "she had had sexual intercourse shortly before her death."

Mrs. Elliot's mouth was now a thin line but, despite himself, Finch could not help admiring the tenacity with which she pressed on with the subject.

"In that case, Inspector, my brother-in-law could not possibly have committed the crime."

Ah, thought Finch, so that's what they were whispering about.

"I don't follow," he said, although he had a very good idea of what lay behind her remark.

She was sitting in a chair opposite him, her knees close together, her hands clasped in her lap. A cup of coffee which she had not yet tasted stood on a table beside her. So well-controlled was she that it was only by a slight tautening of the muscles of her knees, pressing them tighter together and causing an almost imperceptible movement in the fold of her skirt, that Finch was able to guess at her inward tension.

167

"My brother-in-law is not interested in women," she said.

Finch sipped more coffee and watched and waited. She threw back her head.

"We think he may have homosexual tendencies," she said in a clear voice.

Finch almost laughed. There she sat, a well-bred, carefully made-up bitch with as much usefulness and heart as the stupid little toy animal she carted around under her arm, discussing Smith with pinched nostrils and taut knees, as if he were something dirty and discreditable. What agonies they must have suffered out there, she and her husband, deciding which was worse, for Smith to be suspected of murder or to confess to his possible sexual deviation!

All the same, Finch could not help feeling a little thrill of exultation to have this knowledge of Smith and to have this woman sufficiently at his mercy to divulge it. But even as the thrill came he felt himself as much discredited as she was and to cover up this feeling he got up and walked over to the window where he stood looking out through the fine net curtains at the gauzy view of the sunlit street outside.

"Tendencies?" he asked. "Can't you be more specific?"

"Very well."

Behind his back her voice took on an almost clinical crispness.

"About two years ago there was a scandal concerning a boy of about seventeen who was employed in the design office. He was not a very prepossessing young man, rather shy and not very talented: secondary school and one year at an art college, that type. Francis became

168

friendly with him. I don't myself think there was anything, well, criminal about the association. Francis took him to art galleries and theaters and occasionally asked him to his flat, that sort of thing. But it was very stupid of Francis to have encouraged the boy. The people in the factory were bound to gossip. The boy was teased and eventually the situation reached such a point that it could not be ignored. My husband dismissed the boy; his design work, anyway, had never been very satisfactory. He was given a good reference and the whole thing could have passed off quite smoothly. Unfortunately, the boy's mother, a frightful, common sort of woman, came to the office and made a scene. She accused Francis of all kinds of things. My husband threatened to call the police and eventually she went away. Francis refused to discuss it with anybody and in the end we had to try to forget about it. However, it does lead one to believe that Francis is not psychologically the type that would commit that sort of murder."

Finch turned from the window. His face betrayed nothing except official politeness. He held out his hand.

"Thank you, Mrs. Elliot, for being so frank."

She raised her eyebrows at the suddenness of his departure but said nothing. Finch went over to the door and on opening it discovered Michael Elliot loafing about in the hall, biting his fingernails.

"You're not going, Inspector?" he cried, springing forward, hand extended.

The poodle which had been asleep on the landing came running down the stairs, barking and bouncing up at them. Mrs. Elliot scooped it up under one arm.

"I'm sure you can cross Francis off your list of suspects," Elliot was saying with terrible joviality. He even pressed the Inspector's arm as he escorted him to the front door.

"By the way," Mrs. Elliot said, her clipped voice commanding their attention, "how did you find out our address?"

"That's my business," replied Finch, and walked out the door, past the lollipop bay trees, their thick leaves shining in the sun, and went down the street without a backward glance.

14

After the destruction of the garden Smith could not bring himself to work in it again. He could not even bear to walk through the gap in the rose hedge. The briers sprang together; new shoots began to grow across the gap. In the garden the trampled earth remained unraked. Young weeds sprouted up with here and there a bean plant or a seedling lettuce where the scattered seeds had germinated.

Without the garden to attend to Smith had to make a new routine for himself and Cairn. In the mornings he either stayed in the cottage, reading, or he busied himself with household chores: chopping and stacking firewood, cleaning the cottage, and preparing a meal. It was usually a soup made of vegetables and meat which he simmered gently on the oil stove for several hours. Cairn usually slept, curled up on the sack in front of the fireplace, waking up when the smell of the soup permeated the living room.

Several mornings were taken up with shopping. Since the oil van had not stopped that morning at the end of the lane, Smith had resigned himself to walking to Wrexford to buy oil which he needed for both cooking and lighting. As it was too far to carry a week's supply in one journey, he had to make a second trip. When he had the garden to work, he had done the shopping in the afternoons, but now he went in the mornings, buying other necessities, such as meat, bread, and vegetables at the same time and, as he was now reading more, he usually visited a back street junk shop that had a tray of sixpenny secondhand books outside the door.

He returned home from these shopping trips with the book he had bought in his raincoat pocket, banging against his knee as he walked, the full can in one hand and a carrier bag of shopping under his arm and Cairn trotting obediently at his heels.

Thus he built a new routine, busied himself in new ways in the mornings and in the afternoons went for long walks. These were different from the walks he was accustomed to taking when he rambled across the fields to collect firewood or strolled to the outskirts of the next village to give Cairn exercise. These walks were of several hours' duration, covering many miles, and were taken as an escape from the confines of the cottage which he found irksome in the long afternoons.

He left after lunch, taking in his pocket bread and cheese to eat later in the day. He set off across the fields and kept as far as possible away from the roads and human habitation. Sometimes he would pass a cottage or a farm or hear, from a distance, the rumble of traffic along a road but for the most part he was alone in the countryside. It surprised him to discover, although the land everywhere bore signs of man's labor, how meagerly those men occupied the land they worked. It was possible to walk for several miles without seeing another human being.

The wet weather continued but Smith became aware, on those long walks, of the arrival of spring. There was a buoyancy in the air, a growing softness in the landscape. The harsh, wintry outlines of the hedges and trees were blurring over with green as the young leaves opened. The grass had a lush springiness under his feet. Sometimes he would rest, sitting under a hedge or on a gate, and survey the countryside around him, taking in slowly the vista of field and meadow, hedge and woodland, irregularly patched, and above, the sky over which clouds moved, continually drifting, dissolving, and re-forming.

He was aware also of the minutiae of the life about him and could watch for a long time rabbits feeding in a field while Cairn trembled beside him; or observe, a few inches from his face, a spider making a web across twigs, clambering about the intricate net while the wind blew it gently and the glistening fibers swung to and fro.

But it was the evenings that gave him particular pleasure, when the light began to fade and took on a grainy quality, like an old photograph, in which quite ordinary objects, a fence, a distant barn, a clump of trees against the skyline, became more significant than they seemed in the full light, more true to their own particular quality of uniqueness. Birds flew homeward, an urgency in their darting flight. The sky soared away and the earth seemed to crouch closer to itself. The night life of the countryside rustled and whispered in the huddled hedges and close woods.

It was then that Smith turned for home, trudging wearily, the dog at his heels. It was good to reach the cottage at last, to put his hand on the gate and give the familiar shove to open it, to stand on the stone step and run his fingers over the door, feeling for the keyhole in the dark. He turned the key and stepped inside, Cairn padding quickly in front of him to lie down on the sack in front of the fireplace. Smith fumbled on the table where he had left, in readiness for his return, a candle in a white enamel candlestick, a box of matches in its tray. The little yellow flame of the match spurted up in the dark. Cupping his hands round it, Smith lit the candle and then carried the same match to the fireplace to light the fire. The candle flame balanced on the wick and the soft yellow light wobbled up the walls and then steadied. Smith's shadow, as he crouched by the fire, was huge. It trembled on the opposite wall, bending at the shoulders to cross the ceiling. Cairn wagged his tail wearily as the paper caught alight and the twigs began to crackle into flame. Smith laid his hand on the dog's head in acknowledgment and stayed there, crouching beside the dog until he was sure the fire was alight, and then he got up and moved away. There were other jobs to be done. Part of the pleasure of the late return to the cottage was the number of tasks that had to be performed on his arrival home.

Next he lit the oil lamp that stood on the table and drew the curtains across the window. He had made the curtains after the mud had been thrown at the cottage, cutting up an old shirt that was past repair and threading the lengths of striped cotton onto a string slotted through a narrow hem. The string was held fast by two tacks in the window frame and when the curtains were drawn the string sagged in the middle, showing a half-moon of dark glass at the top, but they gave him a sense of privacy.

When the lamp was lit, he carried the candle into the kitchen and lit the two oil burners in the stove, one under the soup that was already cooked and only needed warming up, the other under a kettle of water. He put out a soup bowl for himself and an enamel dish for Cairn, cut bread, and put a pinch of tea in the pot that stood warming on the back of the stove. He drank tea, very weak, without milk.

Cairn usually padded into the kitchen when he heard the rattle of the plates but, as the soup was not ready, he drank some water and went back to the fire. The dog's weariness and hunger and his bedraggled appearance made Smith feel guilty. The afternoon walks were too long for Cairn. He always returned footsore and unhappy, and when Smith spoke to him he showed the whites of his eyes and wagged

174

his tail in an ingratiating, humble way as if Smith had been physically unkind to him and the dog was grateful for the man's renewal of kindness. The dog's humility hurt him, but there was nothing that Smith could do about the situation. He had to get out of the cottage. Walking for hours had become necessary to him and, as it would be as unkind to leave the dog behind, shut up in the cottage, it was something that Cairn would have to learn to suffer.

After they had eaten, the dog and the man settled down by the fire to rest, Cairn lying stretched out with his belly exposed to the warmth, Smith seated in the deck chair. Sometimes Smith read. Sometimes he simply lay back against the canvas and closed his eyes. In a half-waking sleep he would see again in his darkened mind the details of that afternoon's walk: the changing cloudscapes in the sky; the flight of birds; the pattern of branches against the thin spring sunshine.

Later Smith would get up and potter about the cottage, clearing away the supper things and washing the dirty saucepan and plates, tidying the hearth and putting more wood on the fire so that the room suddenly brightened with the new flames. Cairn stirred, lifting his head because he knew this was the time that Smith would bring the brush to groom his coat. The dog lay still while Smith brushed the hair over his belly, gently teasing out the matted knots and the little pieces of twig and dead leaf which were caught up in the fur. Then he sat up while Smith drew the brush down each leg and along his back with big sweeping movements until the brown and black coat gleamed. Cairn did not like having his head brushed but he always submitted, while Smith held him by the chin and passed the brush gently between his ears. When Smith released him he shook his head to get rid of the feeling of flattened fur and then lay down on the sack to complete the toilet for himself, twisting his body round to lick and suck at a hind paw where the fine hairs were matted together between the pads and had inflamed the tender skin.

Smith got himself ready for bed but it was often several hours before he turned out the oil lamp and got into bed. He liked the evenings. He liked to lengthen them out, postponing the time when he would have to scatter the smoldering logs and quench the light. The cottage was at its best in those hours before bedtime, with the darkness shut out behind the curtains and the interior warm and mellow in the light of the fire and the lamp. After those long afternoon walks he found he appreciated the evenings spent at home by the fire.

Finch called to see him on the afternoon of his visit to London. Leaving his car at the lane's end, he walked up to the cottage, picking his way through the deep ruts which seemed always to contain water, no matter if it had not rained for days. He found the gate shut and, shoving it open, went up to the door and knocked. There was no reply, no expected barking from the dog. Cupping his hands against the glass, Finch peered in through the living-room window. The room was tidy and empty. The hearth was swept, the blankets neatly folded on the camp bed.

Although it was obvious that Smith was not at home, Finch could not resist walking round to the back of the house. He tried the back door, which was bolted, and peered in through the little window over the sink. The kitchen had the same tidy but empty look of the living room. A saucepan stood on the oil stove. A shirt hung on a string over the sink. There was a womanly touch about the washing-up bowl left propped up on its side in the sink to drain, with the dish cloth neatly draped over the rim.

It was pointless hanging about the cottage waiting for Smith, who might be away from home for hours, and so

Finch trudged off down the lane to his car, making up his mind to return the following morning.

In the morning Smith was at home. This was obvious to Finch as he reached the gate. The window was open and he could hear the sound of a broom knocking against stone. Cairn anticipated his approach and was barking behind the door before Finch had knocked on it. He heard Smith's voice calling the dog away and then the door was opened and the two men confronted each other.

"May I come in?" asked Finch pleasantly.

Smith stood silently aside and let him enter the room. The Inspector looked about him with one of his quick, searching glances. The broom was leaning against the wall, with a small pile of dust that had been swept together lying on the floor near it. The grate had been cleared of ash but the new fire had not yet been laid. Finch also noticed two new things about the room: the candlestick on the table and the greatly increased number of books on the mantelshelf.

"What do you want?" asked Smith.

Finch parried the question by saying, "Mind if I sit down? I must be out of condition; I find the walk up that lane a bit of a drag."

Smith shrugged, as much as to say, "Please yourself," and Finch seated himself in the deck chair with a sigh, as if pleased to relax, and folded the skirts of his raincoat over his knees. Cairn, who had gone to sit by the hearth, did not know what to make of the situation. He recognized the Inspector but the dog was uneasy, not sure if this man was a friend or not. He sniffed tentatively at Finch's legs and Finch put down a hand and tousled the dog's ears.

"You're quite a nice dog," he said. "A good house dog but not too unfriendly. I like a dog that knows where to draw the line."

"Why have you come?" asked Smith. He remained

standing as if he were hoping the Inspector would not stay long. His reappearance at the cottage made Smith uneasy. He had put up with his own visits to the police station. They had been requested and as such were official and noncommittal. Smith could remain, to a certain extent, aloof, even disdainful, and on that footing he could meet the Inspector with a degree of amused acceptance. But Finch's calling at the cottage was a different matter. There was no common relationship on which to meet, except that of host and guest, and Smith had no wish to play host to Finch or anybody else.

Finch, however, had no intention of being hurried into an explanation of his motives in visiting Smith. He wanted to feel his way. Although he had given this meeting a lot of thought since his return from London, he still had no idea how to conduct it and had come to the conclusion that it would be better, as it were, to play it by ear when the time came; to take his cue from Smith's own attitude. But the man was edgy, Finch noticed, and he wanted to get him relaxed before he came to the point. But how was he to reach that point? He could hardly say to Smith, "I caught a glimpse of myself in a mirror and I thought of you. I feel we have something in common. What is it?"

He could imagine Smith's sardonic smile if such a question were to be asked. And yet Finch knew, if he was ever to get any rest, that question would have to be asked, somehow, in some form. He had been haunted by it ever since his return from London.

Meanwhile he would have to feel his way, use all the tricks he knew, and perhaps some new ones as well. It would be an interview to beat all the others.

"Why have I come?" asked Finch. "Well, now, that's quite a story, but the long and the short of it is I wanted to come, unofficially, that is, to tell you you've been cleared of any suspicion in the Walker case."

Smith gave a short laugh and sat down on the chair at the table. Finch's explanation, which the Inspector had made deliberately naïve, seemed to amuse him.

"I told you I was innocent the first day you came here," said Smith. "Wasn't my word good enough for you?"

Finch smiled back. "We policemen are notoriously untrusting, I'm afraid."

"Well . . ." said Smith, making as if to get up out of his chair, as though the visit was over.

But Finch was struggling to pull something out of his pocket.

"I've got something for you," he said. "I called in at Mrs. Bland's shop and, as I happened to mention I'd be seeing you, she asked me to give you this."

He held out the thin, buff-colored envelope with the typewritten address. Smith took it with an expressionless face and put it on the mantelshelf.

"She thought you'd be anxious to get it," went on the Inspector, watching Smith's face closely. "Said you'd called in a couple of times."

In fact, the story was a lie. He had deliberately gone to the shop in order to collect the envelope so that he could see Smith's face when he received it. Smith turned his face so that only his profile was visible.

"If that's all . . ." he began. But Finch was not to be shifted. He had settled himself back in the deck chair and produced a packet of cigarettes and a lighter.

"Smoke?" he asked.

"No, thank you," said Smith coldly.

"Mind if I do?"

Again Smith shrugged, and Finch, smiling, lit a cigarette and blew a cloud of smoke out of his mouth. He crossed his legs.

"I went to London yesterday," he said in a conversational tone. "Chelsea."

There was no need to explain it further. Smith had understood. He began to say, "How . . .?" and then he glanced quickly at the envelope on the mantelshelf and down at the Inspector. He had understood the meaning of that also. Finch approved his quick intelligence. He felt proud as if Smith had been his pupil and he had been responsible for training his mind to think so perspicaciously.

"Did you tell them why you had called to see them?" Smith asked.

"I hedged a bit on the details," said Finch. "But I had to tell them it was a question of homicide."

Smith gave that short laugh again. His eyes had wrinkled up in genuine amusement.

"That must have shocked them deeply," he said.

"They were taken aback," admitted Finch. "There was a distinct shudder through the room when I mentioned the word 'murder.' I might have used one of the basic Anglo-Saxon monosyllables."

"Did they hasten to wash their hands of me?" asked Smith. Despite himself he was curious. He found himself watching the Inspector's face closely as he spoke as if to catch in its expression some image, however fleeting, of those frigid rooms which had once been so familiar, or some echo of the voices of the past.

"No, no," said Finch. "They were more than fair. They tried to point out that, although they thought you odd, they did not consider you homicidal."

Smith's upper lip lifted in a smile that showed his teeth. It was a strange smile, bitter, intense. His teeth were startling against his beard. It was the first time Finch had seen him smile in this way and show his teeth.

"In fact," continued Finch, "it was while I was talking to them that I realized you could not possibly have killed that girl."

This was not true. It was a conclusion Finch had reached much later, in his office, after thinking about Smith and the Walker case. And, incidentally, he had understood Smith's reluctance to make a statement; he would have to sign with a false name or reveal his true identity.

"Why?" asked Smith. He seemed interested in the thought process by which Finch had reached this conclusion. Finch made a deprecatory movement with the hand that held the cigarette.

"Difficult to explain. But the murder of Doreen Walker smacks of secrecy. It's cheap and furtive. It's fornication in country lanes with a girl who was half drunk on spirits and probably smelled of armpits. You're too"—he searched for the word, looking quizzically at Smith while he hesitated—"fastidious, is that the word? Wary of human contact, anyway."

"Did you learn that in Chelsea?" asked Smith, turning away.

"I deduced it from what I was told," replied Finch. He was treading very carefully now, although he kept the frank expression on his face. It would be a mistake to let on he knew too much; about the dog, for instance, or the boy.

There was a silence. Finch wanted to go on and ask the question he had been longing to ask, but he wondered how Smith would take it.

"Why?" he asked at last, plucking up courage. "Why did you leave and come here?"

Although he felt he knew the answer, he wanted to hear it from Smith's own lips.

Smith did not reply for a moment. He was considering whether to rebuff the question or not. Yet the situation in itself was so bizarre that he was almost inclined to add to it by answering. There sat the Inspector, with his kind, open countryman's face and his shrewd, sharp eyes; a strange mixture of man, cunning, honest, cruel, and yet sensitive and above all, at the moment, desperately curious.

"I prefer to live by myself," Smith said at last. It was only half an answer and he hoped Finch would be satisfied but he was not. He shifted restlessly in the deck chair, which creaked under his weight.

"Why is that?" he persisted.

"I find I am happier," replied Smith. He realized he was in a difficult position. He would either have to answer the man or be rude to him and tell him to go. He did not want to do that. Why not tell him the truth? They would probably never meet again and, although they meant little enough to each other, Smith recognized in Finch someone not unlike himself in intelligence and perception.

"I enjoy my own company," he said. "The life I was living in London was not what I wanted. Unfortunately, it was the only life I knew then. Had I been born into another class I might have found happiness as a carpenter or a farm laborer. Or if I had had the vocation and the training, as a priest or a scholar. As it was, I was sent to a very minor public school and was taught enough to fit me for the career my father had planned for me, in the family business. Did you go to see the factory? No? It's a sort of glorified workshop in Fulham, two stories high, in one of those grimy back streets near the river. They make boxes there, the fancy kind that can't easily be mass produced. The girls sit at long benches, folding the boxes and then lining them with silk or velvet. All day long there's music coming out of a loudspeaker and the smell of glue hangs about the place. I had a sort of office with a glass window overlooking the finishing shop. I used to watch them working and ask myself, Why? Why was I there, supervising them? Why were they there, sticking bits of white and gold cardboard together? They used to sing to the music. I could only hear the voices faintly through the glass but I could see their mouths opening and shutting like fish in an aquarium. They were pathetic, all those open mouths. They were so bored. So utterly, completely bored. And so was I. The triviality, the futility, the pointlessness of it all was sometimes so overwhelming I wanted to shout and smash things. I hated it all. I hated myself. More than anything else, I hated them."

Even though he had been half expecting an answer of this sort, Finch was taken aback by the abruptness with which Smith uttered the last sentence and at the same time disappointed. Is this what he had been looking for ever since the moment he had caught sight of himself in the mirror of that Chelsea drawing room, a man's hate? He fumbled with the buttons of his raincoat as if preparing to leave. Smith was looking at him closely. His eyes were very bright and his teeth gleamed in his beard.

"You'd understand that, Inspector. We are two of a kind, you and I."

Finch sank back into the deck chair. The other man's eyes held him.

"Do I hate?" he protested.

"No, not hate," said Smith, "But something very like it. You despise people. You use them for your own purposes. You jerk them about like puppets and then you despise them because they let themselves be used."

Finch sat with his chin sunk onto his chest. He was thinking about the people he knew: his sister, silently coming and going about the house; Boyce, walking heavily out of the office; Mrs. Bland, almost in tears; the countless numbers of witnesses and suspects, like Meyrick, who had sat and sweated in front of him in interview rooms. Was Smith right? Had he used these people and then despised them? Was this perhaps the answer he had been unconsciously seeking, the key not to Smith's personality but to his own, because he had recognized when he looked into that mirror that he and Smith shared something too deep and too fundamental to be put into words until that moment?

The deck chair creaked. Smith waited, his eyes on the Inspector's face.

"I felt sympathy for you," said Finch at last. "I wanted to understand you, for yourself."

"Perhaps," said Smith. "But you suspected me of this murder out of your own vanity."

He went to stand at the window, looking out at the hawthorn hedge, partly to spare Finch from having to meet his eyes, partly to hide his own feelings.

"We are too clever for our own good," he went on. "We feel with our brains. There is no heart there at all, no real feelings, or very few. We are critical of others because we see them too clearly and so we despise them. I despise and reject them. You despise and use them. We are eaten up with a kind of intellectual vanity that withers all form of human contact. And it was out of this vanity that you suspected me of the girl's murder. Because I was a match for you, or so you considered. Is that not true?"

He turned abruptly from the window. Finch's head was sunk so low on his chest that he might have been a man asleep, or dead. When he spoke it was as if the words had been torn out of him.

"Yes, it's true."

"I think we have both reached a kind of understanding," said Smith, "and I am glad."

He held out his hand.

"I don't suppose we shall meet again."

Finch struggled up out of the deck chair and took the offered hand.

"I don't suppose we will," he said heavily.

Smith went with him to the door. The sun had come out

and the fat, young buds on the hawthorn hedge glistened in the light.

"Good luck with the case," said Smith. He seemed to mean it.

"Thanks," said Finch, "I shall need it."

Cairn accompanied him to the gate, wagging his tail, while Smith remained on the doorstep.

"Nice dog," said Finch again, stooping briefly to pat him. Then he walked away.

15

Meyrick returned home from work late the same afternoon. He cycled up the hill slowly toward the village, pressing down hard on the pedals. He was thinking about the murder. Indeed, he had thought of little else since the day he had first become involved in it. He tried to escape from it in hard physical labor which was his only means to forgetfulness. Working in the fields it was not so bad, but as soon as he went anywhere near the farm, or the wood at the end of the lane, he was reminded of the dead girl's face staring up at him through the hazel twigs. She must have walked up the lane, past the farmhouse, gone through the gate into the wood and along the path . . . He could never complete the picture. His imagination always stopped short of the actual killing. He shied away in his mind from the image of a man's hands reaching out in the darkness for her throat. But sometimes when he noticed his own hands fragments of the incompleted picture would float into his mind, like pieces of a torn-up photograph scattered on a stream. Hands. Fingers. Stretched out. Squeezing. Knuckles whitening. Then he became afraid of his own hands and thrust them deep into his trouser pockets.

There was no peace from it either when he went home. His wife would not let him forget. She went on and on about the murder until he could have shouted at her had he not been afraid of her. Always she came back to Smith. Smith had done it. Smith ought to be hung. It was a pity they didn't hang killers like him any more. What right had a man like that to walk about free?

Whenever he could Meyrick escaped into the yard, to his ferrets; but often he lacked the strength of mind to get up from his chair by the fire and make his escape. She held him with her fierce eyes. He would mumble something noncommittal, trying to soften her anger, only to find it doubled in its fury.

"Leave him be!" she would shout. "Leave him be! The police are doing *that,* right enough. You want to hear what they're saying about him in the village? There'll be trouble, you mark my words, if that Inspector don't soon make a move."

"What trouble?" he asked uneasily.

He did not particularly like Smith but talk like that frightened Meyrick.

But his wife only laughed shortly.

"I'm not saying. Know nothing, that's my motto. But I'll tell you this, it was a bad day when he set foot here and there's a good few now who won't be sorry to see the back of him."

Meyrick sank back in his chair, defeated. Deep down he believed Smith had killed the girl, although he could not bring himself to acknowledge this consciously, even to himself. It was bad enough that he could not stop himself from remembering the dead girl's face or imagining hands reaching out to leave those livid marks on the pale skin. But to identify those hands, to put, as it were, a face above them, bending down over the girl, was a leap of the imagination that Meyrick fought against making. Better to leave the killer faceless, nameless. So when his wife nagged on about Smith he turned away to poke at the fire, trying to shut off his mind so that he would not hear what she was saying. Or, if he could summon up the courage, he would slink out to the yard, avoiding her eyes, to watch the long, creamy bodies of the ferrets scuttle up and down the cage.

That evening the dread of going home was particularly strong. Two things had given rise to this. In the first place, he had been hedging and ditching in the long meadow on the slope above the farm, from which he could see in one direction the rooftop and chimney of Smith's cottage and in the other the massed trees of the wood where he had found the girl. The view of these two places linked them, killer and victim, inextricably in vision as well as mind and he tried to avoid looking in either direction, and to keep his eyes fixed only on his immediate surroundings, by working bent over, and he had in consequence a pain in his back and shoulders that was, in itself, a constant reminder. In the second place, he had (when he returned to the farmyard) overheard Mrs. Collins, the farmer's wife, talking to her husband. Meyrick was in the barn putting away his tools when he heard the sound of the car being driven into the yard and Mrs. Collins, who had been shopping in the village, saying to her husband:

"Mrs. Bland's been telling me she had that Inspector in the shop again this afternoon. Came to collect a letter for Smith and deliver it to him, as he'd be seeing him today, she said."

Her husband mumbled something and she replied sharply:

"That's all very well but it's about time the police made a definite move. They don't seem any further forward than the day she was found and they were traipsing about here half the night."

They moved away out of earshot and Meyrick heard no more but it had been enough to bring the memory of that day flooding back.

He was, therefore, not looking forward to an evening spent at home with his wife who, no doubt, would have the same information about the letter and who could be counted on to talk about it for hours.

Dusk was falling as he reached his house. Meyrick reached out with his left foot to balance on the curb while he got off his bicycle. A square of yellow light from the living-room window streamed out across the path and lit up the boundary fence. The curtains were not yet drawn. But in that very moment of noticing this the light was suddenly dimmed as his wife pulled the curtains across the window. It was in that moment that Meyrick made up his mind. He was not going home. Not yet. He wanted a few hours of peace and forgetfulness. Thrusting off with his foot, he cycled away down the road, the lamp on the front of his bicycle wobbling to and fro as he pushed on the pedals.

The Wheatsheaf was empty of customers. It was too early in the evening for anyone to have arrived. People were still having tea, or reading the paper, or getting ready to go out. Meyrick went into the public bar and ordered a pint of bitter. He rarely went into a pub. He did not like the noise or the smell or the smoke. He had always disliked crowds and, anyway, Mrs. Meyrick would have frowned at the waste of good money on drink.

The landlord was surprised to see him. He was still getting in crates of beer from the store at the back and he came in wiping his hands on a cloth.

"Well, well, you're a stranger," he said.

Meyrick answered surlily and the landlord shrugged and served him. If the man did not want to talk, that was all right by him, was his attitude and he went back to the store while Meyrick carried his beer to a corner table and sat down.

He drank slowly, taking the beer straight down his throat. He did not much like the taste of it but he could think of nothing else to order except whiskey, which was too expensive.

Presently the bar began to fill up. Men came in. Cigarette smoke began to drift upward toward the white plastic light shades. Meyrick shrank into his corner and kept his eyes lowered but they noticed him, laughed, nudged one another, and came over.

"Fancy seeing you here, Mr. Meyrick."

"Given the wife the slip, eh, Reg?"

"What you drinking, mate? Get him another, Percy."

They crowded round and he could think of nothing to say to make them go away.

"Here," said one man, young, with spots and a new, thick mustache, "heard the latest? That Inspector's been to see Smith again."

"Garn," said another. It was the lad who drove the oil van, Colin Edge.

"Straight up," said the first.

"It's about bloody time he arrested that sod," said Edge. "Those bleeding Londoners think they own the earth. If you talk with a posh accent, the bloody police'll lick your boots."

A pint of beer was put down on the table in front of Meyrick.

"Drink up, Dad," advised the youth who had bought it. Meyrick drank mechanically, watching the faces of the men round the table. They had forgotten him and were intent on discussing Smith.

"Still, we showed him," said another youth. There was general laughter which Meyrick did not understand.

"I *do* love gardening," said Edge in a mock pansy voice, one hand on his hip. They laughed again, their mouths wide open, spluttering beer.

"Here, watch it," warned the youth with the mustache, glancing about him. The laughter subsided except for some smothered giggling from a ginger-haired lad. Meyrick's eyes went from face to face.

"What you on about?" he asked abruptly.

"Never you mind, Dad," said Edge, leaning toward Meyrick to stub out his cigarette in the tin ashtray on the table. "What the eye don't see the heart don't bleed over."

"Have a bleeding heart!" joked the ginger-haired youth and there was more laughter.

Meyrick drank again. The noise, the smoke, the beer which he was unused to, all had begun to make him confused. The youths round the table seemed to loom over him. Their mouths were very big and their hands too were enormous, as they lifted their beer glasses to drink or their cigarettes to draw on. They were all hands and mouths and loud voices. The words they spoke clamored in his ears. Meyrick's head was bursting. The beer churned in his stomach. He was suddenly angry and he wanted to shout. He brought his beer glass down with a crash on the table and lurched to his feet.

"Sod him!" he shouted. "That's what I say. Sod him!"

The faces gathered round him in a circle. They swam nearer.

"Sod who, Dad?" someone asked.

"Sod him!" cried Meyrick. He wanted suddenly to be sick. He pushed his way through the circle of faces and staggered to the door and just made it to the yard where he vomited between two parked cars. Afterwards he shuddered and wiped his mouth with the back of his sleeve. Tears stung his eyes and the taste of the vomited beer was acrid in his mouth. Some of the youths had followed him out. They stood a little way off, unidentifiable in the dark.

"All right now, Dad?" someone asked uneasily.

Meyrick shook his head. His stomach no longer churned

but there was a roaring sound in his head and his legs trembled violently.

"Shall us see you home, then?" came a voice.

Meyrick leaned his head on a car window. The glass was cold to his forehead. He wanted to cry. He wanted to say, "I dursn't go home," like a little boy. A sob broke in his throat. Feet shuffled nearer across the gravel and a hand touched his arm.

"What's up then?" asked a voice.

So, because he was ashamed to say what he wanted to say, he said instead:

"I can't give over thinking of her. Her eyes were open. She were staring straight at me."

He was really crying now. Tears ran down his face and he rubbed them away with his sleeve.

"Come on," they said. They heaved his arms across their shoulders and began to walk him up the road, his feet stumbling and slurring. He talked most of the time, incoherently, with his chin resting on his chest. Car lights went past and lit for a moment the grass verge and the hedge.

His wife put him to bed, grim-faced, her jaw working silently. She put the slop pail on the floor beside the bed and went heavily downstairs. The smell of the fluid in the bucket pervaded the little bedroom. Meyrick rolled over to face the wall and tried to remember what he had said on the way home. Fragments of sentences came into his mind and became confused with scraps of remembered images. Long grass lit by a light. Sod him. Tangled brown hair. Sod who, Dad? Smith. Wide-open eyes. He killed her, the sod. Feet stumbling on a road. A boat crashing through thin twigs. He got her. We'll get him, Dad.

Meyrick groaned and put an arm across his face.

16

The following afternoon Smith went for one of his customary long walks. It was late when he returned and darker than usual. The weather had changed again and the promised spring seemed to have retreated. All day low clouds had obscured the sky and there had been a continual fine drizzle. The evening set in early and, as he walked back across the fields, Smith found it was not easy to make out any detail of the landscape. The hedges were dark bulks and the trees showed up against the sky only by reason of the closer density of their darkness. Cairn trailed miserably at Smith's heels, his fine-haired coat heavy with moisture.

Suddenly the dog stopped and whined uneasily. Smith bent down to put a hand to its head and felt, in the darkness, the dog's stiffened neck muscles and raised ears. Smith stood silent himself, listening and peering into the darkness. There was nothing that he could discern to make the dog uneasy except a glow in the sky some distance away, although at what exact point was difficult to determine because a copse at the field's boundary obscured his vision.

"Come on, Cairn," said Smith, urging the dog forward. "It's only a bonfire somewhere."

The dog padded forward again and Smith walked on, keeping his eyes fixed on the glow behind the trees. Cairn's uneasiness had made him uneasy. He could see now that the glow could not come from a bonfire. It lit up too much of the sky and the glare rose and fell with a breathing movement which could only emanate from a big blaze. As he drew nearer to the copse he became aware also of the bitter flavor of smoke in the damp air. Cairn whined again and ran forward and Smith broke into a run after him, stumbling through the darkness, shielding his face with one arm against the low-hung branches as he lurched and fought his way through the trees.

As he emerged into the field beyond it was clear from the direction of the blaze that it was his cottage that was burning. The fire was too far to the west to be Stokes's farm and the shape of the building was wrong. It was the cottage. Even at that distance Smith could make out the outline of the roof and the chimney stack against the red glow of the flames.

Cairn was barking wildly now and running backwards and forwards hysterically, jumping up to paw at Smith's coat one moment and dashing in front of him the next. Smith almost fell over him as the dog ran against his legs, and Cairn yelped piercingly. The shock of stumbling and the yelping of the dog brought Smith to his senses. He stopped, called the dog to heel and, taking the belt from his raincoat, slipped it through Cairn's collar. Then he walked on across the field, toward the burning house. There was no point in running. He could see it was well alight. The smell of the smoke was stronger now and from time to time a flake of burned paper or material floated down and touched his face.

There was a thick hedge of hawthorn surrounding the field and cutting it off from the adjoining meadow which lay directly behind the cottage. The best approach to the house lay down the bank, where the hedge was thin and broken, and then along the lane to the front gate. As Smith drew nearer to the edge of the field his view of the cottage was obscured by the high boundary hedge to his left; only the burning glow remained, lighting up the sky and growing more intense with every step that Smith took. He had no difficulty now in seeing. The grass, the twigs, and the sagging branches of the trees that bounded the lane were clearly visible as the flames leaped upward. The air was warm with sudden gushes of heat and there was a dull and subdued roaring sound like traffic in the middle distance.

Smith found the gap in the hedge and scrambled down the bank. The cottage was clearly in view now, some twenty yards away, and he stood where he was to watch, his gaze riveted on it. The windows poured flame. Even the door was alight, a rectangle of fire that flickered and danced up and down. Only the gate was untouched. Smith was aware, then, of other silhouettes; several people grouped together, standing a little way ahead of him in the lane and, beyond them, the huge bulk of a fire engine, drawn in against the hedge, with the helmeted figures of the firemen, looking like figures from a medieval drawing of the inferno, crouching or leaning across the background of flames. Water, pumped from the tender, arched upward and then fell into the glowing shape of the cottage. All was movement there in the foreground: the water, pouring out in living ropes; the flames surging and sucking; the branches of the trees moving restlessly in the currents of hot air. Only the human figures were motionless, standing or crouching; but there was intensity also in their immobility.

Smith could see it was hopeless. The cottage was too well alight for it to be saved. Even as he watched, the roof at the back collapsed with a great roar, sending a gush of sparks funneling upward, followed by a rush of flames through the opening, that towered above the chimney stack. Cairn gave a yelping cry that was almost a shriek, and two of the watching figures, hearing it, turned to look. One was Stokes. Recognizing Smith, he immediately walked over to him.

"They'll never save the bugger," he said. He meant the cottage. He had to raise his voice against the roar of the flames and the noise of the pump.

"No," agreed Smith.

"Fifteen bloody bob a week rent going up there in flames," went on Stokes. He spat. "You lost much?"

"How did it happen?" asked Smith.

"I heard some lads go by and I've got my own ideas," began Stokes, but the other man, Russell, the policeman, came up at this moment and said warningly:

"I'd advise you to keep them to yourself, Mr. Stokes."

Stokes made a contemptuous noise in the back of his throat and moved away.

Russell said, "It's a great shame about the cottage, Mr. Smith. I hope you're insured."

"I hadn't bothered," said Smith. His teeth gleamed for a second in the light of the flames.

"That's a pity," said Russell. He was surprised. An educated man like Smith should have had the sense to be insured.

"I hope you haven't lost much," said Russell.

"A few books and clothes. Some furniture," replied Smith. His eyes were on the flames, bursting upward.

Both men were silent. They seemed mesmerized by the fire. Then Russell remembered his duty.

"Inspector Finch gave me a message for you, sir. He wants to see you at the police station at Wrexford."

"Why?" asked Smith sharply, turning to face Russell.

"He didn't give a reason, sir, just said he wanted to see you."

Smith did not reply. Although his face remained expressionless, he was bitterly angry. He felt the Inspector had betrayed him. After the talk they had had in the cottage, after all that had been said, why did he still suspect him? Smith regretted ever having let himself be drawn by the other man. He had been a fool to trust him.

Russell was saying, "He said to ring through when you were back and ask for a car to be sent to pick you up. I've got my bike. It won't take five minutes to cycle up to the village and phone."

"I'll walk," said Smith shortly.

"But he said . . ."

"I said I'll walk," repeated Smith. "I don't need a car,"

"Very well, sir," said Russell.

Smith walked away, the dog cringing at his heels. Russell watched him go and wondered if he ought to insist on sending for a car. The man looked dead beat. The dog too. Then Russell shrugged. If Smith preferred to walk, that was his lookout.

When he reached the bottom of the hill Smith turned right along the Wrexford road. The rain was falling heavily now, slanting at an angle directly into his face. At first he bowed against it, ducking his head and stooping his shoulders against the downpour, but the muscles in his neck soon began to ache, so he threw his head back and met the rain face on. It ran down his beard and hair and trickled below his collar. The fronts of his trousers were soon clinging to his legs. Cairn trailed miserably at his heels, his fine coat heavy with water. Cars passed occasionally, in a glitter of light, their wheels throwing up a fine spray-like mist from the wet surface of the road.

On the outskirts of Wrexford Cairn sat down suddenly on the path and would not get up. Smith urged him on but the dog only wagged his tail feebly. In the dim light of the street lamps, which were strung out sparsely here on the edge of the town, Smith could see the whites of Cairn's eyes showing in bright desperation in the soaked hair of his face.

"Come on!" said Smith, snapping his fingers.

Cairn whined and lifted a front paw uneasily but he did not stand. Then Smith stooped down and, putting his arms under the dog's belly, heaved him up into his arms. Cairn lay quiescent in his grasp, his head resting somewhere near the man's shoulder. Smith could feel the heavy rise and fall of the dog's flank against his chest. Carrying the dog, Smith walked the last half mile into the town.

The interior of the police station was very bright and warm and restful. There was a gentle hum from the electric clock on the wall. Someone had stood a rubber plant in a brown pot on the black-and-white tiled floor. The thick leaves shone as if they had been oiled and the glossy painted walls reflected light. The duty sergeant, busy at the desk, glanced up from the report he was writing and caught a glimpse through the rain-starred glass door of two bearded faces, one above the other, struggling together. Startled, the sergeant put down his pen. The next moment the door was shouldered open and Smith came in carrying the dog. Water ran from his clothes and his beard and hair were matted with rain.

He came over to the desk, where he put the dog down on the floor. It lay stretched out, its head on its paws, and appeared to go straight to sleep.

Smith said, "Inspector Finch wanted to see me."

"That's right, sir," replied the sergeant. "I'm afraid he's not in at the moment. He's been called away. He rang through a short while ago to see if you had arrived and to say he might be delayed." He looked at Smith's wet clothes. "P.C. Russell was supposed to phone through for a car to fetch you."

"I preferred to walk," said Smith impatiently. "What does he want to see me about? Is it the murder case?"

He seemed almost agitated. The sergeant, who was not sure himself of Finch's reason for wanting to see Smith, avoided meeting the man's eyes.

"He didn't say, sir. Just said he wanted to see you and would you wait. I think he may be quite late back."

"And what am I supposed to do?" asked Smith. "Wait here indefinitely in these wet clothes?"

"Well, sir, I suggest, under the circumstances, you have a hot shower and get changed. We can find you something dry to wear. And something for you to eat. Have you eaten?"

"No," said Smith. He looked suddenly defeated. "Neither has the dog."

"I expect we can rustle up something for both of you," said the sergeant. He was enjoying the situation in a heavy, humorless way. He called a constable, sent him off to find clean clothes for Smith, organized everything.

"By the way," the sergeant added, in a throwaway manner that did not fool Smith, "you won't have any objection to staying here the night, if the Inspector's held up for a long time?"

"Why not?" said Smith, with weary resignation. "There's nowhere else to go."

The sergeant raised his eyebrows at this but made no comment. The constable returned at this point with a bundle of clothes which he handed over to the sergeant and then he turned to Smith. He was a pleasant young man, who hated night duty, so Smith's arrival was something of a diversion.

"You're very wet, sir," he commented.

"Yes," replied Smith laconically.

"And so's the dog," added the constable. But the sergeant cut him short.

"Take over at the desk, Hunt," he said. "And if you'll come with me, sir, I'll show you where to go."

Smith snapped his fingers at the dog, which stood up, leaving a puddle of dirty water that had run off its coat onto the gleaming tiles. The three of them moved away, an odd trio: the bulky, upright figure of the sergeant, followed by Smith in his old plastic raincoat, looking more weird than ever, his hair and beard straggling; then the dog, last of all, padding heavily in the rear, his wet tail almost brushing the floor.

The basement locker room was bare and functional with cream-painted walls and rows of narrow, gray metal cupboards with air grids in the doors. Beyond was a washroom, a dazzle of white tiles, with a row of washbasins, a urinal, stall lavatories, and three shower units with half-partitions, above which the pipes and nozzles of the shower fittings could be seen. Towels hung down in deathly stillness. The massive, blue reflection of the sergeant passed across a series of mirrors with Smith's head and shoulders always one image behind, looking insubstantial and out of place among all that solid porcelain. The sergeant opened the door of a shower cubicle.

"If you'll leave your wet clothes outside, sir, I'll see they're dried for you." He handed Smith the bundle of clothes. "That's the best we can do. I hope you'll be able to manage."

"Thank you," said Smith.

"There'll be a cup of tea and something to eat afterwards. I'll send a constable down in about quarter of an hour to show you the way. But there's no need for you to hurry yourself."

"Thank you," said Smith again.

"And if there's anything else you need, you only have to ask for it," went on the sergeant. Proud of his organizing ability, he stood like an overanxious host at the door of the shower, blocking Smith's path. Smith looked at Cairn.

"If you have an old towel, I should like to dry the dog," he said.

"Certainly," said the sergeant, with a slight intake of breath, as much to say, I don't know where I'm going to find an old towel, and I've got other things to do anyway, but I'll put myself out to be obliging.

He left and Smith went into the shower cubicle, called Cairn in with him. It was a long, narrow compartment with a slatted bench at one end and a shower tray sunk into the floor at the other. As soon as he heard the locker-room door close behind the sergeant he began to undress, pulling his wet clothes off quickly. He had already given the bundle a quick examination and found it to contain P.E. shorts and singlet, two towels, clean but harsh to the touch as if they had been too quickly dried, white socks and plimsolls. The bundle was wrapped up in a dark-gray dressing gown and, in the center, like a pearl, nestling between the rolled-up socks, was a new cake of soap.

As soon as he was undressed Smith took the soap and stepped into the shower tray. He was unused to the taps and at first the water shot out, too hard and too hot. The fine, scalding spray on his cold skin made him gasp and he lunged forward to adjust the control. Cairn, who was lying partly under the wooden seat, looked up briefly at the man's involuntary exclamation. One eye opened in his wet fur and then closed again.

Feet in boots appeared in view below the partition. There was a discreet tap on the door.

"Your other towel, sir," said a voice, not the sergeant's. Smith, who was soaping and rubbing his hair, called out: "Thank you. Leave it on the floor, would you, please?"

The towel was put down by the partition and the feet went away. Smith called the dog.

"Cairn! Here, Cairn!"

Cairn opened his eyes again. His tail brushed the tiles.

"Here, Cairn!" said Smith, more persistently.

The dog got up stiffly and came to the edge of the tray where it stopped. It would not come any farther. Smith had to seize it by the collar and drag it forward, the dog's back feet slithering unwillingly across the floor. But once under the shower it gave up any attempt at resistance and crouched in the bottom of the tray while Smith rubbed its coat in the fine spray of warm water, coaxing small pieces of twig and taggles of mud out of the wet fur. This complete, he turned off the shower and, naked and dripping wet himself, straddled the dog, gripping it between his knees and drawing his hands along its flanks and under its belly to wring out the surplus water. Then he reached under the partition for the towel and wrapped it round the dog, rubbing and massaging the fur to dry it and to get the warm blood circulating beneath. Smith was shivering. The water had dried on his back and shoulders leaving them stiff and cold.

As soon as the dog was reasonably dry, Smith toweled himself vigorously and then dressed in the borrowed clothes. The plimsolls were too small and he padded out of the shower in his stockinged feet, carrying the shoes, together with his wet clothes and the damp towels. A constable was sitting on a chair in the locker room, smoking surreptitiously, the cigarette concealed in the cupped palm of his hand. He stood up when Smith came in.

"Ready then, Mr. Smith?" he asked, sounding more friendly than he had intended, because Smith had seen him smoking on duty. He dropped the cigarette slyly to the floor and trod it out with a casual-seeming shifting of his feet.

He took the bundle of clothes and towels from Smith, remarking, "I'll see to these for you," and led the way up the corridor, Smith following with Cairn close behind. Both the dog and the man were rough-haired from the shower and the brisk toweling and both walked with the heavy, deliberate movements of the exhausted.

"We've sent out for something for you to eat and drink," said the constable over his shoulder. "I don't know where you'd like to have it. The canteen's closed but we could open it up for you."

"Don't bother," replied Smith. "I just want to eat and go straight to bed."

"Well, if you like, you can have it in bed," said the constable. "I say 'bed' but it's a cell, you do realize that, don't you?"

"I don't mind," said Smith wearily.

"The mattresses are comfortable enough," went on the constable. "No sheets, but you'll be warm enough. There's plenty of blankets. It's down this way."

He turned right at the end of the corridor. They went down several steps.

"Here you are then," he said, pushing open a' door. Smith looked past him into the cell beyond. It was bigger than he had imagined, squarer, with walls tiled in cream halfway up and painted pale gray above. A small window, high up in the wall, probably looked into the basement area. There were no bars but the window was fitted with thick, opaque glass. A bunk bed occupied most of one wall. There was a mattress on it, a pillow, and several dark-gray blankets, folded into squares. A table and a chair stood against the other wall and there was a washbasin in one corner with a lidless lavatory beside it. Light flooded down from a white glass globe, fitting flush against the ceiling.

"There you are," said the constable. He seemed proud of the clean, shining modern cell. "Not exactly the Ritz but better than a lot of places I've had to sleep in. If you'd like to be making up your bed, sir, I'll nip upstairs and fetch your supper.''

Smith walked over to the bed and Cairn followed him. The constable cleared his throat.

''Your dog could sleep in the cycle shed across the yard. It's warm and dry in there.''

''The dog stays with me,'' said Smith, unfolding blankets.

''Oh,'' said the constable. He sounded nonplused. ''I don't know what the sergeant'll have to say to that.''

''The dog stays,'' repeated Smith, ''or I go.''

''I'll tell the sergeant,'' said the constable huffily and departed.

Left alone, Smith made up the bed, tucking in the blankets, and then sat down on the edge. Cairn, who had hung about near its foot, now came up and thrust his nose into the man's hand. The dog's eyes were anxious. It seemed to be asking, ''What's happening? Why are we here?'' Smith gave him a reassuring pat.

Presently the constable returned carrying a brown plastic tray on which were two plates, one with a metal cover over it, an enamel mug of tea, and a knife and fork. He put the tray down on the table. Another constable followed him with a large cardboard box in his arms. Both had the long-suffering expressions of people of whom too much has been demanded. The second constable dropped the box onto the floor and departed silently.

''There's your supper,'' said the other constable. ''And the box is for the dog to sleep in.''

''Thank you,'' said Smith. He hesitated and then added, ''I'm sorry to be a nuisance.''

''That's all right,'' replied the constable, mollified by the apology. ''I thought you could use the dish cover for the dog to drink from. I've put a plate of potatoes and gravy for

204

him and there's an old coat in the bottom of the box, so he won't be cold."

A strange expression passed over Smith's face. His jaw trembled and his eyes screwed up very small. For an awful moment the constable thought he was going to cry. Deeply embarrassed, the policeman went over to the table and began to unload the tray, clattering the plates and cutlery about more than was necessary. When he turned round he was relieved to see that Smith looked normal, only very tired. He even gave a weary smile.

"I'll leave you then, sir," said the constable. "Bang on the door when you want the light out. The switch's outside. The door won't be locked, of course."

He left and Smith went over to the table, calling Cairn to come with him. The dog got up, with a feeble wag of his tail, and Smith put the dish of gravy and potatoes down on the floor for him and then filled the metal cover with water from the tap at the basin.

The dog sniffed the food suspiciously and then began to eat. While he ate, Smith got on with his own supper: a chop, peas, and mashed potatoes. The food had a dried crust over it, as if it had been kept warming in an oven for a long time. But he ate it, nevertheless. He was very hungry. He drank the tea also, although it was too strong and too sweet. Afterwards, he rinsed out the mug and filled it with water, which he drank too.

Cairn had finished his supper and was rattling the dish across the floor as he licked the plate clean. The dog also drank deeply and then sank down on the floor. Smith picked him up bodily and placed him in the box, folding the sleeves of the coat over his back. Then he banged on the door as he had been instructed and got into bed. Almost immediately the light went out. The policeman must have been waiting outside for his signal.

Smith turned on his side, drawing up the blankets round his neck. They were coarse and smelled faintly of dry-cleaning fluid. He tried to sleep, but he had reached that point of exhaustion at which sleep becomes replaced by a sensation of swooning, of spinning away into unconsciousness, and he kept jerking himself awake, reluctant to submit to this vortex of oblivion. Cairn seemed restless too. Smith could hear him shifting about in the box. There were other unaccustomed sounds of the police station, faint, metallic, and hollow echoes.

Presently Cairn scrambled out of the box and jumped up onto the bed. He trod about in the darkness for several seconds, finding somewhere to lie down, and then slumped across Smith's legs. Smith put out a hand and touched the dog's head but there was no response. Cairn had already fallen asleep. Smith lay back and closed his eyes, and very soon, with the dog's heavy body warm against him, he, too, was asleep.

17

Finch was in a quiet, introspective mood after his interview with Smith. His colleagues, misunderstanding the reason for it, thought it was caused by a visitor he had received soon after his return from interviewing Smith. This visitor, a Mr. Digby, had made utterly useless Lamport's evidence by explaining that it was he and his wife whom Lamport had seen standing in the gateway on that Saturday evening. His wife, Mr. Digby explained, had been feeling car sick and, after parking the car at the roadside, he had walked with her up and down the road a few times until she felt better. He remembered standing for a moment or two in a gateway and being dazzled by a car's head lamps as it passed on the road. Digby had no idea why the car's driver had not noticed his own car parked twenty-five yards up the road. The sidelights were on and Digby was sure it must have been visible to a passing motorist.

As far as Finch was concerned, Smith was out of the case anyway and Digby's statement did nothing more than clear up the mystery of the unknown man and woman that Lamport had seen. However, it was a convenient excuse to explain away his mood and Finch did nothing to contradict his colleagues who took this attitude. Only Boyce was puzzled. He had known Finch bad-tempered, gloomy, even at times depressed when a case was not going well. But he had never before known him in this present withdrawn frame of mind. There was a sad gentleness about it that was totally alien to Finch's character. Finch's sister also was surprised by him. Finch telephoned her that evening to say he would be late home, a thing he had never done before.

The following day, the day of the fire at Smith's cottage, Finch stayed in his office, working on the Walker case. Boyce had reported for duty that morning and Finch had sent him home. The sergeant was heavy with a cold caught on the long hours he had spent tramping about in the rain, looking for witnesses. When he left, Finch gathered together all the files he had on the case and stacked them on the desk. He had decided to start again at the beginning. With Smith out of the case as a suspect and Meyrick too, for the Inspector no longer regarded him seriously as being concerned with the girl's death, Finch felt like a man who has been following a thread through a maze, expecting to find the center, and has come, unexpectedly, to a blank end. Intellectual vanity, Smith had called it. Finch gave a wry smile. Very well, he would be humble. He would admit defeat, wipe the slate clean, and make a fresh start.

He had, therefore, spent all that day reading over the statements and reports which dealt with the death of Doreen Walker, beginning with the report of Meyrick's discovery of the body early that Monday afternoon. As he read through the statements he made notes on a separate sheet of paper of possible lines of inquiry which had either not yet been followed up or had been only partially completed. They were pathetically few. Despite the shortness of the time and the enormity of the task, a great amount of investigation had been completed and a large number of people had already been interviewed. This would obviously have to be intensified. The inquiries at the places where Doreen was known to have spent her Wednesday afternoons must be extended. Tobacconists' shops were a possibility, and newsagents', hotel bars and lounges, amusement arcades, and bingo halls. Taxi drivers were another untapped source of potential witnesses, as were newspaper sellers, lavatory attendants, and the amorphous mass of teen-agers that seemed to spend a large portion of its leisure time simply waiting about in cafés or snack bars or on street corners for something to happen.

This aspect of the investigation would have to be intensified and Finch blamed himself for having spent so much time and trouble on the local angle of the case, although he still felt intuitively that the answer to the riddle of the murderer's identify might lie nearer to the girl's home.

Restlessly he got up from his chair to look at the map on the wall.

"All right," he said to himself, "let's carry on with the local angle but let's approach it scientifically. Let's take every house within a mile radius of the girl's home and make door-to-door inquiries. We can leave out Framwell. Boyce has already covered that, but we'll visit every house, farm, and caravan in a given area."

He made a rueful face, imagining Boyce's reaction when he received the news of these intensified personal inquiries.

Finch returned to his desk and looked again at the other suggestions he had written down. The two remaining ideas stemmed out of the first pathology report he had received on the examination of the girl's body. The contents of the stomach had already suggested two lines of inquiry which Boyce had been following up: those at the fish-and-chip shops and at public houses and off-licenses. These could possibly be extended to cover a wider area. There remained two other points in the report which Finch had not yet dealt with; one was the girl's pregnancy. She had probably known that she was pregnant. She might possibly have tried to do something about it. Had she visited a doctor? Or a chemist? Or a back-street quack who might sell her some pills to bring about an abortion? Here, anyway, were three other possible lines of investigation that would have to be followed up in every place known to have been visited by the dead girl.

The second point raised by the pathologist's report was so small that Finch had hesitated before making a note of it. It was the large bruise on the girl's right shin which had been inflicted a week to ten days before her death. It might signify nothing. She might have banged her leg against the counter at work or tripped and fallen in the street. Finch remembered the conductor's evidence, how she had stumbled in her high heels coming down the stairs when she had alighted from the bus at Bell Green. Nevertheless, it was an opening which could not be ignored if he was to keep to his principle of a fresh beginning to the case and an opening which could be quickly tried out by making inquiries of Brenda Parsons or the dead girl's family.

Finch glanced at his watch. The time was 6:15 P.M. If he left now he could interview Brenda Parsons at home, call also on Constable Leach and his wife, who might have something to add to what they had already told him, and then he could go on to the Walkers' house.

He was on the point of leaving the office, was switching off the light at the doorway, when the telephone on his desk rang and he switched the light on again and crossed the office to answer it. It was P.C. Russell, his voice sounding very loud and respectful. Faintly in the background a baby wailed.

"Inspector Finch?" asked Russell. "It's Russell here, sir, from Frayling."

"Yes?" said Finch.

"I didn't want to disturb you, sir, but you did ask me to

let you know if I heard anything about Smith in the village."

"Well?" said Finch. With Smith out of the case, Finch was anxious to get on with this new line of inquiry.

"It's his cottage, sir. Stokes, who has the farm at the end of the lane, has just come up to the village to tell me that the cottage is on fire. I've already telephoned to the fire brigade and I'm on my way down there myself."

"Was Smith in the cottage?" asked Finch.

"I don't think so, sir. Stokes is under the impression that Smith is out with that dog of his every afternoon until quite late. Leastways, he's noticed him several times recently coming home round about eight o'clock and earlier on, at dusk, Stokes noticed the cottage was in darkness."

Russell paused but had taken a heavy breath as if he intended to continue. Again Finch said, "Well?" and Russell took up the story.

"There may be nothing at all in it, sir, but Stokes reckons someone may have been down at the cottage. He heard someone go by in the lane about half past five. His dog was disturbed."

"It could have been Smith," said Finch.

"Stokes doesn't think it was, because about five minutes later he went out into his yard and he noticed the cottage was still in darkness. He can't see much of it from where he lives but he says he can see if there's a lamp lit. He's noticed it before. The light from the windows at the back of the cottage shines out onto the hedge. So if it was Smith who went past, he'd've had time to get home and light the lamp."

"I don't see . . ." began the Inspector but Russell doggedly continued.

"A bit later on, just before six o'clock, Stokes reckons, he heard voices and the sound of footsteps running down the lane past his farmhouse. It sounded like several people, possibly youths, he says. His dog started up again and he kept it up for so long that Stokes decided after several minutes to go out and quiet it. It was then he noticed a smell of burning and saw flames coming from Smith's cottage. Smith used oil for both cooking and lighting, so that's probably why it went up in flames so quickly. Stokes ran out into the road and stopped a passing car and got a lift up to the village."

Finch pinched his lower lip. Stokes's evidence, transmitted by Russell, suggested that Smith's cottage had been set on fire by human agents. Was it accidental or deliberate? If deliberate, then it was arson. Was someone trying to punish Smith or drive him out of the village? If this was so, then it would be a criminal act, open to police investigation. But the case he was concerned with was the murder of Doreen Walker. All the same, he felt a surge of pity for the man and a sense of responsibility toward him. After what had been said between them the day before in the cottage, Finch could not now wash his hands of him. Smith would have nowhere to sleep that night and it was cold and raining again.

"Look, Russell," said Finch, speaking quickly. "I can't come myself. I'm just on my way out. But I want you to go down to the cottage and get hold of Smith. Tell him that I want him here at the police station. You can phone through for a car to pick him up. I'll leave orders for it this end. Is Stokes still there?"

"No," said Russell, "he left after I phoned the fire brigade. He's walking back. I'm following by bike. What shall I say to Mr. Smith when I see him?"

"Just tell him I want him here at the station," snapped Finch and hung up. He had no intention of explaining himself to Russell.

At the desk he stopped to give brief orders to the duty

sergeant. Again he did not explain in detail. He just told the sergeant to expect a telephone call from Russell for a police car to pick up Smith and to bring him back to the station. He was to be kept at the station until his, Finch's, return. The Inspector was about to walk away when, on an impulse, he turned back and added:

"By the way, I want him treated kindly."

"Of course, sir," said the sergeant, and only raised his eyebrows when Finch had turned away.

Outside the rain, which had been a steady drizzle all day, was falling more heavily. Finch ran for his car, cursing the weather under his breath. He thought of Smith again and then dismissed him deliberately from his mind. There was nothing practical that could be done for him at the moment and the investigation of the Walker case must take priority over every other consideration. Finch turned the car and once more took the road that led to Framwell.

The Parsons family was watching television. Mrs. Parsons, fat like her daughter, showed Finch into the living room where her husband and Brenda were sitting on a large settee, eating plums and custard with automatic gestures, their eyes never moving from the screen.

"Inspector Finch is here to see you, Brenda," said Mrs. Parsons. The girl's eyes rolled in Finch's direction. She lowered her spoon.

"I'll turn the telly down a bit while you're talking," said Mrs. Parsons. She went over to the set and lowered the volume. The singer, his voice reduced to a whisper, went on posturing and grimacing. Mr. Parsons, who had given Finch only a cursory glance of bovine casualness, like a cow looking over a gate, leaned forward, straining to hear the sound. Mrs. Parsons lowered herself between her husband and daughter and gave Brenda a shove with her elbow.

"The Inspector wants to talk to you, dear," she said, and

213

when Brenda got up from the settee, Mrs. Parsons spread her bulk across the vacant space with an audible sigh of relief.

"What d'you want?" asked Brenda nervously.

"Your help," said Finch. "Doreen had a bruise on her right leg, on the shin. She must have knocked her leg about a week or ten days before she died. Can you remember it?"

"I don't think so," said Brenda. Her eyes kept swiveling back to the television screen.

"It was about here, on her leg," said Finch, stabbing at his own shin with a finger and forcing her attention. "It was a big bruise. Bad enough to make her limp."

There was dawning remembrance in the girl's face.

"Oh, yes, I remember now. Her leg was ever so stiff the next day. She 'ad a job getting on the bus."

"The next day?"

"Well, after she banged it."

"At work? At home?"

"No, getting into the van."

Brenda put her hand up to her mouth. "Ooh! I'd forgotten about that. Is it important?"

"It could be," replied Finch, deliberately keeping the excitement out of his voice. "Try to remember exactly what she said."

"Well, nothing much, really. We was at the bus stop and when the bus come along, she said, ' 'Ere, give me a 'itch up. I've banged me leg and it don't 'alf 'urt.' And I said, ' 'Ow?' and she said, 'I give it ever such a wallop getting into the van yesterday.' "

"Do you know what van?"

"No," said Brenda, shaking her head. Her interest began to wander back to the television screen.

"What day was this?" persisted Finch.

"I dunno for sure. Could've been a Thursday morning."

"In that case, she banged her leg on a Wednesday?"

"That's right," said Brenda.

"Did she ever mention getting a lift in a van or knowing somebody who had a van?"

"No."

It was clear that Brenda had told him all she knew. Her eyes had taken on an opaque look and she began to fidget. Finch took his leave, refusing Mrs. Parsons' offer of tea. Even before he had reached the back door the television was blaring out again.

Outside, he sat in the car thinking deeply. The scrap of information might mean nothing at all and yet he could not get it out of his mind that it was significant. She had banged her leg getting into a van and this had happened, if Brenda Parsons' memory was correct, on Wednesday, either in the afternoon or the evening when she was known to be meeting a man. What sort of person owned a van? Finch let the word drift about his mind. Van. Garage. Breakdown. Van. Ice cream. Milk. Delivery. Goods. Delivery—goods! Then, shop! The bits began to fall rapidly into place and they formed a pattern so neat and so obvious that Finch hardly dared breathe as his mind raced on. Yes, it all fitted; the Wednesday afternoons, the new packets of stockings and underwear, the bicycle, perhaps even the shoes, Mr. Severall's remarks . . .

He would have to get in touch with Severall. The shop would be closed. Perhaps he was on the telephone at home. Telephone. Leach. The police house would have a telephone and it was only three doors away from the Parsons' house. Finch got out of the car, walked up the road a little way, and knocked at the door of the police house.

There followed three quarters of an hour of frustration. Finch found Mr. Severall's home telephone number without any trouble and the shopkeeper was able to give him

215

the name of the man. He was unable to supply the man's address but suggested that the Inspector get in touch with the man's employer, a Mr. Weeks, who had a business in Southend. Finch telephoned to several people of the name of Weeks, listed in the Southend directory, before he found the right one. Mrs. Weeks answered the telephone. Yes, indeed, her husband did own that particular firm but he was not at home. He was spending the evening at the Conservative Club. Finch rang the club and, after some delay, Mr. Weeks was found and came to the telephone. He had a rich, fruity voice. Finch imagined him, prosperous in a dark suit, with plump hands and a softly jowled face.

Finch identified himself and asked him if he employed the man whose name had been given him by Mr. Severall. Mr. Weeks replied that he did.

"Could you tell me his home address?" asked Finch.

"Not offhand," replied Weeks.

"Then could you get it for me?" asked Finch. "You must have records in your office?"

"Now?" asked Weeks, sounding scandalized. Finch could almost see him puffing out his cheeks in annoyance. "Is it important?"

"Yes, it is," replied Finch. "I wouldn't have troubled to telephone you this evening, Mr. Weeks, if it could be left until the morning."

"Very well. I shall be at least half an hour before I can phone you back. My office is the other side of town and I shall have to go home first to collect the keys."

Finch thanked him, gave him Leach's telephone number, and hung up.

While he waited he rang the police station at Wrexford to ask about Smith. The duty sergeant told him that Smith had not yet arrived.

"I shall probably be late," said Finch. "I want him kept there until I get back."

216

"Very good, sir," replied the sergeant.

The curtains in Leach's little office had not yet been drawn. Finch looked at the rain sliding down the darkened glass.

"All night, if necessary," he added and hung up before the sergeant could reply.

Mrs. Leach had made tea and Finch drank it in the living room. He was preoccupied and spoke little. Leach sat at the table writing out a report about a stolen car while Mrs. Leach sat comfortably by the fire knitting. The little blue shape on the needles had grown since Finch was there last.

"Leggings for my grandson," said Mrs. Leach, holding it up for Finch to see.

"Very nice," said Finch.

"Are you married?" she asked.

"No," said Finch, and added, "never seemed to have the time."

There had been a girl once, the sister of a colleague, Kate, with brown eyes and an infectious laugh. She had married someone else in the end.

"Who looks after you then?" asked Mrs. Leach. Her husband looked up, disturbed by her questions.

"My sister," replied Finch. "She's widowed."

A silence fell. Finch drank his tea. Presently the telephone rang. It was Mr. Weeks with an address, in Roxleigh. When he rang off, Finch quickly consulted the telephone directory. The man was on the telephone but the Inspector had no intention of ringing him. He went back into the Leaches' living room, briskly buttoning up his raincoat.

"Things moving?" asked Leach, noticing the Inspector's purposeful walk.

"I hope so," replied Finch.

Roxleigh was a small town midway between Wrexford and Southend. The address that Weeks had given him was in a housing estate on the outskirts, a postwar estate, mostly bungalows, with small front gardens. All the roads had the names of trees. Maple Avenue had nothing to distinguish it from the others. Finch drove slowly along it, looking out for number 17, or Ambleside, as it was listed in the directory. The street lighting was poor and the rain, slanting down onto the windscreen, did not make vision easier.

At last he found it and drew the car into the curbside, and, repressing an urge to get out of the car straightaway, he sat still for several minutes, composing himself and thinking of what he was going to say. He had only a theory to go on. No evidence. No witnesses. Nothing. A chance remark only had brought him to this man's address. It might be another blind alley, leading nowhere. But the theory fitted the facts, or at least some of them. And yet the facts had seemed to fit into the theory of Smith's guilt.

Finch climbed slowly out of the car and locked the door. You despise people, Smith had said. You use them and then you despise them. Finch put the keys into his pocket. A quotation from the New Testament came into his mind. St. Paul, was it? Something about that without charity you are like sounding brass or a tinkling cymbal. It had been read in assembly in the grammar school at the beginning of every term. In the seconds as he walked in the rain from the car to the front gate of the house he recalled the school hall, the tall windows letting in the sunlight in great oblongs, catching the gilt paint on the roll of honor board on the wall and the folds of the dark-red curtains on the platform, outlining the round-bellied water carafe on the table, with its downturned glass over it, which was never used. For some reason he had always associated the words "tinkling cymbal" with the water carafe.

He walked up the short path to the front door and rang the bell. There was a light on in the hall, shining out through the ribbed-glass panels in the door. After a few

218

moments' delay the door was opened by a woman, wearing a coat which she had obviously only just put on as she was still adjusting the collar; a tired, nervous woman, thin-faced, anxious, and in a hurry.

"Mrs. Viner?" asked Finch.

"Yes?" she said, struggling to free her collar which had got folded in at the back.

"Is your husband at home?"

"Yes."

"I wonder if I might have a word with him."

"Well—what do you want to see him about?" She was anxious not to offend him and yet a little suspicious of admitting him into the house.

"I'm from the police, Mrs. Viner," said Finch. "There's a matter I'd like to discuss with your husband if I may."

Strangely enough, she wasn't surprised. She opened the door wider to let him in and said:

"I expect you've come about that trouble at the office. My husband's been ever so worried about it."

"Quite so," said Finch. He did not know what she was talking about but thought it best to appear to agree with her. She opened the door leading into the living room, explaining as she did so:

"I'm just popping round to my sister's for an hour. Derek," she added, "here's someone from the police. I'll leave you two together. I was on my way out when you rang."

Finch stepped inside the room and met the eyes of the man who was sitting by the fire and had, just at that moment, looked up. Derek Viner was in his early thirties, undistinguished-looking except for his mouth, the lower lip of which was full for a man and gave him a boyish, slightly sulky expression.

" 'Bye then," Mrs. Viner was saying. "I shan't be later than ten."

" 'Bye," said Viner automatically. His eyes remained fixed on the Inspector's. The expression in them had changed from surprised anticipation when Finch first walked into the room to wariness when his wife had mentioned the word "police." Then he had glanced down. He was holding in his hands a child's red plastic lorry and had been testing the wheel-drive mechanism when Finch entered.

Finch looked about him quickly. The room had a pleasant, cluttered air. It was an all-purpose living room, with a dining-room alcove, the furniture of which was rather too large for it. There was a child's high chair standing in one corner, with a plastic bib draped over the tray. The other end of the room, where Finch was standing, was the sitting-room area. It contained a three-piece suite covered in worn, red fabric, a coffee table, and a television set which was not switched on. From the children's toys and clothes scattered about, Finch guessed that the Viners had three children, a boy, an older girl, and a younger child.

The two men waited. It seemed to be a tacit arrangement between them. Finch stood, taking in the details of the room; Viner sat, eyes lowered, running the wheels of the toy lorry across the palm of his hand. Presently they heard what they had both been waiting for, the sound of the front door closing behind Mrs. Viner.

Then Finch said, "Do you mind if I sit down?"

"Help yourself," said Viner, without looking up. Finch lowered himself into the armchair across the fireplace from Viner and tried to draw the man's attention.

"Smoke?" He held out his cigarettes.

"No, thanks," said Viner. "I just put one out."

Finch lit his.

"Well?" said Viner suddenly, putting the lorry down on the floor beside his chair.

"Mr. Viner, we're making inquiries into the death of a girl called Doreen Walker. She worked at Severall's. I believe you may be able to help us."

Viner said unexpectedly, "I recognized you when my wife said you were from the police. I was in the shop that time you called. I thought you were a customer."

Finch thought back quickly and remembered the occasion. He had waited in the shop while Mr. Severall gave an order to a traveler. Then the man had left. There had been a green van parked outside.

"I didn't recognize you," said Finch. "You call at the shop fairly regularly, I believe."

"Usually once a fortnight. I'm rep to a firm that sells women's clothing."

"Yes," agreed Finch. He himself had found out this much. He continued, "So you knew Doreen Walker?"

"Yes, I knew her."

"How well did you know her?" Finch went on.

Viner was silent and Finch waited. He was not sure what his next move should be. Viner seemed to have gained some confidence. The frightened look in his eyes had gone but the expression in them was veiled. He avoided looking at Finch and began to feel in his pockets as if searching for something. At last he got up and looked along the mantle-shelf and found what he was searching for, a packet of cigarettes. He took one out, lit it, and sat down again.

"I've changed my mind," he said. "I need a fag after all."

He drew on it deeply.

"I asked you a question," said Finch, with a touch of severity.

"Yes, I heard you," said Viner. He looked across at Finch with a strange expression on his face. Finch found it hard

221

to analyze what was in that expression: appeal, certainly; a touch of cunning; a bright-eyed look which suggested an odd amalgam of defiance and shamefacedness.

He went on, "But I don't have to say anything unless I want to. You can't make me say anything."

It was at this point that Finch was certain. There was no need for him to look any further. Viner was the man who had killed Doreen Walker. But could he be persuaded to confess it? Or would he deny it, and go on denying it, until the police had built up a case against him? It would be laborious work, even though Finch now knew the man's identity. Viner seemed to have done a thorough job in covering up his traces.

A feeling of utter exhaustion swept over Finch. It was not only physical fatigue, although the investigation had been tiring. It was more a kind of moral collapse; a realization that the old cunning had left him. He was sitting there with the cards in his hands and for once in his life he did not know how to play them.

Viner was watching him and a little smile had begun to touch the corners of that full lower lip. The sulky look had gone. He seemed amused, perhaps even triumphant. Finch suddenly saw himself as he must appear to Viner; a middle-aged man in a shabby raincoat, gray-faced and heavy-eyed with fatigue.

"No, Mr. Viner," he said heavily, "you don't have to say anything."

He added, almost to himself, getting ready to heave himself out of the chair, "It's not a pretty business, hunting down a man, but it has to be done. You see, I saw her, lying dead in the wood, under the bushes, so I'm committed. I keep remembering her face."

It was said as a sort of apology, an explanation, offered for God knows what motive. Viner's eyes had not left

Finch's face. Hardly a muscle moved and yet in the space of time it took Finch to speak those words the smile became fixed into a ghastly grin and the bright-eyed look turned into an expression of horror. Suddenly his head fell forward and he bent over so that his face was almost hidden between his knees.

"Oh, Christ Jesus, what a mess," he whispered.

He remained stooped over like this in silence for several seconds. Presently he roused himself a little and raised his head to look at Finch. Finch was reminded of an animal, terrified, surrounded, peering out at its captor from some dark hole in which it had gone to ground.

"You won't make me look at any photos of her?" Viner said. "I don't want to see any pictures."

There was a rising note of panic in his voice.

"No," said Finch gently. "You won't need to see any photographs."

Viner dropped his face again between his hands so that all that remained visible was the top of his head with the brown, springy hair.

Finch leaned forward and spoke softly. It was the tone of voice he might have used to coax a frightened animal out of a corner.

"There's no need to be afraid, Mr. Viner. Come on now. Tell me how it happened. You'll feel better if you talk about it. You met her at Severall's, didn't you?"

Viner again remained silent for a moment, the smoke from his cigarette trickling upward. Then he sat up and, resting his elbows on his knees and his forehead on his fists, he began to talk.

"Yes, I met her at Severall's. She was working on the ladies' counter then, at the far end of the shop, and every time I came I used to take the new delivery of goods through there—mostly stockings, some clothes—and we'd

223

have a bit of a joke together. No harm meant but I knew what sort of a girl she was. You can pick that type out a mile off. Anyway, one day old Severall heard us laughing and ticked Doreen off about it—told her to get on with her work. I felt sorry for her and a bit—well—guilty. I was partly to blame. Anyway, the next time I came in he'd moved her onto the haberdashery counter and when he wasn't looking, she said, 'It's all your fault.' She was looking fed up. That was before Christmas and I didn't get a chance to speak to her much after that. I was busy doing extra deliveries and the shop was crowded every time I went in."

"But you met!" prompted Finch, for Viner seemed to have exhausted that part of his story.

"Yes, we met," he said bitterly. He threw the end of the cigarette that he had hardly smoked into the fire. "By chance. I was in Southend one afternoon. I'd gone back to the warehouse to collect some extra stock. She was walking down the High Street. I pulled up. She said it was her half-day and she was going to the pictures. I couldn't take her out then, I had some deliveries to do, but I said, 'I'll treat you sometime, to make up for getting you into a row.' She said, 'When?' She was eager for a date, all right. It should have warned me off. Like a fool I fixed up to meet her the following Wednesday afternoon. I didn't want to be seen out with her, so I said I'd meet her in the country somewhere. I'd got some deliveries to do round some village shops. I told her where I'd meet her. I forget the place now . . ."

"Bell Green?" suggested Finch.

Viner gave him a quick glance. "There's not much you don't know, is there? Yes, it was Bell Green. I parked the van off the main road, in a side turning, and she walked up the road from the bus stop to meet me. I did the deliveries and she sat in the passenger seat, except when we came near the village, and then she'd climb into the back of the van. She didn't seem to mind. In fact, she seemed to enjoy it.

"We met the same the next Wednesday. That was at Maxstead. We had a narrow squeak that afternoon. The old biddy in the shop caught a glimpse of her. She'd followed me out to the van. I had to pass Doreen off as my wife and ask the old girl to keep quiet about it as I wasn't supposed to carry passengers."

Finch made a mental note to follow up this piece of information. At the moment Viner seemed willing to tell everything, but he might deny it all later.

Viner was saying, "Doreen was already getting a bit fed up with just driving round while I did deliveries. She said couldn't I take her out somewhere else? I was already hooked." He looked at Finch and gave a little shamefaced laugh. "Nothing much up till then, just a quick cuddle at the side of the road. But I knew she was hot stuff and I couldn't give it up. I wanted to go on and have a bit more. My wife's all right, Inspector, don't get me wrong, but she's not the type. Never has been. Doreen was, though."

Even now there was an excited overtone in the man's voice. He ran his tongue over his full lower lip. Sexual vanity, thought Finch, can destroy a man as much as any other kind.

"So you started taking her out to places like Brentwood and Romford?"

"That's right. I altered my delivery schedule around. Did the country deliveries another day and fitted in some of the local towns instead. She'd catch the bus or train, have a look round the shops, and then I'd meet her outside the cinema. We pretended we weren't together. I had to be careful. A lot of people know me and I didn't want to be seen with her and word get back to my wife or to the office that I was meeting a girl. I was knocking off early from work as it was."

Finch understood this. Viner had a strong streak of vanity which would make him think along these lines. He was the sort of man who would not see himself as just another face in a crowd.

"I'd give her the money and she'd buy a ticket. Then I'd wait a bit and buy mine and we'd meet up inside the pictures. After a bit, though, she got fed up with this. She wanted to go to London. I took the afternoon off and met her up there. The next week she wanted to be brought back in the van, instead of catching the train home. I was getting worried. I was taking more and more time off and getting behind on my deliveries. I was sure sooner or later some of my customers would start ringing up the office to complain. I was worried, too, that somebody'd see us. And another thing—Doreen began asking for things. It was my fault, in a way. I put the idea into her head by giving her a pair of nylons—they were samples. But it soon got that every week she expected something, stockings, undies, a jersey. Then she started hinting she needed money to buy other things. I gave her thirty bob toward a pair of shoes, one week. The next week she'd seen a handbag she fancied. I was taking stuff from stock and having to fiddle the books. I knew I'd have to finish with her and I made up my mind I'd tell her I wouldn't see her again.

"I'd been meeting her for some time in the evenings. It was Doreen's idea. The back row of the pictures is all right but you have to be careful. So she said, 'What about meeting me one evening?' And she gave one of those smiles. I knew exactly what she meant—she was game if I was. I used to go out, anyway, on a Wednesday night, round to the pub. That was my evening out. The wife has Thursdays. Like tonight, she goes round to her sister's. Doreen wanted it to be a Saturday. She fancied going out of a Saturday evening, so I told the wife I'd made arrangements to help a customer do his books every Saturday evening. I said there'd be a few quid in it for me and I'd buy her a new coat with the proceeds, so she didn't kick up a fuss about me being out two nights a week.

"I'd meet Doreen just outside the village where she lived. I have the use of the firm's van in the evenings, although I have to pay for the petrol. She'd come on her bike and I'd put it in the back of the van and then we'd drive off somewhere quiet and park."

He gave a little, excited laugh again.

"We were quite well organized. I kept one of those air mattresses in the van and when we'd found a place I'd lift the bike out and then we'd blow up the mattress. I kept a bottle of gin in the back, too, and some paper cups. I used to nick them from the tea machine at the warehouse."

He sounded proud of this small act of thieving.

"Sometimes I'd stop and get fish and chips and we'd eat them in the back of the van when we'd parked. Anyhow, like I said, I wanted to finish with it. I was spending too much on her and she was getting to want more and more. She was nasty with it sometimes. There was the business with the bag. It cost nearly two pounds. I said, 'Well, Doreen, that's your lot till next Christmas,' trying to tell her in a joking sort of way that I wasn't going to keep on putting my hand in my pocket. And she said, 'You'd be surprised how often Christmas comes round,' or something like that, and she wasn't joking.

"I saw her on the Saturday night and I'd made up my mind to take her out for the last time the next Wednesday afternoon. I tried to give her a bit of a hint, to sort of prepare her for it. I said, 'This can't go on forever.' And she said, 'Who says?' And I said, 'Well, it stands to reason, I'm

227

married.' Then she said, 'You should've thought of that a bit sooner.' I was worried, I can tell you. I guessed she'd try to make trouble and I made up my mind I'd tell my wife about her, make a clean breast of it. Then, if Doreen threatened to tell Joan, I could say, 'She knows about it already.' It'd take the wind out of her sails.

"Well, that Sunday morning, Doreen phoned up, here, at the house. She must have looked my name up in the directory because I'd never even told her I was on the phone. My wife answered it and said, 'It's for you. It's a Miss Walker.' I had the shock of my life. Doreen said, 'You've got to meet me tonight. The usual time. And stop off at the fish-and-chip shop on the way.' Then she rang off. Joan was looking a bit suspicious so I had to make up an excuse. I didn't want to tell her about Doreen then, not on a Sunday morning, with the kids running about. So I said it was the girl from the office and they wanted me to go over that night to help out, as they were having trouble with the accounts. And Joan said, 'What, on a Sunday?' So I had to say something to make it sound pretty serious, so I said, 'They think someone's fiddling the books and they want to check up while the office is empty.''

So that's what Mrs. Viner meant by trouble in the office, thought Finch.

"Anyway, I drove over to meet her," went on Viner. "I picked her up as usual outside the village and we drove to a lane we knew of about two miles up the road. I'd stopped to buy fish and chips, like she said. We parked and got into the back of the van and started eating them. I asked her why she wanted to see me—was anything the matter? But she just said she'd fancied the evening out. I didn't say anything at the time but I was pretty mad with her and I made up my mind definitely that I'd have to stop seeing her. We had a couple of drinks. Doreen had about three, I think, more than usual, and she was a bit tight. I hadn't meant to make love to her. I wanted to show I was cross with her for phoning me up but—well—she was more than willing, so we did.

"Afterwards she told me. She said she was pregnant and she wanted the money for an abortion. About a hundred pounds, she said. I told her, 'Don't be daft. I haven't got that kind of money.' She said, 'You'd better find it then because if you don't I'm going to the police.' I said, 'Why?' and she said, 'Because I'm under age. I'm not sixteen yet.' "

"I swear to Christ I had no idea. I thought she was at least eighteen. I got in a panic. I said she wasn't a virgin when I had her first. She started to shout back at me. She was sitting up with her back against the side of the van. She said, oh, God, dreadful things. I knew she was pretty foulmouthed, but I'd never heard a woman say the things she said to me.

"In the end, I lost my temper. I simply wanted to shut her up. I put my hand over her mouth and she struggled to get her hands out of her pockets to hit me. She was kicking out with her feet. I hit her on the side of the head. I must have hit her harder than I thought, because she fell over sideways. The next thing I knew I had my hands round her neck and her head was lolling back, all loose. I knew I'd killed her. Funnily enough, I was quite calm then. I sat in the van and thought for a bit. I thought I might get away with it. If nobody'd seen us together, who was to know it was me? I carried her up to the wood and put her under some bushes and then went back to the van. Her bike was still propped up against the side. I didn't want to leave it. I knew I'd handled it and my prints would be on it. So I put it into the back of the van. It was then I saw her shoes and handbag. She'd taken her shoes off while we were making love. I thought it would be best to dump them with the bike.

"I drove home. The road goes over the river at Hunt-bridge. It was dark and there was nobody about. I parked the car and threw the bike and the other things, her bag and shoes, over the bridge. The tide was high and I knew they wouldn't be seen in the middle of the river, even at low tide. Then I went home. I thought I'd get away with it. But, honest to God, I didn't mean to kill her. I only wanted to stop her from saying those terrible things."

Viner was trembling now. He had leaned forward again, his head sunk into the palms of his hands. Finch looked at his bent head.

"I'll have to take you in and charge you, Mr. Viner," Finch said.

"Christ Jesus, what a mess and all for that bloody little whore," the man replied.

18

The next few hours had a nightmare quality of unreality. Although Finch was sharply aware of what was happening, he had the slightly disengaged feeling, probably brought on by fatigue, of being an onlooker as well as a participant in the events; a feeling such as one has sometimes in dreams.

This did not, however, prevent him from performing his job efficiently. He telephoned to police headquarters in Chelmsford and asked for a woman police officer to be sent to collect Mrs. Viner from her sister's house. He obtained the address from Viner, who looked up briefly from his crouched attitude and answered automatically, like a well-rehearsed child telling its address. After that Finch telephoned Boyce, giving him only the barest circumstances.

While he waited for their arrival Finch made tea in the kitchen, hunting about in the cupboards for the things he needed. A serving hatch gave access to the dining area and he opened it a little way so that he could keep watch on Viner. Finch did not think the man would try anything violent, like attempting to escape or trying to take his own life, but the Inspector was too well-trained in official procedure not to take this precaution. Viner was still seated, with his elbows resting on his knees and his head in his hands. As he watched him, Finch tried to analyze his feelings about the man. He had no sense of personal triumph nor of relief that this part of the investigation was completed; no personal dislike for him either as an individual or as the killer of Doreen Walker. Instead, he felt inside himself, wherever it was that emotions take their root and flourish, only a kind of empty space, hollow and clean, in which there was nothing but a calm acceptance. Viner had taken another person's life; it was his, Finch's, job to arrest him; that was all. For the first time in his life Finch felt he had some conception of what is meant by the word "justice." It was something far larger than he had ever before been able to imagine; above personality; above man; above the laws which men make. It was too pure and vast even to contain pity, although it was only through compassion that mankind could understand and interpret its vast, impersonal abstraction. And, looking at Viner through the narrow opening in the hatchway, Finch himself felt compassion; not pity; this was too weak and mean a word to express the sense of common humanity that Finch realized he shared with this man. But justice remained above compassion and justice had to be served first.

Finch made the tea and carried it through to the living room on a tray. They drank it together in silence. Viner seemed to have reached a point of numbed acceptance. He took the proffered cup and sat drinking, his eyes on the fire.

Boyce arrived soon afterwards, looking flushed and smelling of camphorated oil. He and Finch held a whispered consultation in the hall, while Boyce tried to blow his nose without making too much noise. While they were still talking, the woman police officer arrived with Mrs. Viner, who had been told merely that her husband was to be arrested. She was already on the edge of hysteria and Finch was glad to see that the officer had had the sense to bring the woman's sister with her. When Mrs. Viner heard what the charge was to be she broke down completely. The next ten minutes Finch preferred to forget. A doctor was sent for and Finch hurried Viner out of the house, while his wife screamed and sobbed behind the closed bedroom door. The noise had awakened the children and their frightened wails were added to the woman's agonized cries.

It broke Viner. He was white-faced and shaking as Finch, his hand on the man's arm, led him out to the waiting police car.

It had been arranged that Finch and Boyce would travel back with Viner, leaving Finch's car for the woman police officer to drive back later. Finch put Boyce and Viner into the back and himself sat in the front next to the driver. As they drove away Finch noticed that the presence of the police cars had excited the interest of the neighbors. Faces were pressed to windows and two or three, more brazen than the rest, were standing on their doorsteps, despite the rain, for a better view.

It was then that Viner began to cry. He wept bitterly for several minutes. The three policemen, horribly embarrassed, pretended they could not hear him. Boyce coughed several times and kept on blowing his nose. Finch stared stolidly out the window, while the driver, after one quick, involuntary glance into the rear mirror, kept his eyes fixed on the road ahead.

Presently Viner stopped crying. There was a muttered remark from Boyce, who appeared to be offering him his packet of paper handkerchiefs. Finch heard a muffled, "Thank you."

Then the driver made a comment to Finch about the rain, simply for something to say, and Finch said, "Yes, I feel sorry for the farmers."

He thought then of Smith and wondered if Russell had given him the message.

After that the four men were silent. The car swept on

through the rain, the windscreen wipers ticking to and fro.

At headquarters Viner made a statement which took four hours to write down and transcribe. While they waited for it to be typed, Finch sent out for tea and sandwiches. He had already sent Boyce home. The sergeant had left reluctantly but there was no point keeping him out of bed any longer. He was thick with cold and obviously running a temperature.

"Go home, Tom," Finch told him. "Take a few days off. I can manage here."

"But I'd like to stay," Boyce protested. "See it through to the end."

"It's all finished for now," said Finch, "bar the formalities."

Boyce gave him a quick look.

"Are you sure *you're* all right?" he asked. "You've seemed a bit off color recently."

"Only tired," said Finch. He did feel tired. He rubbed one hand across his eyes.

"Well, take it easy," advised Boyce, "or you'll be cracking up next,"

Finch smiled and touched him on the arm.

"You'll do, Tom," he said. It was the nearest he could get to an expression of his gratitude. Even so, Boyce was embarrassed.

"I'll get off home, then," he said gruffly.

At three o'clock in the morning Viner's statement was read over to him and he signed it. Afterwards Finch formally charged him with the murder of Doreen Walker and he was committed to the cells. All of this was carried through in an atmosphere of impersonal calm. It steadied Viner, who behaved with remarkable control. It was only when he was being led away and looked back over his shoulder at Finch that his face betrayed what he was really feeling. His full, lower lip trembled and his eyes held a pleading, frightened expression. Then the door closed.

Lapped by waves of fatigue, Finch went slowly up the stairs, like a man wading through deep water. His office was at the back of the building, an ordinary enough room, furnished with the regulation desk, hard chairs, and filing cabinets. Finch entered, switched on the light, and, standing just inside the room, took off his raincoat and jacket, which he hung on a hook behind the door, and then his shoes. These he carried in his hand, dropping them on the floor beside a battered armchair which he himself had introduced to soften the room's official atmosphere. They lay abandoned, one turned on its side. Loosening his tie, he went over to the handbasin, concealed behind a curtain, and washed under the running tap, throwing the water over his face and head. Then he switched off the light and settled down in the armchair, wrapping himself in a gray army blanket which was kept folded on the chair seat.

Despite his discomfort he usually slept well under these circumstances, when a case had kept him late at the office and it was not worth going home. That night, however, he could not settle. Viner's arrest had disturbed him. He could not forget the man's face or the sound of the woman's crying behind the closed bedroom door. For several hours he dozed only fitfully, waking up, it seemed, every few minutes, aware of the sounds in the building, the smell of old dust in the cushions of the chair, the noise of an occasional car going past. At last the gray light of morning began to seep into the room and Finch, abandoning all attempts at sleeping, threw back the blanket and went over to the window to survey the morning. Just discernible in the thinning darkness were the wet slate roofs and the clustering

235

chimney pots of the surrounding buildings. Smoke trickled upward. Here and there a light burned in a window.

Finch turned away, rasping his hand across his chin. He needed a shave. Then he remembered that he had taken the razor he always kept in his desk drawer to Wrexford, in case he had need of it there. There was no means of making tea either. In a somber mood he washed briefly and went out, slamming the door behind him.

His equanimity returned, however, on the drive to Wrexford. He liked the early morning. The roads were empty. Nobody was up and about yet. He felt most strongly a sense of belonging, of roots that stretched back into the past, to ancestors who worked those fields, in the days of the red deer and the wild boar, when spring was indeed a miracle and harvest a time of rejoicing. His spirits began to rise.

Presently he passed a farm laborer, wearing an old army greatcoat, a haversack on his back, on his way to work, cycling along with slow deliberation. The man reminded him of Meyrick and from Meyrick his thoughts turned to Smith. Finch wondered if Russell had found him and if the man would be waiting for him at the police station. There had not been time, after his visit to Leach's house on the previous evening, to telephone a second time to find out if Smith had arrived or not.

Smith, meanwhile, also was awake. He was not sure what time it was. He possessed no watch and the thick glass over the cell window let in so little natural light that it was difficult to judge. But he guessed it must be morning. There was a gray quality about the light and the sounds he could hear outside in the corridor were the sounds of a place coming back to life after the night. Doors slammed. There was the sound of footsteps and voices.

Cairn still slept, stretched out across Smith's legs, and

Smith did not want to wake the dog. He lay back, listening to the noises and the dog's regular breathing and thought over what he must do. He had already come to a decision concerning his own future. There remained one problem.

Presently the dog's weight became oppressive. Carefully Smith began to move his legs, trying to draw them out without disturbing the dog. He managed to extricate one but Cairn suddenly rolled slightly, shifting his body as he did so, so that his weight was now lying directly across Smith's other leg. Smith waited, one leg drawn up, the other still extended. He had managed to half sit up, resting his weight on his elbows, and in this semiupright position he could now look down on the sleeping dog. It lay sprawled out, its head resting on the blanket across Smith's thigh, its belly turned slightly, so that the little curling hairs, still rough and springy from the shower, were exposed. Its ears, in sleep, were completely flaccid, soft and drooping forward. Even its tail was asleep, spread out limply like a ragged banner.

In a sudden excess of emotion Smith bent forward and gathered the dog in his arms. It woke, grunted, struggled for a moment and then lay still but its tail was beating, sweeping across the blankets in the old rhythm of love, and its eyes that looked up into Smith's face were very bright.

Wrexford was just beginning to stir as the Inspector drove through. A few people, dark, huddled shapes, stood patiently at the central bus stop, waiting for the early-morning workers' bus. They might have been waiting for the tumbrils. The police station was more lively. The cleaners had been and gone away, leaving in their wake shining floors, emptied wastepaper baskets and the faint odor of soapy water and disturbed dust. The lights were still burning but already they had a pallid look.

Finch went up the steps, pushed open the glass door at

the top, and went inside. The sergeant, who had been on duty all night, was tidying up the desk with the ponderous movements of a man who will soon be going home and intended to make the job last out until he did.

"Did Mr. Smith turn up?" Finch asked him.

"Yes, sir. He stayed the night. Do you want to see him now?" the sergeant replied. "I don't know if he's awake yet."

Finch hesitated and then said, "Any chance of getting breakfast for two? Something substantial?"

"I expect something could be arranged, sir."

"Good. Have it taken into my office and then ask Mr. Smith to join me. I shall be leaving today and I want to get my things cleared out."

Although he said nothing, the sergeant exuded curiosity.

"Yes," said Finch irritably, "we've made an arrest."

He immediately regretted his irritability and added, "I'll see you get the report. After all, its thanks to your cooperation that we've been able to clear this case up."

It sounded heavy and glib to Finch's ears but the sergeant looked pleased.

"Just doing our duty, sir," he said. "But I'm glad it's all settled. Not a nice case, not nice at all. I'll see about that breakfast."

"Thank you," said Finch, and as he walked away he made a mental note to thank personally every person at the station. It would seem to be worth the trouble.

While he waited for Smith's arrival Finch emptied the drawers of the desk and began to stack the files on the Walker case on the top. Now that Viner was in custody he intended conducting the rest of the case from headquarters. He was still busy with this task when Smith came into the room, Cairn at his heels. He was dressed in his own clothes which had been brought to him dried but not ironed. This gave him a rumpled air, as if he had slept in his clothes all night which was accentuated by the roughness of his beard and hair, still untidy from the previous evening's soaking and which, in absence of a comb, he had not been able to tidy. His face, despite the night's sleep, looked gray and hollow.

He stopped just inside the room.

"Why do you want to see me?" he asked.

"Sit down, then we can talk," replied Finch.

"I want to know why you want to see me," Smith persisted. There was a rising note in his voice.

Before Finch had time to reply there was a knock at the door and a police constable entered with a tray. The smell of hot egg was very strong. The constable stood in the doorway, aware of an uncomfortable atmosphere in the room, unsure what had caused it. He was himself made uncomfortable.

"Put the tray down over here," said Finch, pushing aside the stacked folders on the desk. Some of them began to slide sideways and he had to lunge forward before the slipping pile turned into an avalanche of paper. Picking them up, he dumped them on the floor. The constable put down the tray and left.

"Breakfast!" announced Finch, waving a hand. He looked pleased as if he had just conjured it up out of the air. He drew up a chair to the desk.

"I want an answer to my question," said Smith.

Finch paused, his knife and fork in his hand, and looked up at the other man. Smith was bristling with suspicion. His eyes were cold and met Finch's in a hard stare. Despite his shabby, even ridiculous appearance, which would have put any man at a disadvantage and made him feel ill at ease, Smith managed to remain in charge of the situation. His pride and sense of self-assurance were unimpaired.

"I wanted you to come here because you had nowhere else to go," said Finch simply. Then he pointed at the other plate with his fork and, bending his head, began to eat his breakfast.

Smith drew a chair up to the desk and sat down opposite Finch.

"Thank you," he said.

Cairn, who had come to sit at Smith's side, looked up with bright eyes and began to make little pleading noises in his throat.

"I forgot the dog," said Finch. "Will he eat bacon?"

He lifted the rasher from his plate and looked at Smith quizzically. Smith suddenly smiled.

"I think he will. He can have mine too."

Finch fussed about, cutting up his own bacon and Smith's onto a saucer, breaking up a slice of bread and moistening it with some milk from the jug. All the time the dog watched eagerly, his tail beating gently on the floor. Smith watched, too, with a curious expression on his face.

"Here, Cairn," said the Inspector, bending down to put the saucer on the floor beside him.

The dog looked up quickly into Smith's face.

"Go on, eat," said Smith. Cairn rose and walked round the desk to eat from the saucer at Finch's side.

"So you lost everything?" said Finch, as if picking up the thread of a former conversation.

"Yes," replied Smith.

"Do you know how it happened?"

The Inspector was eating quickly, putting food into his mouth and chewing energetically, washing it down with quick gulps of tea.

"Probably an accident," said Smith. "There was an oil lamp in the cottage as well as a stove. It would be easy to knock one of them over in the dark."

"And what will you do now?" went on Finch. He had already finished his breakfast and was wiping round his plate with a piece of bread speared on his fork.

"I'm not sure," said Smith, although he had already made up his mind.

"You won't go back to London?"

"No. That's finished with."

"I've finished here," said Finch. "A man was charged last night."

He watched Smith's face closely for his reaction. Smith smiled faintly.

"Did that please you?"

"Yes, it did," said Finch sharply. "I'm too old a dog to learn new tricks. It's my job and this is where I belong."

He indicated with his hand the office, the files, the map on the wall, the whole world of police investigation.

"But," he added, "there was no sense of triumph. Only a kind of compassion for the man, and for the girl he killed."

He paused expecting Smith to say something but, as the man remained silent, Finch continued:

"It's not easy to learn compassion. It's too late to begin all over again. I shall have to do the best with what I have; myself, my job, the people I'm involved with. Something may be salvaged."

"The phoenix rising out of the ashes," said Smith.

"A bit charred round the edges and not able to fly very far or very high," said Finch, grinning at the ineptitude of the simile as applied to himself. Smith suddenly pushed back his chair and stood up.

"I'm leaving too," he said. "There's nothing to keep me here any longer."

"Where will you go?" asked Finch.

"I don't think that matters. But, unlike you, I can't take

up the old threads. There is nothing left of them. Besides, it was all so dishonest."

"Dishonest?" cried Finch uncomprehendingly.

"Yes, and cowardly. I despised the old life but I had neither the courage nor the honesty to break with it completely. One thread remained, a golden thread, a lifeline—the money that came with such reassuring regularity every Friday morning, the wages of the past."

"But you were entitled to that money," cried Finch, distressed by the note of bitterness in Smith's voice.

"No. Because with it I was no more independent than a child in a tree house is independent. I was only pretending to be free. Will you do two things for me?"

"Of course," said Finch.

"Will you write to my brother and explain. I feel I owe that to him. It wasn't his fault that we couldn't be friends."

"Yes, I'll do that," said Finch. "And the other thing?"

"Will you find someone to take the dog?"

"Cairn? You aren't going to leave him behind?"

Cairn, hearing his name, sat up, wagging his tail, and Smith looked at him.

"I must. I can't take him with me. It would be unkind. He's used to a fire and regular meals. He would only be unhappy."

"I'll take him," said Finch, on an impulse.

"You?"

"Yes," said Finch. "I've always wanted a dog."

This was true. He was thinking also of his sister. Her life must be very lonely. A dog would be company for her and she liked animals. Besides, Finch thought, Cairn would be a tangible reminder of Smith.

"Thank you," said Smith. He began putting on his plastic raincoat.

"I'll come with you to the door," said Finch.

Cairn, seeing Smith put on his coat, began to whine expectantly.

"Sit," said Smith firmly. "Stay."

The dog sat down, watching the two men and lifting one front paw.

"I'll take him home this morning," said Finch. "I can drop him off at the house on my way to Chelmsford. He'll be well looked after."

"I must go," said Smith, turning abruptly.

As the door shut behind them the dog began to whine, and Finch was reminded of Mrs. Viner, crying behind the closed door. Smith's profile was set and taut.

Finch walked with him to the steps that led down into the street. A pale, watery sun was struggling to shine behind low, thin cloud that was blowing along like smoke. The shops were not yet open but the town had already the animation of a new day.

"Good-bye," said Smith. He did not put out his hand for Finch to shake.

"Good-bye," said Finch. He added, "And good luck," but he doubted if Smith heard it. He had run quickly down the steps and was already walking away with a long stride. He reached the corner, turned it without looking back, and was gone.

A true story of murder and obsession
that shocked a nation

UNHOLY MATRIMONY

JOHN DILLMANN

Twenty-six-year-old Patricia Giesick was on her honeymoon in New
Orleans, taking a midnight stroll with her husband, when she was
tragically killed in a hit-and-run car accident. Her parents were
devastated – she was their only child – but there seemed nothing to
substantiate their wild claim that Patricia's death had been
orchestrated by her husband. That is, until John Dillmann of the
New Orleans Homicide Department decided to investigate . . .

It was only a tiny discrepancy in the evidence that gave Dillmann a
lead. One question led to another, and very soon he uncovered a
massive life insurance fraud. Then he met the strange, sinister
Reverend Samuel Corey, a genuinely ordained vicar who also
turned out to be a well-known massage-parlour king and shady
business associate of Patricia's husband. But Jim Giesick, who
alone held the key to Dillmann's investigations, had mysteriously
vanished. Just how Dillmann managed to track him down and
unravel one of the most twisted and premeditated murder plots ever
devised, when everyone thought it was an unsolvable case, makes
for an electrifying, engrossing, real-life drama.

0 7474 0300 7   TRUE CRIME   £3.50

INTRUDERS

BUDD HOPKINS

IT COULD EVEN HAPPEN TO YOU . . .

They come from far across the universe . . . their purpose: genetic
research. Their unwilling guinea-pigs: human beings. It sounds like
science fiction, but it is incredible, chilling fact . . .

Through extensive interviews and analysis – closely monitored by
top psychologists, doctors and scientists – experienced UFO
investigator Budd Hopkins has recorded the astonishing testimony
of the men, women and children abducted and experimented on by
these alien travellers. The truth of their story is painfully clear; their
scars – physical and emotional – tragically real.

Could the ordeal of so many ordinary people be yours too? The
witnesses in this book come from all walks of life – and no-one is
exempt. INTRUDERS is a gripping, haunting document and a
profoundly disturbing prophecy that will ignite passionate debate on
a subject that no longer exists in the realms of the imagination.

0 7474 0144 6   NON-FICTION   £3.50

An undercurrent of murder . . .

THE DARK STREAM

June Thomson

The small, peaceful Essex village of Wynford was the sort of place featured on postcards of genteel rural England. So when Stella Reeve was found drowned in the stream which skirted the little community, everyone was sure it was just a tragic accident.

But to Inspector Finch, there was a taint of violence about the scene. He couldn't rationalise it but he could sense it almost as if it were an odour in the air. But even if his intuition was sound he'd need a very clear head to follow the swirling, shifting eddies of motive, intrigue and guile which lay behind this extraordinary case . . .

'Neatly plotted and trimly told' *Punch*

Also by June Thomson in Sphere Books:
SHADOW OF A DOUBT
SOUND EVIDENCE
TO MAKE A KILLING
A DYING FALL

0 7221 8441 7   CRIME   £2.75

P.D. JAMES
A Taste for Death

'An astonishing novel of range and complexity . . . she writes like an angel. Every character is clearly drawn. Even the cameo parts are full of sympathy. Her atmosphere – whether that of a family quarrel or a deserted church – is unerringly, chillingly convincing. And she manages all this without for a moment slowing down the drive and tension of an exciting mystery' THE TIMES

'A cunningly compulsive work . . . with a breathless, bravura finale of heart-pounding suspense'
SUNDAY TIMES

'She writes with an extraordinary delicacy about the seedy side of reality . . . she is a wonderful stylist'
PETER LEVI, TODAY

'A major and magisterial book' DAILY TELEGRAPH

'Meticulous in detail and nuance' OBSERVER

'Compelling' SUNDAY TELEGRAPH

0 7221 5222 1   CRIME   £3.50

Don't miss P. D. James's other bestsellers

The Skull Beneath The Skin
Innocent Blood
Cover Her Face
Unnatural Causes
Shroud For A Nightingale
An Unsuitable Job For A Woman

Death Of An Expert Witness
The Black Tower
Non-Fiction
The Maul And The Pear Tree
(with T. A. Critchley)

Deadly gamesmanship in the ruthless world of
championship golf . . .

BULLET HOLE

Keith Miles

For Alan Saxon, the British Open Championship is a crucial
tournament. He's on top form and being tipped as a winner.
But his game is rudely interrupted by the appearance of a
young, pretty golf groupie who ends up naked and dead on
his bed. And she's not the only problem. Someone wants
Saxon out of the Open. But who? Which of his competitors
is so desperate to win that he'll stop at nothing? Not even
murder . . .

'A golfing Dick Francis'
GOLF WORLD
'A compelling story . . . as thrilling as holing a
25 yard putt'
DAILY MAIL
'A racy novel . . . good fun'
GOLF WORLD

0 7221 6039 9   CRIME   £2.95

FOR THE FIRST TIME EVER, A MEMBER
OF THE KRAY TWINS' FIRM SPEAKS OUT

MURDER
WITHOUT
CONVICTION

JOHN DICKSON

Ronnie and Reggie Kray were a formidable
partnership, possessing a charisma that was
glamorous but deadly. Celebrities, film stars,
con-men and killers were attracted by the Twins'
curious mix of charm and violence, whose reign of
terror in the mean streets of London's East End
continues to exert a compulsive fascination.

Now, John Dickson, a close and trusted henchman of
the Krays for many years, tells the inside story of their
notorious gangland underworld. He describes the
murders, the extortion, protection and gambling
rackets; the Mafia connections; entertaining the
famous; the increasingly erratic and senselessly
violent behaviour of the Twins and their final
dramatic arrest at a time when they had built up so
fearsome a reputation that they were convinced they
were invincible.

This, the first inside account of the gang that
dominated the East End of London for most of
the 1960s, reads like a thriller, but is based
entirely on fact.

0 7221 2948 3   TRUE CRIME   £2.99

A CLASSIC CRIME THRILLER . . .

THE SENTRIES

ED McBAIN

Jason Trench had had it up to here with the way those Commies were giving his country the runaround. If the politicos weren't going to get up off their fat butts and do something then he sure as hell would. He wanted action *now*.

Jason wasn't just some patriotic fruitcake who'd seen one too many John Wayne movies. Jason had a plan. He had forty-two loyal men behind him and they were even crazier than he was. He didn't need speeches or slogans.

He had guns. And he used them . . .

0 7221 5762 2 CRIME £2.95

Also by Ed McBain in Sphere Books:
JACK AND THE BEANSTALK
SNOW WHITE AND ROSE RED

A selection of bestsellers from SPHERE

FICTION

JUBILEE: THE POPPY CHRONICLES 1	Claire Rayner	£3.50 ☐
DAUGHTERS	Suzanne Goodwin	£3.50 ☐
REDCOAT	Bernard Cornwell	£3.50 ☐
WHEN DREAMS COME TRUE	Emma Blair	£3.50 ☐
THE LEGACY OF HEOROT	Niven/Pournelle/Barnes	£3.50 ☐

FILM AND TV TIE-IN

BUSTER	Colin Shindler	£2.99 ☐
COMING TOGETHER	Alexandra Hine	£2.99 ☐
RUN FOR YOUR LIFE	Stuart Collins	£2.99 ☐
BLACK FOREST CLINIC	Peter Heim	£2.99 ☐
INTIMATE CONTACT	Jacqueline Osborne	£2.50 ☐

NON-FICTION

BARE-FACED MESSIAH	Russell Miller	£3.99 ☐
THE COCHIN CONNECTION	Alison and Brian Milgate	£3.50 ☐
HOWARD & MASCHLER ON FOOD	Elizabeth Jane Howard and Fay Maschler	£3.99 ☐
FISH	Robyn Wilson	£2.50 ☐
THE SACRED VIRGIN AND THE HOLY WHORE	Anthony Harris	£3.50 ☐

All Sphere books are available at your local bookshop or newsagent, or can be ordered direct from the publisher. Just tick the titles you want and fill in the form below.

Name_____

Address_____

_____

Write to Sphere Books, Cash Sales Department, P.O. Box 11, Falmouth, Cornwall TR10 9EN

Please enclose a cheque or postal order to the value of the cover price plus:

UK: 60p for the first book, 25p for the second book and 15p for each additional book ordered to a maximum charge of £1.90.

OVERSEAS & EIRE: £1.25 for the first book, 75p for the second book and 28p for each subsequent title ordered.

BFPO: 60p for the first book, 25p for the second book plus 15p per copy for the next 7 books, thereafter 9p per book.

Sphere Books reserve the right to show new retail prices on covers which may differ from those previously advertised in the text elsewhere, and to increase postal rates in accordance with the P.O.